WRECKED

A Gus Dury novel

by

TONY
BLACK

DOCKYARD PRESS

For Barry Graham

Among them, as always, were good men and straight, men honestly without work, victims of a society ravaged by avarice, sloth, stupidity, and a God made wrathful by Babylonian excesses.

—William Kennedy, *Ironweed*

WRECKED

CHAPTER 1

THINGS were on the up.

Sort of.

Couldn't say I was closing in on the Seven Series Beemer, but at least I had wheels. How long they stayed attached to the motor was a whole other story.

'So what's the problem?' said a beer-gut, shoving a wedge in his sky-rocket that could settle a few rounds at Bilderberg.

'It leaks oil, by the bucket. I drove it here with the temp in the red the whole time.'

Hands.

I got shown palms — and they looked suspiciously clean for a man claiming to be a grease-monkey. 'Never leaked when it left here, mate.'

Did I tell him I wasn't his mate? No. Better to keep something in reserve at such a delicate stage in negotiations.

He leaned on the wing of my new Golf — well, new to me, Jimmy Savile was wining and dining with Prince Charlie and Sir Cliff when this one rolled off the line. 'Look, mate, you got a nice little run-around there. If it's a bit greedy for oil then you should keep it topped up.'

'It's a leak. If I pump any more Castrol in there it's going on my boots.'

A shrug.

I got shrugs and a shake of the head — guys like him, it's as if they think life's a contest for the world's biggest bell-end. He sprung off the car, turning to walk away.

'Well, that's what they call "buyer beware," son.'

I didn't like the *son* bit at all. And it came with a sneer.

'*Caveat emptor* ... that's what you're giving me?' I shoved it back at him, he looked perplexed. 'It means buyer beware.'

He stopped, weighed me with his eyes but had no answer. He took a step closer, his gaze never leaving me. He kept about an inch of air between his beer gut and myself, but I wasn't playing ball, said, 'Have you ever heard of *caveat rectum?*'

'What?' That look of the scoobied, the thrown.

'*Caveat rectum* — that's where the buyer investigates the seller's arsehole with his Doc Martens because he's so fucked off with his purchase.'

Swear, I felt that beer gut retract — maybe he sucked in a breath.

He pulled back his shoulders. I saw that he thought about it, having a go, like, but retreated. I heard Michael Caine saying, "You're a big fella, but outta shape". This was far from a full-time job to me, but when the radge was on I could do a good impression of the bold Carter.

'You got the paperwork?' he said. 'Sure have. And pay close attention to the date I drove it away.' I handed over the document wallet and watched him flick through. 'And you'd be Gus Dury?' 'That's my handle, don't wear it out.' He closed the wallet and crossed hands. His expression was inquisitive now. 'Why do I know that name?' 'Because you recently offloaded this piece of shit on me, perhaps?'

He watched me, his stare cold.

4

'*What?*' I said.

'Just wait here a moment, please.' His demeanour changed. He turned, began to traipse back to the portacabin. If he was trying to rattle me, he'd succeeded.

There was a big window on the cabin, barred over and plastered with sale signs, but I could still see him inside. He checked over the details in the document wallet again and then started tapping at a keyboard. I kept watching as I sparked up a red top. This lad was hunting for something — I thought it might be a get out, a way of spiking my claim, until he picked up the phone and looked even more pensive.

I turned away from the portacabin, concentrated on my tab and a manky seagull sitting on another rusting VW, a Polo this time, and I bet it came with quite a few holes. I kept a guard on beer-gut. The hardy stance had gone now. He was staring at me, clearly reciting my vitals down the line to an interested party. So now he was sussing me out, but who with? The DVLA? Plod? The Leith Massive?

The thought made me shudder — my rep hadn't improved much lately, I'd only seen more loss of cred. I was shocked to see his grimace slide as he returned the phone to its cradle. He almost skipped down the steps towards me, a wide smile pasted over his face.

Maybe I still had some friends. Maybe it was just the Leith address. Maybe I was fooling myself.

'Sorry, mate,' was his opener. A forced laugh erupted. 'I saw the name and thought I recognised it ...'

'You did,' I nodded. I wanted to talk about the car, but the conversation had clearly moved on in his mind. I was intrigued but my dander was still racing about the Golf burning oil and, along the way, my coin.

Said, 'Look, can we talk about the motor?'

'What?' He appeared genuinely stunned. 'Maybe you could just follow me into the office.'

'For a refund?'

'God, no. I have a very interesting proposition for you, Mr Dury.'

And that is how it always starts.

The road to bruised knuckles and heartache. The sob-stories and the bad turns taken by people who should really have known better. We should all know better, shouldn't we? I certainly should have in the past but things were different for me now. Christ, I had my job back. I had a measure of the fabled sobriety for once. Did I really want to go back over the past?

'No, you look ... and don't call me Mr Dury, I hear that and I think you're confusing me with my father, which is not a flattering comparison. I'd sooner talk about this bloody oil leak before we go any further.'

'Sure. Of course, just consider it sorted. I'll put the Golf on the ramp today and the lads will soon have it purring like a pussy cat.'

I had my doubts, considered asking for it in writing.

'This way, come on, Mr D— I mean, Gus.' He indicated the portacabin door, he'd left it open and the grubby, yellowed venetian blind was rattling in the breeze, scaring more manky seagulls into flight. 'Come on, come on.' He set off, mumbling, 'Fancy you walking in here today when I've been after a man with just your particular talents since ... well, we can get into that.'

Knew I would do just that. And more besides. But my focus was slipping towards the craziest about-turn I'd ever seen on a car lot. Salesmen usually only put on the charm when they want your money. This one was definitely after something but I had no clue what it was.

I crushed the cig under my boot and went inside.

'Take a seat.' He cleared a plastic chair of a pile of mouldering Auto Traders and pointed downward.

I dusted the base of the chair with my hand and sat. He was rubbing his palms together as he stood before me.

'Coffee … er, tea?' he said.

Declined. My shots weren't up to date, so thought it best. 'Can you get to the point?'

'Of course, yes.' His fat arse slid onto the desk, dislodging a lava flow of windscreen sale stickers. He was clearly nervous, perhaps even a little perturbed. I found myself glancing at the door but wondering all the while when my car was going on the ramp.

'Okay. Okay. So, it's like this Mr—'

'Gus,' I cut in.

'Yes, Gus. I've lost something.'

Your mind, perhaps? I held schtum, he still had all the cards after all.

'Go on.'

'I looked around …'

'But couldn't find it?'

'That's right.'

Was going to be pissed if *it* was a set of car keys after this build up.

He went on. 'A friend of mine, well, I asked him what to do. And he said, what you need is someone who does this kind of thing, y'know, professionally.'

'A professional *finder*?'

'A detective.' He almost whispered the word, like it was too politically incorrect to utter.

'And so you priced them up and thought, fuck that! Which is where my name came in.'

'Oh, no. No, no.' He slid off the desk, his lardy arse still wobbling as he shuffled nearer to me. 'You've got me all wrong. It's not that kind of thing I'm looking for, not a ...' he weighed hands in the air, like he was trying to juggle water, 'it's more of a, you might say, unconventional loss. Yes, that's it, not through the proper channels, so to speak.'

I was getting the picture, even if he was drawing it for me in crayons.

'Let me get this straight. You lost something and you need to find it, so a friend gave you my name as someone who might help.'

'Yes.' He nodded. There was a twitch above his eye and a line of moisture forming on his upper lip that caught my attention.

'Now, if I'm picking you up right, this loss of yours wouldn't be anything a reputable firm would even be remotely interested in finding.'

He kept quiet, only wetting his dry lips with a grey tongue.

'And so you come to me, as a man well-known for sticking his face in the fan.' I paused, my lungs still seemed to call for tobacco, so I sparked up again. 'Which makes me think this loss of yours would be far from above board, possibly verging on the illegal, am I right?'

'I don't think illegal is the correct term.' He flustered, running the back of his hand over his mouth as he gazed out the dirty window at the contents of his dodgy car lot. 'But I would be keen to avoid entanglements with the law, that is fair to say.'

I drew on my tab, the small room was filling with smoke. He fidgeted before me and then retreated behind his desk to withdraw a battered, oily fingerprinted cheque-book from the drawer.

'I could pay you, Mr D—'

'I don't think so.'

'What? Are you turning down good money?'

'Turning down this job of yours.'

'But ...'

'No buts, bud.' I uncrossed my legs and leaned forward, the plastic chair let out a loud creak. 'You see, I might not be the best detective in the world, or even Leith for that matter, but I think I have just about enough savvy to suss when someone is feeding me a line. And right now, I'd say you were full of more bullshit than a farmer's foreskin.'

Beer-gut recoiled. Stupefaction replacing every other hint of an expression on his face. There was a moment, a millisecond or so, when I thought I might be prepared to go to the mat with him over his proposition, perhaps even tease the proper facts from him, but it passed. Truth was, I couldn't summon the interest to give a shit about what was really going on inside his mind — my guess was a gerbil on a treadmill was turning the cogs.

The cheque-book was raised again, like a limp white flag he hoped would come to his rescue. 'I could pay you. I could pay you a decent sum.'

It got my goat to think of him offering me a cheque when I knew he was holding a wedge as thick as *War and Peace*, Parts I & II, in his pocket. I got up and opened the door. 'Thanks for the offer, but, as tempting as you make your bullshit sound, I've moved on from this kind of thing.'

I walked out. The portacabin rocked on its pins as he bolted, fatboy-fashion, behind me. 'What about my ... *loss?*' He stayed in the doorway, a spit of rain had started to fall.

'Looks like more on the way ... rain I mean.'

'But, Gus, can you come back and talk. At least hear me out. Please.'

I gazed at the sky, black clouds rumbling in signalled a heavier downpour — it'd be falling in stair-rods in no time. 'When can I come back for the Golf? The sooner being the better.'

'Tomorrow. I'll have it ready for you then if you like. Will we say about noon?'

A cold easterly bit, I looked about, confident a courtesy car wasn't going to be an option. 'That'll do.'

'It'll be ready, I promise.' He stuck out his hand, I thought at first it was to shake but he grabbed my sleeve and patted my arm. 'Just have a think about my offer, will you do that, please?'

I didn't like to see a man pleading, so I just left him hanging there, a dick in the wind, so to speak. I dowped the red-top and put the collar up on my Crombie as I headed into the smirry rain. The brisk wind was chasing empty take-away boxes down Fort Street and onto Ferry Road. I was pissed off at the walk ahead to my Easter Road flat but at least my car was coming back to me, hopefully minus the slug's trail.

CHAPTER 2

I was back in the workplace. The last time I was here it was brutal. The lifeless corpse of the newspaper industry, having already been picked over for scraps, was having the marrow sucked from its bones. It was hard to watch colleagues being bent over by corporate gimps, but I'm sure some of them actually enjoyed it. They were still there after all, still taking it up the farter.

I wasn't allowed to call myself a journalist. Was now a "content provider", or as I preferred, a prestitute. I didn't even have an office, just a website to upload to and a boss on the end of an iPhone. Standards were non-existent but that was fine because I had very few of those left anyway.

Seemed to me like the whole game was fixed for everyone now. It might have been working for a few real-estate magnates in London, and was definitely working for the likes of George Soros, but try preaching that in the engine room. The bloke in Tesco jeans wanted change and he didn't care who was selling it. There were pitchforks in the post, you could sense it. They were already rioting in France. If it kicked off here, I'd be joining them, but I did worry if we had enough rope and lampposts in the country.

I fired over my latest piece and settled down in front of the gob-unit. I was flicking, retching over the sight of fucking Jedward in the Big Brother house, when the phone went.

'Gus, it's Terry.' I checked the clock, he was starting early tonight. Normally he left his calls till my eyes were closing and my kip beckoning.

'Yeah, all okay?'

'I just got the piece — it'll do — but I'll need you to churn out another one right away. There's been a magnitude seven earthquake in the Philippines, which should be great for our clicks.'

Terry wasn't a hack and was lacking something that was once a vital prerequisite for the job: an interest in humanity. He wanted eyeballs on the site and people being tragically killed or made homeless really beeped his jeep.

'Terry, it's nearly midnight.' It was no surprise to me that I had to remind him that his staff weren't just another app on his phone.

'Yes, I know that, but I run a 24-hour news service, you knew that when you took the job.' I was waiting for the "Money never sleeps" speech.

'Terry, I've been on the go since early doors, if I don't get some kip I'll be propping up my eyelids with matchsticks.'

A gap on the line, then a sigh, 'I didn't have you down as a clock-watcher, Dury.'

I resisted the urge to slap him down, said, 'If I was, Terry, I'd have knocked off about seven hours ago.'

A huff. Followed by a tut. 'You get your beauty sleep then, Dury. I'll find someone else to write up the quake.'

'Night-night, then.' Terry or his wife Jayne would write it up in their usual sub-*Beano* comic style and make every reader want to gouge their eyes out with spoons. It wasn't my problem, though I knew Terry would have plans to make it so.

'Let's talk tomorrow, Gus,' said Terry.

I put down the phone and flicked off the telly. Was heading for bed when my mobi pinged back at me. It was a text from Hod.

— *You up and about?*

— *Barely. Long day.*

— *I heard. Just coming back from gym, you about for five?*

— *Yeah, suppose so. But just five. Shattered.*

Fair play to Hod, at least he texted before dropping in, or calling, at the witching hour. That was the difference between friends and bosses. It seemed like I was totting up more complaints about Terry by the day.

The sound of knocking on the door came like a road crew had rocked up. I lunged, swung open the door. 'Fucksake, you trying to wake up the whole stair?'

'Too loud?' said Hod.

'Worse than Vanessa Feltz's wardrobe, mate.' I ushered him in.

'Shit, I should tone it down.' He helped himself to a bottle of Beck's from the fridge. He knew I kept them there, not to drink, but to test my willpower. I figured if I could keep alcohol under my own roof, and still avoid it, then I could keep the demon at bay. At least that was my thinking, I'd tried everything else so I might as well give it a shot. So far, it seemed to be working; I was dry as a pie.

'I ran into Bruce today,' said Hod, settling down on my sofa and stretching out his legs, exposing hairy ankles beneath his joggers.

'Bruce, you mean Windae Willis?' Bruce was the latest name that had been conferred upon Peter Willis, a former school friend of ours whose first job had been a window cleaner, hence the original tag of Windae Willis. The moniker had worn out at some stage, obviously after the release of *Die Hard*, and he'd been called Bruce ever since.

'The very same,' said Hod, sucking down the Beck's.

'And? … I mean, I'm sure there's a reason for you coming round after midnight, other than to raid my fridge.'

He sat up, 'Yeah. He was asking about you, he wanted to know if you were still, y'know, in the biz?'

'You know I'm not.'

'Well, I know you're sick of Terry and June.'

'Jayne. Though it's a fair match on other fronts.'

'So, are you?'

I started to feel a little more awake than I had five minutes ago. Perhaps it had something to do with putting two and two together on Hod. I'd known him for years, and he was a big-time adrenaline junkie. What really got Hod excited, more than anything else, was tagging along on my jobs. Officially, he liked to claim he was there to assist but the real reason was that he liked nothing more than a good pagger.

'What the hell are you up to, Hod?'

'Nothing.'

'You can't kid a kidder. C'mon, what's Bruce been saying to you?'

Hod put down his beer and laced his fingers together in front of him, it looked like he was constructing a point to focus his thoughts on. 'Well, I don't hear from Bruce that often, as you know.'

'Neither do I.'

'So, it was a bit of a shock to see him waiting for me outside the gym. I never even recognised him, he had to clothesline me to get my attention.'

'He turned up at the gym?'

'Yeah. I mean, he obviously knew he'd get me there. Said he'd seen me going in and out a few times, he lives down in Newhaven, at the new flats on the shore.'

I didn't know where Hod was going, but I had a few alarm bells ringing. 'Okay. So what did he want?'

Hod unclasped his fingers and sat back in the sofa, 'Well, he said he'd given your name to a friend of his who was looking for someone like you.'

'Wait a minute. Would this be a car dealer down at Newhaven by any chance?'

Hod reached for his beer, 'No idea, he never said.'

I watched Hod fire down the remainder of the Beck's and sink further into the sofa. 'Don't get comfortable,' I stood up, fully aware of the purpose of Hod's visit now. 'I'm about to crash out, gonna hit the hay.'

Hod rose to face me. 'So, are you back in action? Because if so …'

'No, mate. I'm not back in action. I have a job already. And to be honest, after your previous sojourns into the role you'd be the last man I'd be asking to ride point.'

'Oh, come on. That's unfair.'

'Is it? Do I list the arrests? The floggings? The misadventures? Or, how about, the seedy run-ins with gangsters, multiple thugs, hot-heads, men with guns! The list goes on, Hod, you're a walking disaster and about as useful a wingman as fucking Cheech is to Chong.'

'Okay, no worries.' He moved for the door.

I was surprised how well my talk had went, but maybe I'd gone too far. 'You mean that's it? No put up? No argument? Just, "Okay"?'

'Gus, I think we both know we're getting a little too old for this racket. You're probably right, we should avoid all excitement at our age.'

I laughed him up. 'Yeah, and reverse psychology won't work either, mate.'

'As you say, Gus.'

'Don't wind me up, Hod. I'm not falling for your Jedi mind tricks ...'

'I know. And I'm in full agreement.' He opened the door, walked into the stairwell and turned round, raising his index finger towards the ceiling. 'Gus, sorry to have bothered you, I'll let you get some sleep.'

He'd overdone it now, said, 'Fuck off.'

'I'm going.'

'And, I'm not taking on a job, even if it's for a friend of Bruce's.'

'I hear you.'

'I mean it. Get going.'

'I'm gone already.'

I slammed the door behind him, but could still hear Hod mumbling to himself as he headed down the hall towards the front door.

I'm eight, no more.

I know that because I can hear my baby brother crying.

My mam is crying too, sobbing. I know it's worse than that, though. The sobbing hides the screams she's trying to hold back, hold inside her. There's fear there too, I can feel it inside me as well.

I'm on my knees in the back garden. It's a nice day, sunny. The sky's a shade of blue I hardly recognise, it's the colour of holiday brochures and cowboy films from America. The sky looks strange above my head, like it doesn't belong, doesn't go with the sounds of crying and screaming and the intimidating bellow of my father's voice.

'Give me it!' he yells. 'Hand it fucking over or I won't be responsible for my actions.'

He always says that. But it doesn't mean anything. Even at eight I know what he's responsible for.

I start to dig in the ground with my fingers. My nails break the hard-packed soil after a while but it's brittle and dry. My fingertips get sore, the earth pushes its way under my nails and soon they start to bleed. The pain becomes unbearable but I can't stop.

'What have you done with it?' I hear my father yell again. His voice is growing frantic. I know when he gets like that it cannot last. Someone always gets in the way of his anger, sacrifices themselves for the rest of us.

'I'll fucking hammer you!' He strikes my mother and she screams alongside my brother Michael, the babe in her arms.

I stop digging and freeze. For a moment I can't draw breath, my heart beats so hard I can feel it in my chest and I think it will soon jump out of my mouth and into the hole below.

I look down. My pathetic scratchings have barely moved the topsoil. I reach down for the jam jar full of pennies beside my handiwork. The pennies are for the baby's christening, it's all mam has talked about since she came home from the hospital with the baby. And now he wants those pennies for drink.

'Run, Angus!' I hear my mum, she's nearer, I turn and see her at the backdoor. My father is pushing past her, a great scowl cutting his brows like a battle wound.

'Stay put!' he tells me, his voice so full of threat I can hardly move. But, I do.

I turn from him, back to the ground, and snatch up the pennies. They feel cold inside their glass shell but my hot hands throb around them. For a moment I wonder what to do, do I run for the gate? Do I try to make it over the wall?

'Gus…' he shouts, I know he senses my desire to run. I clasp the pennies tighter, hide them under my jumper.

'Gus…' I hear his steps now. I know if I run I will save the pennies for Michael's christening but I also know he will take it out on Mam and the others.

'Gus…' I hear his voice ringing in my ears, he's so close I can feel the ground trembling beneath me. My hands start to tremble too and then I feel it spread all over.

There's a loud pop as the jam jar slips to the ground. The pennies clatter and wheeze over the jagged shards of glass and the flat of the soil. For a moment I watch the sight in a kind of slow state of disbelief, did it really happen? I know it did when I hear my father's roar.

'Gus…'

'Gus…'

'Gus…'

'—*What?*' I was bolt upright in bed. The sweat streaming off me as I kicked back the duvet and leaped to my feet.

Shakes. I slapped my arms to try and wake myself. But, something worse, I was spooked.

I flicked on the light and looked around, wondering if I really was alone.

I got back into bed. But I kept the light on. And why wouldn't I? When I can still hear my father's voice ringing in my ears, calling my name.

CHAPTER 3

My bed felt uncomfortable as I woke — got up and headed for the kitchen. I'd been told to avoid coffee, whilst coming off the sauce, because it could trigger another addiction. It didn't take much to sell me on the idea, given I was usually revved up without the caffeine. So, tea it was.

The skyline beyond the window was a jagged grey smear, bearing down on the horizon. The picture was near drained of all colour, like the classic Lowry view with miserable matchstick men and women. Why did I stay here? There were other parts of the world with sunshine and blue skies, just what was it keeping me in Edinburgh? I seemed to be asking myself that more and more now. A change was coming.

The nightmares were another new worry for me to puzzle over. They'd first cropped up, infrequently, about a month ago but had started to intensify now. I thought I was coping with them at first, brushing them aside, but last night's one was a new low. A vivid, haunting reminder of the worst times of my life. My father's brutality stalked me not just for the hurt he caused me, but for the wounds I'd watched him inflict on others.

'Gus...' I could still hear his voice in my ears. The heavy timbre, the raw roar I remembered him using on the football pitch. It was like a warning siren that had been installed in me all those years ago; it didn't matter how long it had been since I last heard it, the fear it lit was still the same.

When they buried my father I thought I'd chucked all the thoughts I had of him in the casket. I'd been through enough by that stage, trying to figure out just what his problem had been. The conclusion I came to was far from a definitive answer but it sufficed, it was: who gives a fuck? Rattling those thoughts around inside me had solved nothing then and I doubted they'd solve anything now.

I put the cup in the sink and made a start on the day. I showered and dressed in a new pair of grey 501s, a black T-shirt and a matching black hoodie with a red Nike swoosh at the breast. I was booting up the laptop to see what fresh bollocks Terry had sent me work-wise when the landline rang.

'You up and about, then?' It was Hod.

'Isn't that self-evident?' After last night's chat, I should have predicted round two wouldn't be far away.

'Just checking.' I heard some shuffling at the other end of the line, then, 'So, what are you up to today?'

'I'm about to check my workload, then I'm picking up my car from the garage at noon.'

'Want a lift?'

I thought about the offer for a moment, it would be a distraction from work, which was probably just what I needed. 'That would be grand ... cheers, Hod.'

'Right. Sorted. I'll see you about twelve, then.'

He hung up, sounding almost perky, which didn't ring true for Hod at all. Since getting his building firm running again he'd gone from workaholic to total slacker almost overnight. He was a typical type-A personality — always looking for his next Everest but once he'd climbed it the crash to earth could be brutal.

My inbox had a heap of stories from Terry for rewrite, they were all garbage — just celebrity gossip. Ed fucking Sheeran had a new album out — I bet it sounded just like the last one and had all the heart of a styrofoam cup.

I also had a stack of press releases written by school-leavers that would once have required me to spend hours on the phone fact-checking. Fortunately, no one cared these days whether your facts were right or wrong. We lived in the post-truth era and the public were happy enough to stay anaesthetised by any slop you put in front of them. Who was I to buck the system? I made a 'to do' list of the day's workload and did what everyone else does before lifting a finger nowadays — checked Facebook.

Truth told, I bloody hated Faceache, with a passion. But it documented a sort of societal atrophy that didn't make me feel so bad about my own steady decline. It was like the worst of train wreck television, I mean, who gave two fucks what your lunch looked like or whether you had a new integrated dishwasher? It had turned us into mouth-breathing morons, all looking for anything to distract from the painful process of thought. Because these days, thought really was the one thing you wanted to avoid.

I scrolled away, emptying great lumps of my life into the process. Time I'd never get back. Time that could have been better spent doing just about anything other than sitting in a room, on my own, pretending to be social. There was one nugget of good news I did manage to unearth in the process, though. U2 had cancelled a concert due to Bono's sore throat. Anything that shut that gobshite's yap for a few minutes was worth celebrating in my book. I may even have smiled at the screen.

The banging on my door meant one of only two things, either Desperate Dan was in town or Hod had arrived. I looked at the clock and sighed at the amount of time I'd wasted in Zuckerberg's alternative reality. I rose and headed for the door, snatching my Crombie from the peg as I went.

'To what do I owe this honour, Hod?' I said.

'What else am I going to do all day, rattle about the house?'

Was glad Hod's Bedsit-land by the Sea empire was back to top form — restarting the housing market Ponzi with quantitative easing was a truly beautiful thing. I was less welcoming of the fact that it meant Hod was now hanging around my door like a fifteen year old trying to persuade me to duck out for a fly fag every five minutes. 'I have a job to do, y'know.'

'That job's a *carry on* and you know it.'

'Terry and June, as you call them, pay my wages, mate.'

'There's other ways to earn a crust.'

'Is this you picking up where you left off last night? Because if it is, my answer is still the same.'

Hod pointed the key at the Hilux, the blinkers flashed. On the way to Newhaven I kept a lit tab dangling from the window and tried to avoid chatter. Hod seemed antsy, like he was hoping to use the enclosed space to torture me into submission. I was scanning Leith Walk when I clocked on to a familiar figure.

'Holy shit!'

'What is it?' Hod turned towards me, the traffic had slowed to a halt.

'Over there.' I pointed to a shapely form, outside The Bed Shed, pushing a pram.

'Is that Amy?' said Hod, his voice rising towards a shrill disbelief.

There was no mistaking her, very few matched her in the looks department, especially from this angle. 'It's her all right.'

Hod pressed the horn and waved. I slapped down his arm. 'Fucking pack that in!'

'Sorry.' He tipped his head towards Amy, 'She didn't see me. Look, she's going in the big bed shop.'

I watched her negotiate the door with the giant pram, an old Silver Cross number, she struggled a bit but eventually a salesman came over and helped her out. It didn't look a comfortable process for her — truth told, I don't think I'd ever seen Amy look so bloody miserable in all my life. I wanted to jump out and give her a hand but something told me she wouldn't thank me, that I'd only be adding to her woes. As Amy got inside the store and turned her back on the street, the traffic started to ease again.

Hod put the truck into gear. We were past the Foot of the Walk and through the lights onto Great Junction Street before he spoke again.

'You okay, mate?'

'Yeah. Why wouldn't I be?'

'Well, it's just, you've gone a bit quiet.'

I flicked my tab out the window and sparked up another one. Something was irritating me about how keen Hod had been to flag down Amy. 'Did you know she had a nipper?'

'Gus, does it matter now?'

'Well, yes actually, because I'd like to know if my friends are lying to me.'

'I wasn't lying.'

'Well what do you call it? You obviously knew my ex had a child. Is she married now, or what?'

'Gus, I'm gonna pull over.'

Hod parked outside a greasy spoon caff, a rain-worn chalkboard outside yelled *bacon rolls for £1.50*. Neither of us needed to discuss Hod's choice — the laminated menu in the window told us that the place suited us both perfectly. Inside our PVC chairs wheezed with the weight of us, a comforting sound that yelled "home turf". I opted for tea and potato scones and watched a waitress in a powder-blue tabard, a face battered beyond her bad fifties, slouch off without a single word being spoken to us.

Hod was the first to break the hallowed silence. 'Mac met Amy in town a while back … she was still carrying then. He got the whole story or thereabouts but he asked me not to tell you.'

'Why?'

'Because you've just got your shit together, Gus. Mac thought, we both did really, that if you heard Amy had been in trouble you'd, y'know, flip.'

My tea came, a white mug with scratches cut in the rim from a million washes. 'What do you mean trouble?'

'Gus, do you really want to get into this? I know you remember — you have a tendency to go haring about like a lunatic when you think someone close to you has been hard done to.'

I sipped my tea, it was bitter, seemed to fit my mood. 'I just want to know. And you've kept this from me for long enough, whatever your reasons, so just cough it up and stop pussyfooting around.'

Hod leaned back in the wheezy chair and spoke, 'It's the same old story, when you split up she met some arsehole on the rebound and he knocked her up. I think she was expecting him to stand by her but he fucked off to Spain with another girl and left Amy to pick up the pieces. That's it, that's all I know.'

'Name?'

'I don't know his name and neither does Mac, far as I know. Look, what are you planning — a trip to Spain to re-educate him in more gentlemanly behaviour? Dream on, son.'

I gazed at Hod's face for a moment, he was staring into his mug and likely wondering what he'd just done. It was the face he wore to my alcoholics' intervention and the one he wore to every other one of my descents down the greasy pole of life. I had a solid coil of hot wire twisting in my gut, but it hadn't been put there by him.

Hod and Mac had my back. They always had my best interests at heart and I was grateful for that. But, hiding Amy's troubles from me was different. I felt like I'd let her down, like I should have been there for her, and I wanted someone to blame for that because the other option was something I wasn't prepared to face. I knew I could have tried to help her but I wasn't there when she needed me most and that scolded me.

I looked out the window and watched the stream of punters padding the streets. Everyone I saw was a potential enemy to me, everyone I stared at had the potential to cause harm to someone I cared for and there was nothing I could do about it. The anger twisted tighter and tighter until I got up and walked straight out the door.

CHAPTER 4

I didn't open my mouth again on the way to the car lot. Hod tried to speak a couple of times but I shot him down with glowers. We were in a state of perfect silence as we entered the gates and that kept up until I spotted the beer-gut owner trotting down the steps to greet us with our old friend Bruce in tow.

'Tell me you're kidding me,' I said.

Hod was locking the Hilux, looked up. 'Oh. Looks like Bruce dropped by.'

I wasn't buying it, especially after the earlier deception I'd uncovered. 'And you expect me to fall for that, do you? Jesus, Hod, you've planted Bruce here to help twist my arm ...' I was cut off by the pair's arrival.

Bruce spoke first, 'Gus, how goes it my old amigo?'

'Windae Willis, haven't seen you in donkey's.'

'You know me, like to keep a low profile.'

The lot owner stuck his hand at Hod. 'Lovely vehicle you have there ... My name's Andy Wallace, call me Wally.'

Bruce fired up again. 'Wally's been looking for a man like you, Gus ... Did you fill him in, Hod?'

Hod grimaced. 'No, he filled me in, Bruce.'

'What?'

I settled the conundrum. 'Hod's already told me that you're a friend of Wally's, Bruce.' I started to look around the lot, 'I don't see my car, is it ready?'

'It's just getting valeted. It'll be with us in a moment,' said Wally. 'Would you like to come in the cabin and wait?'

Like I had a choice.

The portacabin was cramped with the four of us squashed in there. Wally offered drinks but was rejected all round. I could tell at once that the plan was to try and kettle me into a corner and make it difficult to escape.

I took out my mobi and started to scroll. Nothing but endless emails and texts from Terry and Jayne asking why I hadn't filed anything yet. I was still carrying the anger from this morning's Amy revelation and the messages only added fuel to the inferno. I pocketed my mobi and found myself making eye contact with Wally.

'So, Mr Dury, did you get a chance to consider my proposition?'

'What did I tell you about calling me that? ... No, I mean, yes. But the answer's still no.'

Bruce sparked up, offered me a tab from a pack of B&H. 'Ah, sorry about that, Gus. I didn't realise you were back in the old journalism malarky when I recommended you to Wally.'

I lit my tab and nodded. 'Journalism's maybe too glamorous a term, but malarkey's on the money. And, yes, I'm out the investigative work right enough.'

'I did tell him that,' said Hod. 'But weren't you saying something about it being a friend of yours that was missing, Bruce?'

'More of a neighbour really, it's Wally's buddy. Maybe you could tell us the story, Wally?'

'If you don't mind, Gus?'

'We've time to kill.' I looked out the window, there was no sign of my car.

Wally kicked off with a yarn about how he met Lee Donald, his all-time top salesman, and general dogsbody from what I could gather. He ladled on the stuff about him being a great worker and the kind of bloke who would do anything for anyone, all you had to do was ask him. I was waiting for the bit about his charity work with the homeless and how he regularly donated to food banks, but thankfully, it didn't come. Either way, Lee Donald sounded too good to be true, which in my experience meant he definitely was.

Where Wally became more vague was the actual reasons why he wanted to get hold of Lee in such a hurry. That Lee had taken off without a word to anybody seemed to be the official line but I wasn't wearing it. There was no family, hardly any friends — apart from Wally, and his neighbour, Bruce — and no clue as to where Lee might be, or why he might have just disappeared.

'C'mon, Wally, are you sure this Lee character hasn't nicked off with your takings?' I prodded.

'What? Why would he do that?' said Wally, he locked his brows, but the rest of his face remained frozen in a sort of shock.

'What I'm getting at, Wally, is that from past form I know people disappear in this city when they don't want to be found. And the reason, generally, they don't want to be found, is because they've done something to someone.'

'No. It's not like that. Lee's a good lad, a decent bloke, I'm genuinely worried that something's happened to him. I can't sleep thinking that he's lying at the bottom of a ditch or something.'

'Why don't you try the police, then?'

'I've been to the filth, the bastards don't want to know. They said people take off all the time and that he's a big boy. They couldn't give two shits.'

I was squinting at Wally, trying to figure him out when my mobi started to ring. It was Terry. 'I better take this outside.'

'Where the bloody hell's all my copy?' Terry was fuming.

'The celebrity chatter you sent over earlier?'

'Yes, Gus, the new content that's supposed to be on the site hours ago!'

'Well, I had to go and collect my car, it's been up on bricks and I can't work without it. I'll get on the gossip stuff soonest.'

Hod appeared at the doorway and started to descend the stairs towards me. When he reached my side I could tell from his face that he could hear Terry bawling me out.

'Now, Gus, this is getting ridiculous. I pay your wages and what's more I know from contacting your previous employers that you have form for this sort of bad attitude.'

'Whoa, back-up there, Terry, what do you mean you contacted my previous employers?'

'I'm sick and tired of this nonsense from you, Gus. I am about an inch away from kicking you out the door and ...'

I cut him off. 'And so you thought you'd go and stir up some shit from my past to see if you could find any likeminded pricks to back up your plan to sack me?'

'What did you just say to me?' This was a tone of Terry's I hadn't heard before.

'I said that you're the type of arsehole that, not content with treating his staff like dogsbodies, actually goes as far as to rake around in their past work history to see if there's anything you can find to complain about there too. What were you hoping to find? That I had another boss who was an arsehole like you and that you could maybe get together and see who was the biggest arsehole of the lot? Terry, what you need to get into your head is that paying someone for their labour isn't the same as buying them outright. You're not a fucking slavemaster, you don't own me 24/7. What you do own is a ridiculous joke of a webzine that you think, somehow, gives you the status of a media magnate to rival William Randolph Hearst. Cop on, man! And when you're done with that, and still have the energy, you can take my job and shove it up your arse, sideways.'

Hung up.

As I slipped the phone in my pocket I caught sight of Hod's open mouth breaking into a face-splitting grin.

'Go, Gus.'

'The man had it coming.'

'I'd say he's got it now.'

'For all the good it'll do him, those types never learn.'

My Golf, bright and gleaming, pulled into the lot. As I made my way over to collect the keys from the driver I was followed by the others.

Wally seemed happy with the valeting job. 'You see, I told you, Gus, it'd be purring like a pussycat.'

Hod leaned over the door and spoke, softly, 'You realise you're going to have to find a way of paying for this motor now that you've packed in your job.'

I revved the engine — it never sounded sweeter.

'Give Wally the nod, would you?'

'I take it we're on then?'

'Well, what else am I going to do with my time?' Open days on my calendar had a way of turning into lock-ins at the pub.

Hod tapped the sill and nodded to Wally.

Wasn't sure what I was getting myself into, or whether it was simple anger displacement, but when was I ever wise?

CHAPTER 5

I couldn't call Wally the most reliable, or trusted, employer I'd ever had but after Terry he came over as agreeably as Gandhi. He sprung for expenses, upfront, and even countered my disdain for the offer of a cheque with a few fresh sheets pulled from his doorstop wad. Everything was Kool and the Gang. I was holding folding, back in work after the shortest lay-off on record, and looking at a case the boyos over the Atlantic might call a slam dunk.

Shoved the niggling concern that was rattling about in my gut right out, and made a start on finding Lee Donald. They called him Donnie but something told me he was a million miles away from the Osmond lad with the same name. The picture Wally had supplied showed a chancer with a broad grin, enough gel in his hair to make Nick Cotton stare, and a goldie-lookin' chain only a car salesman would think improved his appearance. There was a word that came to mind when I clocked his photo but Hod beat me to it.

'He looks a bit of a cock.'

'A bit? I'd be checking his feet to make sure he wasn't balanced on football-sized bollocks!'

Hod and I rarely disagreed on these things. We did disagree on how to find Donnie, though. After he pleaded to tag along I informed Hod he could consider himself "on call", as in I'd call if I found myself in desperate need of a burly nut-job who was prone to punch first and ask questions later, otherwise I was flying solo.

The picture of Donnie that Wally supplied was torn in two, it was clear that someone had been cut out but Wally had no comment on that, said it was the way he found it in Donnie's desk drawer. Scribbled on the back of the photo was Donnie's address. It was a fairly up-market flat for the Shore, but still the kind of place people went for when Stockbridge was just a notch out of reach.

I parked the Golf next to a black MX-5. When I got out I spotted another MX-5 — by the looks of things there were quite a few hairdressers living in this block. The buzzer on the back door had a *Services* button, I tried my luck and found it was still working for me — this was Edinburgh, couriers could still be delivering at 11pm — why was I surprised?

The stair was clean and sparse, not even a bike chained to the balustrade. You could really rate an Edinburgh neighbourhood by the state of the stair. In Morningside they had a thing for occasional carpeting, Yucca plants on Moroccan tables and the odd Colourist print on the walls. Down the Shore, it was potluck depending on how militant the stair committee was. Donnie's place was minimalist, verging on the spotless. My Irish granny would have said the place had "notions".

I took the shining steps — not even a dust ball kicking about — all the way to the third floor. The door to the flat appeared closed but when I applied a little pressure to the handle the wood separated effortlessly from the jamb. The sound of clunking and scratching from the dangling lock on the other side told me that something wasn't right. A quick look at the splinters on the floor, accompanied by a couple of bent screws, and I knew a jemmy had been in the hood. Donnie clearly hadn't been the last person to check-in at his place and whoever had been definitely wasn't the Avon lady.

Broken furniture.

Smashed telly.

A microwave in the living-room, so buckled that, by the looks of it, had been thrown from the kitchen.

The floorboards were bare and smashed glass crunched underfoot as I walked. Donnie was lucky — if I can use that word — not to have had very much furniture, because what was left had been well and truly wrecked. This was a purposeful going over. An angry statement of worse to come, for sure. Trashing a property this thoroughly was like therapy for a particular type of thug who was disappointed not to be distributing actual bodily harm.

So, somebody wasn't happy with the bold Donnie, that was a given.

I tried a few cupboards in the kitchen but only found crappy kids' cereal and pop tarts — the man obviously lived like a student. The cutlery drawer was tipped out, spoons and forks scattered all over the floor, but there was nothing for me to go on.

In the bedroom the mattress and duvet were cut to shreds, likewise the pillows. Down feathers danced about my Doc Martens on every step, like I was in some dodgy 80's music video. I opened a chest of drawers, hoping for anything, but there was nothing inside except stale air. There were a few items of clothing tipped to the floor — shirts, jeans, boxers — but no bags. I wondered if Donnie had been back and packed up a few things for a quick getaway?

The bathroom cabinet was empty too, not a toothbrush or a tin of Lynx. There was a full bottle of toilet duck but looking at the kip of the loo rim I'd say that had been there since he moved in. I was puzzled. My thoughts freestyling until the rattling of the bathroom window brought me back to Earth.

It was a small window with a single latch that was dangling into the street. The ledge was wet, we'd had some rain lately, and as I got closer I saw the wall was soaked, a moisture trail all the way to a squelching carpet.

I leaned out the window and saw there was a drainpipe running beside the ledge, all the way to the back green. The flat was three floors up but it wasn't beyond belief that someone could shimmy all the way down. Especially if their life depended on it.

I tried to see what was on the ground — there was an enclosure for the bins and the rest was a neat lawn that ran up to a more unruly border with the neighbouring block of flats.

It was one of those pictures. Something bothered me but I couldn't make out what. There was the bin depot, the beautifully shadow-striped lawn, and the jungle of a border. All that registered, but something wasn't right. There were broken branches on the ground, the long grass there was trampled. Had there been a scuffle? I decided to head back to the stairs for a closer look.

On the way out, closing the door behind me, I spotted a thin man with a laundry bag putting a key in the door of the flat opposite.

Said, 'Hello, there.'

He nodded, looked more than a bit scoobied. Neighbourly chat was a dying art in the city. Who needs real people to talk to when you have a flatscreen telly and an internet connection?

'I'm a friend of Donnie's, I was wondering if you'd seen him of late?'

'Who?'

Pointed to the door I'd just left. 'Donnie … Lee Donald, your neighbour.'

'I'm sorry, I don't have much to do with him.'

'What about the other neighbours?'

He eased inside his door, clutching the laundry bag to his chest like a child with a giant teddy bear, almost hiding behind it. 'No. I wouldn't know about them either. People tend to keep themselves to themselves in here. Everyone works, you know how it is. You hardly see anyone, only coming and going.'

Nodded. 'What about a disturbance?'

'Disturbance? No. I wouldn't know about that. Ask the factor, he files all the complaints.' The scrawny man went inside and closed the door, one of the laundry bag's handles got trapped and the door sprung again but was quickly slammed shut. I wondered if he drove an MX-5?

Welcome to the modern world. Everyone so ensconced in their own little compartmentalised kingdoms, so stuck to their multiple screens, that they don't even know who is living next door. Society was sowing seeds of deep division; we weren't made to live like this. I pondered the fate of all the families that lived in Leith, it took me back to my childhood, the flash reminder promptly told me to bury a thousand questions at once.

I trotted down to the back green, jamming open the outside door with my Zippo lighter. The grass was wet, squelching. The green didn't seem to have been used in a long time. No footprints, no signs of activity at all. Of course, coming out here might mean meeting the people who lived under the same roof, which wasn't a prospect worth entertaining.

At the bourne of the yard, where the smooth lines bled into rugged and untrammelled bushland, it was a different story.

Standing beneath the bathroom window of Donnie's flat I could see the route he might have taken down the drainpipe. I followed the path out to the tree-line and looked beneath the scrub. There was nothing there. I don't know what I was expecting to find — Donnie's crumpled and decaying body from a three-floor fall perhaps?

I stepped back from the wet branches and, getting nowhere looking down, decided to look up.

And there it was.

A small black holdall, what might have once been called a weekend bag, hanging on a branch.

It was out of my reach. At least twelve-to-fifteen feet above my head. I picked up one of the damp, fallen branches and tried to unhook the bag but it wasn't long enough.

I envisioned a desperate Donnie trying to perform this same rescue in a hurry — perhaps a couple of burly pugs in hot pursuit — and giving up in favour of saving his neck. I would have done the same thing, being very fond of my neck the way it is, but now I had time on my side.

On the third attempt at lobbing the wet branches I dislodged the bag, which being lighter than it looked, fell cleanly into my arms.

CHAPTER 6

'*I just don't know where to begin ...*' Elvis Costello, prophetic as ever, started on the speakers as I put in the car key.

On the road back to my flat in the East End I had some time to ponder what I'd just locked in the boot. Donnie's holdall, from what I'd seen of it so far, looked to be a hastily packed affair, but I didn't feel right digging into it out in the open.

The whole scene had me a little shaken. Wally hadn't mentioned anything about Donnie being on the run, but the way things looked he was definitely legging it, and at full pelt. It wasn't the filth he was fleeing either. That, I reckon, I could handle. You knew where you stood with plod, but the hardy lads were another story entirely.

In this city, when someone takes enough interest in you to turn your furniture into sawdust and send you shimmying down the drainpipe it's safe to assume that serious people have been pissed off.

I hoped Donnie found enough time to pack plenty underwear because by the look of it, I'd say the lad was currently dropping his arse, with some regularity. This wasn't going to play out as easily as I first thought. I cursed Hod for yanking me back into the world of Edinburgh's knuckle-breakers with grudges. I knew I shouldn't bother, though, it was a decision I'd entered into with my eyes open. Wally had fed me a line, for sure, but I'd known about that from the moment he opened his trap.

Coming off the top of the Walk and onto London Road Costello started on 'Peace, Love and Understanding.' The line "What's so funny about that?" always made me smile because the song was a favourite of my ex-wife's. I shuddered to think about Debs — it was the second time today that she'd entered my thoughts. Or to be more specific, the child we'd lost together was on my mind again.

I flicked off the CD and took the car down Easter Road, parking up on Rossie Place. I tried to block everything out, get in the now, but I'd never been very good at burying my emotions. I tended to be a lot better at drowning them. I grabbed Donnie's bag and headed for the flat, crossing the road early to make sure I'd avoid the offie.

The flat was cold and gloomy, matching my mood.

The curtains — open wide to the street — exposed me to more of the world than seemed advisable in my current state of mind. I thought to close them but resisted. Locking out reality had been what I'd done with drink for way too long. I was starting to accept that, if I wanted to stay sober, it meant facing up to the things I'd previously hidden from.

Call it my own version of pop psychology if you like, but nothing else had worked for me. A bottle of scoosh and a few tins of Mick Jagger numbed the pain, even worked as a valve for the anger, but lately something else had come into play: mortality.

At some stage in every drinker's life comes a realisation, screamed from a body that can no longer cope. What you got away with before is no longer possible. Of course, some carry on. Go all out. And I've been to those meetings with the ones who have swapped interior plumbing for exterior fittings. It's never pretty, and something to be avoided whilst the will still has, at least some, strength.

I turned on the table light, tried to banish the doom, and took up Donnie's holdall. The zip stuck a little, being out in the elements will do that, but eventually opened without too much fuss.

Inside, sitting on top, was a black T-shirt. Not folded, more like bundled in there. More T-shirts. Some socks and jocks. A pair of unworn Converse All Stars. A toilet bag with an orange Bic razor. Tube of toothpaste. Badger brush. Spare razors.

A pile of junk was building on my coffee table.

Grey Adidas joggers was the last item to come out. Was about to chuck the joggers on the pile of junk when I spotted a zipped pocket with something inside. A black diary, also well-worn, with a few pages coming away from the spine. It seemed to have been used as a telephone directory, all names and numbers added in block capitals, like it was important to be clearly legible for the reader. I glanced at a few names but didn't recognise any — put the diary down.

The rest of the bag was empty, except for one more small item. At the very bottom of the bag was a photograph. There were two men and a girl in the picture: a Christmas scene in a heavily-tinselled home with a tree and presents on the floor. I recognised the men — Wally and Donnie — but I had no idea who the young woman was.

I eyeballed the scene for a moment or two, then slipped the photograph in the back of the little diary and returned both to the table.

Was booting up my laptop, to see what else I could unearth about Donnie when my mobi started.

Ringing.

'Howdy, squire. Any joy on the case?' It was Hod.

'Are you shitting me? I just got started.'

'All right, calm down, just checking up.'

'Yeah, well don't. I told you I'd let you know when, or if, I needed you.'

Hod let out an audible sigh. 'Did you check on his pad?'

'Totally wrecked. And I mean wrecked.' I let the tone of my voice sink in for Hod. He seemed to catch on that I knew Donnie's disappearance wasn't as straightforward as Wally had made out.

'You think he's been worked over too?' said Hod.

'No idea. There was neither hide nor hair of him. I'll tell you this much though: Wally better hope I find him before whoever else is on the sniff, because I don't think they're the friendliest.'

'Sounds to me like Wally's not revealing the whole story … And also like you could do with someone at your back.'

I laughed him up. 'Yes and no, Hod. And by that I mean, *yes* Wally's been at it and *no* I haven't caved on my earlier plan to keep you at arm's length.'

'But …'

'But nothing, mate.' I said. 'Tell you what you can do for me though. There's a photo I picked up from Donnie's stuff, and there's a girl in it. Brown hair, maybe mid-twenties, does she ring any bells?'

'Not with me. Have you asked Wally?'

'No. Maybe I'll do that. Maybe it's not important.'

Hod steered the chat again, 'So what's the next step?'

He was angling now. 'I get back to work. Bye, Hod.'

Hung up.

I stared at my phone for a moment. My finger was twitching, that way when you can't quite decide to make the call or not, when, 'Fuck it…'

I scrolled down my contacts and found Amy's number. I was likely to regret this but something possessed me, pushed me towards pressing *call*.

The icon changed to a jingling receiver and I put the phone on speaker. The tinny noise of the line connection bounced off the walls, fair rattled my nerves. There was a jumble of thoughts racing through me, chief among them: What would I say?

I didn't find an answer and then my thinking shifted once more: What the hell would *she* say? It had been some time since I spoke to Amy. We hadn't parted on bad terms. It was more a case of my immaturity; a bitter irony considering the age gap between us had all the years stacked on my side. You could say drink played a part too, but when did it never?

I was nearing panic mode, a constriction in my throat that threatened to strangle my efforts at speech, when I was thrown a get out.

The line died, cut to voicemail.

I pressed *end call*.

For a moment I felt enormous relief, and then I found myself wondering if Amy had seen my name next to the incoming call and decided to ignore me? It didn't feel like something Amy would do — she had always been so forthright about her interest in me — but I didn't know. The next thought to arise was that perhaps she had every right to ding me now, after all, what kind of a friend retreats as far as I had?

I was more concerned than ever about Amy now. And worse, I was worried that she didn't even know she had someone who cared anymore.

I pocketed my mobi because the sight of it on the table only reminded me of my own bloody stupidity.

CHAPTER 7

Every time I went on Faceache I was reminded of the fact that Zuckerberg kept the camera on his computer covered with a piece of Blu-Tack. There was a meme kicking about of the gawky geek, in his usual gimpy-casual T-shirt — sans logo, of course, because there was getting down with the sheeple and there was actually promoting brands other than FB to them — a PC behind Zuck had the camera obscured. It said it all to me: the man snooping on billions of us doesn't like being snooped on.

Still, Faceache was here for now, though if you thought it wasn't going to crash and burn eventually, then I had a Myspace account to sell you. I pulled up Donnie's page and took a deck. It was an eye opener.

My own stream was full of virtue signalling about Trump and the Tories. Boomers with no skin in the game commenting on a future they wouldn't see. By the time the real shit hit the fan they'd have cashed in their chips. It was refreshing to see the faces occupying Donnie's page were blissfully unaware of anything occurring outwith their own group of friends. It was mainly piss-ups. A beer-fuelled bowling night at the Sheep's Heid seems to have been a proper gas for the lads. I was going through the photos when I spotted someone I thought I recognised.

'Aye, aye,' I double-clicked on the image. 'Oh, I know you all right.'

It was the girl from the photograph I found in Donnie's bag earlier. She looked a little subdued, not exactly getting into the swing of things but it was a rowdy lads' night out so I gave her a pass. The girl was wearing a super-heavy Arran jumper indoors and seemed to be drinking orange juice, which made her stick out a bit further. The other girls nearby looked legless, like they'd be carrying their shoes and squatting in the gutter for a piss on the way home.

I thought about checking Donnie's friends list for this mystery girl but there was more than four-hundred friends on his dashboard and it seemed like a big ask, especially when I could get the same result by asking Wally. I kept scrolling but it was all more of the same. Drinking, trips to the footy, the occasional crashed-out dude with a cock and balls marker-penned onto his forehead, that sort of thing.

The last entry on Donnie's page was from a week ago at a drinker in Leith called The Buck. I couldn't say I knew it, though I knew of it. Even in my shambolic, drunk, swilling about the streets state, The Buck was a fair schlep from my manor. Going by Donnie's Facebook page though, it seemed to me he was a bit of a regular at this drinker.

I checked the time, had a couple of hours before the punters would be piling in. Any that were in post already would be insensate, part of the furniture. I closed up the laptop and looked for something to eat. Bread breaking out in blue spores and a can of Barr's Cream Soda didn't impress me. I guess it'd have to be the instant noodles, then.

* * *

The Buck reminded me of a particular type of pub that was rare these days in our tarted up and pimped out capital city. I remembered my old man knocking back pints of heavy, sometimes black and tans, in great thick, double-glazed tankards. Those pint jugs made a reassuring sound when clattered down on the bar, which was usually solid hardwood, stained black by the bucketloads of beer it'd been soaked in, day in and day out.

Cannis Dury was a regular feature in those old drinking dens. Just like the yellowed walls and the thick pall of smoke that hung over proceedings. My father seemed, to me, at home there. Mam would send myself and my brother to drag him home for his tea, or to extract rent money from him if the landlord — a bastard in a black homburg — appeared.

Cannis wouldn't exactly welcome us, he was never a welcoming man, never that. But in those old pubs with the stained-glass windows and the frosted-glass snugs he was approachable in a way he never was at home. Perhaps it was the presence of other people, witnesses that might change their opinion of the mighty Cannis Dury if he was to be seen felling a child with a back-hander. Or perhaps he was just that bit happier there, away from home, away from his family.

For years his ways had bothered me. I didn't know why my father drank or battered us all and I never found the answer. For a long time I simply didn't care, I just wanted to wash him out of my mind and I found the drink he was so fond of worked for me too. Something like a calcified hatred formed over all those memories and I truly believed that the barrier could never be broken but something was changing.

As I looked around the bar, it was like he was there in the room with me, just like the times I'd wake from nightmares re-running his brutality. I wanted to shake out the old hurts,

47

watch them fall onto the hard floor and stamp them down but I knew that wasn't going to be an option. Only the drink had kept them at bay before and facing the smug chops of Captain Morgan before me I was sorely tempted.

'This isn't your local.' I turned to see a battered face, creased like an old hankie. The blue nose, wreathed in broken veins, twitched as he cued up another gambit, 'I'm saying, what's that you're drinking?'

'You offering to buy me another?'

'That'll be right ... It looks like water.'

'It is.'

He tutted. Shook his head and returned to his wee goldie. He didn't lay eyes on me again.

The rest of the bar shared the old boy's demographic. Dole moles and off-duty cleaners. A couple of wifies in anoraks — dating back to the seventies — who looked like they were just stopping off on their way to the bingo. I tried a few with Donnie's picture but got nothing but head shakes. I was starting to feel weary when a big biffer in a black leather waylaid me by the cigarette machine.

'What's that you're showing around?' he said.

'A picture of a local man, used to drink in here ... he's missing.' I held up the photograph.

The pug took the picture in a hand full of sovereign rings and had a look. He didn't seem overly interested, passing it to the barman after a glance, 'You know this joker, Davey?' he said.

The barman was leaning on the bar and only needed to alter his line of sight to see Donnie's image. 'Who wants to know?'

'Yeah, that's a good question,' said the pug, towering over me, 'Who wants to know?'

I sensed any more questions might end with me wearing the imprint of four sovies on my face so eased off. I lied, 'He's just a friend of mine, nobody special.'

I picked up the photo from the bar and headed outside. I was sparking up another tab when an old woman in baffies came out of the bar behind me.

'Can I grab a light, son?' she said.

I was always a sucker for oldies. 'Sure thing.'

She was smoking Super-kings, must have been no less than eighty, and raking the whole street with a cough like a howitzer. I liked the cut of her jib, went for broke. 'Do you recognise this bloke, my dear?'

She took up Donnie's photo and started to nod instantly. 'Och, of course, that's Lee Donald.'

'You know him?'

'I knew the Donalds when they were living up our close, but that's a few years ago now. Lee's doing well for himself.'

'He is?'

'Oh, yes. Big motor — a Jag — and everything. You still see him driving about now and again, don't think he lives too far away. He was in young Morag's chippy on the London Road just the other night there.'

I wanted to pick her up and give her a bear hug. She was one of those Leithers that would talk all day and all night, non-stop.

'What chippy's that?' I said.

She looked scoobied. 'There's only the one, son ... Aldo's, my grand-niece works there at night.' I thought she had stopped but it was just a pause. 'Donnie goes in with that lassie of his. He stays in the big car and sends her in every night around half-seven. I don't think he wanted to leave the car because there's some dafties around there and, y'know, with a car like that it could get damaged or even pinched.'

I nodded. It was like encouragement to her.

'Mind you, Lee Donald would know all about the dafties from round here — it's not that long since he was one of them himself. I think he must still be friendly with a few of them, I quite often see him talking to them out the window of that big flashy motor of his.'

She was getting into her stride when the big lad in black leather appeared again. I dowped my cig on the cobbles and took a step back just in time to see a second lump appear. This one was attached to an English bull terrier on a choke chain and neither looked like they were off to the park to throw a ball about.

'Is this muppet bothering you, Ina?' he said.

He didn't get an answer, only shrugs. He'd broken Ina's stride but he wasn't about to break mine. I nodded my thanks to the old girl and headed back to the car.

I'd parked further away than seemed wise now, as I stretched out my steps. I could hear the dog barking, and one quick turn showed me the jaws closing like a steel trap. I picked up the pace, crossing the road to the street where I'd parked. I probably had twenty or thirty yards on them but a good two-hundred yards to the car.

'Fuck ...' I had a slim chance of outrunning the muscle-bound biffers but a voice in my head, sounding not unlike C3-PO, was telling me the odds of outrunning the fighting dog were the same as successfully navigating a meteor storm: precisely 750-1.

CHAPTER 8

I heard the dogs barking, they were getting louder, which meant closer. I adjusted the threat level accordingly — legged it, full pelt. Pain shot through my thighs as my unused muscles screamed in protest. It had been a long time since I'd taken any kind of exercise; you could say I was one of those people who didn't like getting out of breath. Bollocks, you could say I didn't like getting out of bed if I could help it.

As I made it to the car door, my heart was pounding. I rifled my pockets for the keys to the Golf. Did that whole pat-down thing, slapping my hips and chest. That nugget off the telly started singing in my head: *"Where me keys? Where me phone?"*

Yelled out, 'Just fuck off now!'

The tune died as I found the car keys in my Crombie pocket. I got the door open and was stepping inside when I felt a dart hit the back of my calf.

'Jesus ...' I looked down to see a blur of white attached to me, shaking my leg out of its socket. The pain was intense.

I raised my right foot, brought a heavy blow down on the dog's head. I repeated the move three or four times and the dog slunk off whimpering. 'Get yourself to fuck.'

There was another parcel of teeth and jaws propelling itself towards me, but I got the door closed in time to avoid

51

any more injury. As I turned over the engine the two beasts jumped at the driver's window taking bites out of thin air. Their slobbering covered my window in frothy, white spit but I was glad to be on the other side of the glass.

I nodded to the bouncing beasts. 'Good luck with that, lads.'

I gunned the engine, put it in first, as I spotted the two pugs pegging it in the rearview. They looked about as fit as me, and were carrying a fair bit of weight between them. I was relieved to hear the tyres spin as I let out the clutch, could have given two shits if I drove over the dogs.

At the end of the street I chucked a quick right and headed deeper into Leith. I didn't care where I was going, so long as it was far away from anything with jaws like a mantrap.

'Close one,' I told myself. Hod was right, I was defo getting too old for this caper.

I had a mad idea to take up some kind of cardio fitness, but then a craving for nicotine struck and wiped out the thought. I sparked up a red top and it seemed to settle my thoughts. My leg was bleeding all over the place, I felt the blood pooling and squelching in my boot. I needed to stop and sort it. Mac's barber's shop was the nearest place, so I headed for his street and grabbed the first park going.

I was hobbling, not a full-on limp, but it was hard to put my foot down. When I did, the blood escaped through the lace-holes in my Docs. I thought of the Haye v. Bellew fight, and Haye's brutal Achilles injury — was I dragging myself around like that? — Felt like I'd gone a few rounds.

The bell clanged as I limped into Mac's shop.

'Bugger me,' he yelled out, 'look what the cat dragged in ...'

'Er, it was a dog, actually.'

Mac was cutting a bloke's hair, he shrugged and made a bemused face. The bloke in the chair kept his eyes on the razor in Mac's hand; didn't blame him, I'd be doing the same.

'Where are you going?' said Mac.

'Out back, you got a first-aid box?'

Now Mac noticed the trail of bloody footprints leading from the door.

'Jesus, Dury, you're trailing claret all through my shop ...' He motioned the customer that he was finished and the bloke took off the barber's apron, dumped it on the chair.

I headed through to the small cubicle that passed for a toilet and removed my boot. It came off with no effort as the laces were soaked in blood and beyond useless. I tipped the boot towards the sink, what looked like a quarter pint of my blood and sweat poured out.

'Dury, you okay in there?' said Mac.

'Just give me a minute.' I lifted my calf into the small sink and let the cold water tap run. The white porcelain turned red, then pink, then returned to white as the blood went down the plughole.

I could see a small puncture above my shin, like an entry wound from a knitting needle. On the other side of my calf was a more ragged, jarring wound that looked like a bad attempt at filleting salmon. I squeezed the skin together and another red overflow poured out.

'Shit.'

'What is it?' said Mac.

I edged the door open, 'Take a look for yourself.'

'That's gross. In a good way, mind. I'd be happy if that was my handiwork, leave a cracking Mars Bar so it will. What happened?'

'It's this job for a friend of Bruce's. Some pug set his hounds on me.'

'Bruce, you mean Windae Willis?'

'Some mate of his has gone missing. It sounded like a straight forward enough gig, but now I'm not so sure.'

Mac eased out the door, 'Come on, I'll dress that leg for you, but it's going to need stitches.'

'Brilliant. Just what I wanted to hear.'

Mac brought through the first-aid box and put some cotton wadding on the open wound. The blood started to appear quickly through the bandage as Mac wrapped it round my leg. The throbbing started in earnest when he tightened up the bandage.

'That'll hold it for now, but you'll need to get to the Royal and get that closed up properly. Probably need some jabs too, I'd say.'

I tossed Mac my car keys. 'You're due a lunch-break. I'll ride shotgun.'

On the road out to the Royal, Mac delved. 'Windae Willis, now that's a name I haven't heard in many moons.'

'He's one of the old school crew. Never left town, so he crops up now and again. Decent bloke, no badness in him.'

Mac spun the wheel, turned left to avoid queuing traffic at the junction. 'And Bruce put you onto this job?'

'Well, you could say Hod put me onto this job.'

'Hod? Jesus, don't tell me he's Ramboing it up.'

I was sitting in the back to elevate my leg, to stop the blood spilling out like a waterfall. 'Hod's bored. He's built the business up again and now he's looking for adventure … and whatever comes our way.'

'Boy's born to be wild for sure. Hope he's not leading you astray.'

My mind turned back to the day when I spoke to Hod about Amy. I wanted to chin Mac about keeping their little secret. Mac was always easier to read than Hod, he had an intrinsic honesty that made it impossible for him to bullshit you. I went for broke, 'I saw Amy the other day.'

Caught Mac's eyes shifting in the rearview mirror. His expression changed, his face growing longer somehow. Was it shock?

'Look, Gus, I wanted to tell you,' he said.

'Tell me what?'

'About Amy, and the bairn.' We caught some red lights, Mac pulled on the handbrake and turned to face me, 'I just, y'know, how do you bring something like that up?'

'Pick up the phone maybe ...'

He was taking the confrontation hard. It started to guilt me, said, 'Look, what does it matter? I know now.'

The lights changed. A car's horn blared behind us. Mac shot the finger out his window and pulled away.

'Are you going to get in touch with her?' said Mac.

'I don't know. I tried to call her last night, it was difficult.'

'The longer you leave it, the more difficult it'll be.'

He wasn't wrong, but I didn't acknowledge it. The Amy situation was complicated, would require proper handling. I didn't know if I was ready for that kind of baggage. The way things were shaping up, I'd have my hands full with other stuff. I shelved the thought as we reached the carpark of the Royal.

'By the way, have you got any plans for tonight?' I asked Mac.

'No. Why?'

'Thought you might fancy a trip to Aldo's.'

'The chippie?'

'The very same. Thought we could bring Hod along too, make a night of it.'

'Christ, Gus, you make it sound so enticing, it's very hard to refuse. Will you throw in a pickled onion?'

Laughter, it made my leg hurt. 'I'll throw in two!'

'Aldo's chipper it is then,' said Mac, 'I can hardly wait.'

CHAPTER 9

The receptionist on accident and emergency looked like she could have named every *Pop Idol* winner of the last ten years. She was tatted, blue-haired and had a ring through her septum with a silver ball that was obviously irresistible to her tongue. I got an eyeful of powder-blue hair — it was being threatened at the roots by rapid black growth — as she ignored the lengthening queue by scribbling on a stack of Post-it notes.

'Excuse me,' I kept my tone low. She looked up, her gaze was utterly vacant. I reckon I could have listed every original thought she'd ever had on one of those Post-its. 'I have a bad wound ... dog bite actually.'

She stared at me for a moment, letting my words sink in, then she turned to her computer terminal and punched a few keys. A printer on the desk spat out a reel of paper. The blue-haired girl took the paper and circled a number in the corner with her pen. 'Current waiting times are displayed above the desk. Follow the yellow line on the floor when your number's called.'

I took the paper and retreated to the seating area. Mac followed, rolling his eyes up in his head and twirling a finger beside his ear.

'What is it with kids these days?' he said. 'I swear each generation gets softer in the head.'

'It's everyone, Mac, we're in the Kali Yuga.'

'Y'what?'

'The end times, you know, before we enter the new Dark Ages. We've all been brainwashed, gaslit, taught to believe the important things are the footie scores and what Liz Hurley's wearing to Cannes this year.'

'I blame the parents.'

'I blame Farcebook, it's like an echo chamber. It's turned everyone into wooly-minded hippies, repeating all the shit they see there like it has some meaning.'

'I can't even talk to these young ones, though. When they come into the shop I'm scoobied for conversation.'

'It's because they've never known anything else. They've grown up with their beaks in phones, being battered by the mainstream media's political correctness. Everything's wrong-think to them, I'd hate to be a kid today, it'd be like living in a straitjacket.'

Mac nodded, 'Imagine that. And only fucking Ed Sheeran to listen to.'

We laughed a bit too loudly for the waiting room; the girl with blue hair shot us a glower. 'Watch out, Gus. Smurfette's gunning for us now.'

More laughs. This would have to stop. The buzzer chimed and the screen changed, we were saved by the bell.

'Y'know, Mac, I don't think Smurfette had blue hair.'

'You're right, she was a bottle blonde, now I think of it — bet the collars didn't match the cuffs.'

Laughter, and tears this time. 'Stop now. It only hurts when I laugh, y'know.'

We followed the yellow line through to the doctor's surgery. A hipster with a full Ned Kelly beard was waiting for us, the only indication he wasn't there to rob the place was the stethoscope round his neck.

I didn't say it, for fear of sounding like my mother, but I thought it: doctors seemed to be getting younger these days. He took my blood pressure and washed out the wound, then confirmed the worst.

'I'll have to sew you up, sir,' he said.

Did I trust a bushranger sticking a needle in me? It didn't look like I had a choice. I gave Dr Ned the nod and settled into the reclining couch.

'I think maybe ten or twelve should do it,' he said.

'Stitches?'

'Yes. You'll have a nasty scar for your troubles too, I'm afraid. Can't do anything about that … This was a dog you say — what breed?'

'Well, I didn't check with the Kennel Club, but I don't think it was a poodle.'

'Cross perhaps?'

The first of the stitches went in, I nearly bounced off the ceiling. 'Well, it seemed pretty *cross*, yeah. Maybe I got it on a bad day.'

The doc grinned. 'I'll give you some shots, to be on the safe side.'

I wanted to ask if they would be Glenmorangie or Talisker, but I didn't think my joking was going down too well.

'Great, thanks.'

'Now, just hold still … we'll be done here in a moment.'

Mac was flicking through a Reader's Digest when I returned to the waiting room. He looked up and seemed eager to get away, rising quickly and striding over to me.

'How did it go?' he said.

I was leaning on the front rail by the reception area. The blue-haired girl had been replaced by a smiling ginge, who seemed altogether more suited to the job. I nodded to her and grabbed a hold of Mac's shoulder.

'Thank you now,' I said.

The receptionist gave us a wide grin as I hobbled, hanging onto Mac for dear life, towards the carpark. The sun was out now, dancing on the car roofs, and drying out the wet road. It felt good to be out; any time I was heading in this direction from hospital was a win for me.

Mac opened the back door again and let me get in. It took an age for me to settle in a position I felt sure wasn't going to burst my stitches on the first emergency stop.

'You quite comfortable now?' said Mac.

'Yeah, but don't go haring it home.'

'Christ, I'm surprised they never gave you a wheelchair if you're that bad.'

'They offered crutches, but I turned them down.'

'Why?'

'I didn't think they were a good look. And besides, they'd be a distinct disadvantage tonight at Aldo's.'

'So we're not just going for a chippie, then?'

'Did you honestly think that, Mac?'

'Gus, with you, I don't know what to think, mate.'

'Well, there'll be no chippie I hate to inform you. This will be a straight-forward kidnapping.'

'*Wha*—?'

'If everything goes to plan, that is. If not, well I suppose chips aren't off the table after all.'

Mac was back to drawing a target on me via the rearview mirror. 'So, do I need to get tooled up for this, then?'

'You mean a shooter? Shit, no.'

'But you said it was a kidnapping.'

'Yeah, we'll be doing all the kidnapping, mate. Or to be more precise yourself and Hod.'

'And how does that work, exactly?'

'Well, it's like this — Bruce's missing pal, Lee Donald, has been seen at Aldo's Chippie a few times before. And he drives a big fuck off Jag, so he shouldn't be too hard to spot. Now, hopefully he doesn't get too jumpy and your good-self and Hod can get a grip of him sharpish, without any fireworks going off, and we can all pass go and collect a nice fee when we return Donnie to Bruce's contact.'

'And who's that?'

'A bloke called Wally, a car salesman.'

'We're working for a fucking car salesman?'

The thought had struck me already. 'He's probably sound, being a friend of Bruce and all that.'

'Jesus, Gus. Have you learned nothing in all your years?'

'Well, it could be worse.'

'How? How could it be worse than working for a car salesman?'

'Could be working for a politician.'

Mac squinted, his face seemed to be hardening into a concentrated look of derision. 'I hope you know what you're getting us into, Gus.'

'I do,' I lied, 'of course I do. Trust me.'

Mac didn't respond.

CHAPTER 10

I navigated the stairs with all the grace of Gaza, not the destroyer of Scottish defences, I mean the later day, well-soaked version. Could have sworn my leg wasn't that bad, and really it wasn't, it was only when I placed my foot on the ground that the whole leg caved. Was a bit of a drawback to the old walking, like being shitfaced without ever touching a drop.

'It pains me to say it, but I've seen you a lot worse,' said Mac.

'Thanks, I'll use that to restore my injured pride.'

Mac let me settle down on the couch, leg elevated, then went to poke about in my kitchen.

'Thought you were off the sauce, Dury?' he yelled.

'I am.'

'Well, all you have in your fridge are bottles of Beck's.'

Couldn't be arsed explaining my theory about how it tested my will power, so went with, 'Hod drinks them, you can help yourself.'

I heard the cutlery drawer slamming and then Mac appeared in the doorway. 'Are you sure you're going to be fit for this caper tonight?'

'It's not me you need to worry about, it's Hod.'

'What do you mean?'

'He's got that look in his eye, y'know, the one that says life's too short.'

'Holy fuck. That's all I need, he's bad enough when he's just pumping iron. He's a total radge when the mood's on him.'

'Yeah,' I wagged a finger at Mac, 'but he's our radge!'

Snorts, some beer evacuated Mac's nostrils. 'Like anyone could ever control him.'

Knew he was right, but my focus was on tonight's plan. I started to run through my idea of how things would play out, got as far as the stakeout at Aldo's chippie when the sound of a battering ram began on my front-door.

'You expecting plod, Dury?' said Mac.

'That'll be Hod. Go let him in before my door's in splinters on the floor.'

Mac returned with Hod — who was rubbing his hands together, excited as a child at Christmas. Mac rolled eyes, made his fucksake-face and went to grab a brew for the new arrival.

'So, tonight's the night,' said Hod.

'Jesus, will you calm down, you're like a dog with two dicks.'

'I am calm, what are you on about?'

Mac handed over a bottle of Beck's, Hod took a heavy pelt, then, 'It's just adrenalin, by playtime I'll be Mr Frosty — trust me.'

Laughs, loud ones. 'Said the spider to the fly.'

Hod glanced over to Mac, who was still wiping his eyes from the last retort. '*Wha*—?'

I reined it in. 'Hod, in all seriousness, man. You're not known for keeping things on the down-low.'

Shrugs. A vague acknowledgement. Hod threw himself in a chair and started tapping the beer bottle on the arm. 'By the looks of things it's not me we need to worry about. What's the story with the stitches?'

I filled Hod in on the day's antics. My trip to The Buck. The pugs with dugs. The hospital. He took everything in, only breaking his focus to slug beer, then he leaned forward in the chair.

'I thought Bruce said this Donnie bloke was sound as a pound.'

'Well, that's my take, but it's not the hot take in Leith. Donnie, by the sounds of it, comes across as a bit of a player.'

'How do you figure that?'

'The gabby wifey I spoke to said he was seen about the streets in his flashy motor. She said he seemed to be pretty friendly with the young crew.'

Hod smirked, 'And you thought, he's more likely dealing to the young crew.'

'Exactly. How else is someone working in Wally's hot car lot going to spring for a new Jag?'

Mac was growing more curious. He pulled his chair closer to our little huddle.

'I'd say he's defo dealing. But do you think Wally's in on it too?'

Hod answered, 'Does it matter to us? If we snatch Donnie at Aldo's tonight and hand him over to Wally, then it's payday.'

Mac didn't look so sure. He started to plane the stubble on his chin with the back of his hand. 'I don't know. All seems a bit suss to me. What do we know about this Wally dude, apart from that he's a friend of a friend.'

Shrugs. All round.

Hod was getting agitated, rocking back and forth in his seat. It was the thought of missing out on some action. If there were the chance of a pagger on the cobbles outside Aldo's tonight, he wanted to be there. 'Well, I say we go ahead with the plan as it is. If Wally turns out to be dodge, then we run a mile from the next job he offers us. I don't see the point in packing this one in because we have a few butterflies. Gus's done all the groundwork and he's got the scars to show for it.'

Mac nodded.

'Wally won't pay out without the goods. He's got a point, mate.'

I had my doubts but I gave him the nod. 'Okay, but if there's any sign of plod or anything else to give us some more doubts we drop this.'

'Like a hot potato,' said Hod, he locked his fingers and stretched them out till the knuckles cracked. 'You won't regret this.'

I turned to Mac. 'Where have I heard that before?'

Aldo's chippie was within walking distance of my Easter Road flat. If I'd had the gable end, I'd be able to see what was on Aldo's menu tonight. Not that it mattered, he was well known for his deep-fried pizza. It was one of those joints were tourists went for the Edinburgh delicacy: the deep fried Mars Bar. They took photos of themselves with this rancid shite and Aldo posted them up in the shop. Apparently, it was so popular he was now taking requests. The deep fried Creme Egg was the latest coming contender.

'How did you find out about Donnie going to Aldo's?' said Hod. He was shifting from foot to foot, shuffling to stay warmed up. It was dark now, save for the street lights and the neon storefronts. Hod's shadow cast a formidable presence against the London Road tarmac.

'I told you, I found a gabby old wifey outside The Buck,' I said.

'Oh yeah, the one that spotted him in the Jag.'

'I think she has a granddaughter or something that works in Aldo's, there's some connection anyway because she said he's been turning up every night at 7.30pm on the dot.'

'Funny time to go.'

'Not really. Think about it. If you don't want to be seen, then 7.30 cuts out the rush-hour.'

'But the chips would be overcooked … hate it when they go all crispy like that.'

He got the look. 'Maybe Donnie has other priorities right now.'

'Yeah, you're probably right, Gus.'

The streets were empty, all around. A bloke sitting in the chippy reading an *Evening News* but I couldn't see his coupon to clock him. Did another recce of the main road and nodded to Mac, in position over the road at the mouth of the close. Things looked quiet, too quiet. I was beginning to get antsy, wondering where Donnie's Jag was, when the bloke in the chippie started to fold up the paper and I recognised him right away.

Said, 'Hod, look who it is.'

Hod lumbered away from the road's edge and back to the shadows. His mouth drooped before he spoke, 'That's fucking Sharky.'

'No kidding it is. What do you reckon he's doing?'

'Getting chips.'

'At just the same time as us? At just the same time that Donnie's been seen turning up every night? Dream on.'

'When you put it like that.'

I turned away from Hod to see Sharky checking his watch. He wasn't waiting on any chips, or a fucking deep-fried Creme Egg. I'd known Sharky for some years, he was a local knuckle-breaker. He'd picked up the name inside, on account of his eyes being so far apart that they almost looked as if they were sitting on the sides of his head, bit like a shark. The tag fitted because he was an apex predator all right, at least he had been since he started working for Jonny Ladd.

'This is not good,' I told Hod.

'Nope. Sure it isn't. You know Sharky works for the Bad Ladd, I take it?'

'Oh, I'd heard all right.'

'Not a man to be messed with.'

'Definitely not.'

Hod looked away, turned to face the street. He was silent for a moment, then quickly turned back to face me. 'Is that a car?'

I looked up London Road. A black saloon was coming towards us, slowing down. The blinkers went on and the front passenger door opened. A young girl stepped out, avoiding the puddles, wrapping a long woollen cardigan around her front. She looked familiar, but only in a vague way. The guy behind the wheel of the Jag, though, that was defo Lee Donald. He looked edgy as all hell, whipping his gaze from left to right.

'Too late to change the plan now,' said Hod.

'Too fucking right.'

We moved into position.

CHAPTER 11

The plan was, there was no plan.

Clocking Sharky had thrown what little effort we'd made out the window. I watched Hod set off down London Road, he was just past the Art Gallery, on the bend, when he started to tug at his collar. *Yeah, that works, mate, totally inconspicuous.* He lumbered on, like a man who was looking for a fight. I couldn't watch. Everything yelled disaster to me. I felt a grim churning in my guts that said this didn't end well.

I watched the girl in the long cardigan go into the chip shop. From my angle, I couldn't put the bead on Sharky. I knew he'd be well aware who the girl was, he wasn't the type to miss homework. Something started me thinking, if Sharky knew what I knew, then there was a reason why he'd positioned himself inside Aldo's and not on the cold cobbles. I upped my pace.

From the edge of my vision I spotted Mac. He was walking parallel to me, just passing the Artisan drinker on the other side of the road. I felt a deep craving, a call to put this entire farce to bed with a bar full of wee goldies. The image played before my eyes, but I told myself those days were over. I was moving on, and I couldn't take the whipping of the next day's hangover.

As I reached the chippy Hod was crossing the road, approaching Donnie's Jag from the rear. For a moment I hesitated, my hand on the door handle. Were we really doing this?

'Get a grip, man,' I told myself.

I glanced up to see Donnie had spotted Hod now. The chunky shape, the upturned collar, the shifty gait. It said it all. I saw Donnie's pallor change, he turned around to get a better look at what was approaching from behind.

Big mistake.

Mac was in position.

He yanked open the driver's door. Donnie didn't know whether to shit or get off the pot as Mac grabbed his car keys. Hod was reaching for the passenger door when I made my move on Aldo's.

The place was like a sauna. You couldn't see outside, the one massive window was covered in condensation. There were a few people spattered about. A group of jakies, like stray dogs, barking over a bag of chips. Some teenies with a tinny mobile singing along to Ariana Grande lyrics about wrist icicles and dick bicycles. And there was Sharky, stony faced, leading cardigan girl back towards the door.

I stood in his way.

Sharky eyed me with a caution that looked wholly alien to him. He was a strike first, ask questions later type. For a moment, as we faced each other down, I swear to fuck I heard Ennio Morricone's score playing somewhere.

Sharky sensed the opposition to his plans and gripped the girl's arm tighter. I grabbed a glance in her direction and caught the terror mounting. She was already in tears. Fear written in magi-marker all over her face.

'Don't think the girl wants to go anywhere,' I said. The words started to echo inside my head.

'Get out the way,' Sharky sounded business-like, this was 'fries with that' to him. Another day at the office.

'I don't think so.' Where I got this front from, I've no idea. I felt a twinge in my bandaged leg and remembered I wasn't Arnie. Sharky sensed the weakness immediately.

The pain came like a shotgun blast.

One flat-footed kick to my knee that folded my leg like a hinge. I fell, face-planting on a red and white chequered tablecloth that brought a shower of salt and pepper shakers, brown sauce bottles and a vinegar dispenser, down on my head.

As I lay on the floor, the throb of wounded pride overtook the agony of my damaged leg.

'Fuck, they're gone!' I managed to my feet, well, one foot. Hobbling to the window, I wiped a porthole in the condensation.

Sharky was out of sight. Gone. And the girl was gone with him.

I tipped my forehead onto the cold windowpane and cursed.

Outside I scanned the street for Mac and Hod. Hoped they'd at least had some better luck than me. There was no sign of Lee Donald's Jag. I was dripping blood into my boot again. Knew I'd burst some stitches, or to be more accurate Sharky had removed them for me.

'The fucking kip of you,' I blasted myself. Was still shaking my head when a black Jag pulled up to the kerb. Mac was driving, as he let down the passenger's window I clocked Hod and Donnie in the back seat, either they were getting close or that was a headlock Hod had on Donnie.

'How'd you go?' said Mac.

'I fucked up.'

'You fucked up. How?'

'Let's just say … totally.'

Hod leaned forward, made some bid to be filled in, but was flagged away by Mac.

'I saw the girl,' said Mac. He nodded to the backseat, 'She's his steady, so he says. He's none too happy at the moment.'

'Did you see where Sharky went?'

'I was about to ask you that.'

'Fucking hell. What a mess we've made of this.'

'*We?*' Mac slapped the wheel of the Jag, 'Don't lump us in with your fuck-ups, Dury. See that lad sitting in the back there, he pays our wages tonight.'

I looked down, butted my head on the door's rim. There was a puddle running the length of the gutter, a stray chip poke floated below me. I wanted to join it.

'You should get Donnie over to Wally's place,' I said. 'That's what we agreed with him. I'd join you, but I'm dripping claret from this leg wound.'

'*Wha*—?' said Mac. He tried to peer into the street to see what I'd managed to do to myself this time.

'Let's just say, Sharky sensed my weakness and went for it. I'll fill you in later. Right now, get to Wally's and deliver the goods. God knows we've earned a drink on this one.'

Mac's stare made his eyes look cold, serious. 'A drink?'

'Just a figure of speech.' I tapped the roof and watched the Jag pull out and head up Abbey Mount towards Wally's place.

Walking was a trial. I could just about manage it by placing a hand on the nearest building to steady me. When I got to the lights, just outside the laundrette, I knew I was going to have to hop across the road. I tried to make my pogoing look as natural as possible, but it couldn't be done. I felt like, and surely was, a complete fucking tool.

By Easter Road my gait was so distorted I must have looked like some time-warped 80s rap nut trying to relive the glory days of Hammer Time.

I cursed myself for ever being born.

Knew I deserved every inch of my humiliation. The leg was a mere inconvenience, a side show. The main attraction, playing in 3D every time I closed my eyes, was the sight of Sharky grabbing onto that young girl.

I stuck my key in the door and went inside. I was waiting for a wallop, a crack to the skull of some description. But it never came. The stair to my flat was empty, though nothing like as empty as I felt inside.

CHAPTER 12

'I'll skin his fucking arse,' he yells.

My father, roaring drunk, is back from the pub. I watch my mother try to placate him. The baby's crying and the noise seems to bring its own tension with it. Mam holds the child closer, she swings her shoulders to try and settle him and her whole body sways. I watch but it makes me feel sick.

Fish fingers and beans. That's what I'm thinking about. *Doctor* Who has just finished and *Planet of the Apes* is on the other side now but I'm thinking about my tea that I just bolted.

'I'll do it, I swear, I'll crack leather over his arse.' My father stomps the floor, he has to grip his trousers because he can't find his belt.

'The little bastard's hidden it!'

He thinks I've taken the belt, thinks I've outsmarted him. He's enraged that I might have hidden his belt to avoid another whipping.

A crash. The little round table with the glass top falls to the floor. The glass shatters into tiny pieces. The noise makes the baby scream louder.

I see the fish fingers. The big plateful, smothered with beans. I know I ate them too fast because I wanted to watch the Doctor, it's the one with the long scarf, he's my favourite.

Mam shushes my baby brother again. 'There, there …'

'There fucking there,' roars my father. 'Put that bairn down and find my belt.' My mother puts the baby in the playpen and near runs for the door. My father walks over to me, stands between the television and myself?

He towers over me. I'm terrified. What am I, eight? How could I defend myself?

'I know you took it,' he says, swaying now. 'Think you're smart, smarter than me, don't you.'

They're always saying I'm smart.

'He's a bright boy, your Gus.'

'Good head on them shoulders.'

They all say it.

But he hates to hear it. It draws the attention away from him. I know that even though I'm just a child. He wants to be the one they fuss over, the Mighty Cannis Dury, the football player that's feared on every pitch he sets a foot on.

'So where is it?' He wipes the frothy spittle from the edges of his mouth, still swaying, still grasping his trousers by the waistband.

'Well? Are you going to tell me, or do I have to whip it out of you?'

My heart races. I can taste the milk I washed down the fish fingers with. It's in my throat, rising. I'm going to vomit. I know it, and it'll give him just the excuse he needs to beat me.

'No,' I say the word so softly, I wonder if I've said it at all.

'What was that?'

'I said no.'

'No what?' His one free hand forms a fist.

I'm shaking. I can't stop it. My stomach contracts sharply and I vomit. The lumpy liquid smells of fish, it lands squarely on my father's shoes, splashing his trouser legs.

'Jesus Christ!' he yells. He reels, forgetting he has to hold up his trousers, as the folds gather round his heels, he starts to stagger backwards.

'Cannis!' It's my mother. She holds up the lost belt, the cause of all our upset, 'It was on the toilet floor, you must have dropped it.'

Her words pull him front, it's all too much for him, the trousers gathered at his ankles tackle him to the ground. The television breaks his fall, I see the plug yanked from the socket and there's a little explosion and sparks in the back of the telly.

'Cannis!' Mam yells again.

He's flat out. The television below his great back. There's a strange smell in the room, a mix of sick and blown fuses and scorched carpet. Mam runs to him, makes little smacks on his face but he's cold. She calls his name, again and again. I hear my brother start to cry once more. The place is a mad house. I want to tear my hair out to try and make sense of the scene before me.

Do other people live this way?

Does everyone fear their father so?

Why does Mam even care?

I want him to be dead. I want him gone from our lives forever. I don't want to feel the fear anymore. I don't want to be sick or panic or be scared anymore.

'What's going on?' he grumbles, his voice a stupefied drawl, his gaping mouth drools.

'Thank God you're not hurt,' says Mam.

'What?' His gaze floats over weary eyelids, then his head flops backwards. He starts to snore, he's passed out right in front of us. The chaos vanishes too as I watch his felled body move with the suck and swell of his breathing. I run from the craziness. I run from my mother's cries, 'Gus ...'

'Gus …'

'Gus …'

I try to run faster but my leg hurts. Why? What's wrong with my leg?

'Gus …'

'Gus …' my Mam's voice rakes the street, seems louder than ever.

'Gus …'

'—*Mam?*' I shout myself awake.

I'm in bed. My feet feel strange, wet. I yank back the duvet.

I've bled all over the bed.

The bandage that was on my leg has unfurled itself. The blood-soaked remains of the bandage are looped around my legs and feet.

'The fuck is this?'

I start to kick out.

There's anger. Real hurt and pain.

But none of it's for my leg.

Never had I felt more like taking a drink. That in itself should have set an alarm off. But I was following different road markers. The older I got — the more my sorely punished body told me I needed to stop drinking — the more I wanted it.

The addiction owned me. The neural paths were well worn, wouldn't be replaced. When I encountered a problem, I took the easy option, drowned it with drink. That had been my way for more than twenty years now, my art was well practiced. And it didn't matter how expertly I identified the triggers, because I knew they were still there.

I rose from my bed and tried to put some weight on my bad leg. It was a trial, like shrapnel shooting through my shins. I grabbed the calf, some dried blood flaked off in my hand.

'Christ on a cross,' I mumbled to the cold and empty room.

I needed to shower but the cupboard in the corner sang out to me. I yawed painfully over the exposed boards and grabbed the handle.

It was an old press; these flats had been sub-divided so often it might once have been a pantry. Deep and shelved. I stood back and stared at my clandestine work.

Every shelf was covered with a bottle of some description. Mainly spirits.

Beefeater gin.

Absolut vodka.

Black Heart rum.

The middle shelf heaved with whisky.

The Famous Grouse.

Macallan.

Johnnie Walker — red and black labels — I'd have to work on the blue, I still had a ways to go.

I stared, longingly.

For maybe nine months I'd built up this store. Every time I passed an offie, and I was holding folding, in I'd go and add to the collection. It was a strange sensation, when it came over me. It was as if I was still drinking, but not touching a drop. I'd sit in an old bentwood chair, open the cupboard door, and just stare inside.

What was I doing?

Did I even know the answer to that?

Sometimes, I toyed with the idea that there was an alternate reality where another Gus Dury was tanning the lot.

Utterly carefree. At other times, I pondered the day when I'd crack the seal on the first bottle. I'd get so involved in these fantasies that I could almost feel the foil wrapper folding in my hand, the bottle-top slackening. The taste, oh sweet Lord, the taste.

I continued to stare but no answers appeared. Somewhere, at a very deep level inside me, there was an answer. A full understanding, replete with all the knowledge I sought. But I wasn't there yet, nowhere like it, that was my current take away.

All I knew, as I stared into the abyss of those rows of bottles, was that some part of me had been left unevolved by the years of drink. My emotional development had been retarded; perhaps that's what I'd always wanted.

I would drink to forget, to allay social anxieties, to blind myself to the real world. To ignore the child I'd lost with Debs. To ignore the child I was when my father ran wild. There was no shortage of fuck-ups on my part and the game of life had no problem adding to the list.

I reckoned I'd started drinking in all seriousness at around 14 or 15 years old. I didn't even consider attempting to put the cork in the bottle until my mid 30s. By my reckoning, that meant I had lost at least twenty years of natural emotional development.

This was heavy stuff, but it was the way my thinking was going. An alkie in their 40s has a lot of self discovery to catch up on. I had a hell of a lot of emotional development to go through, well, that's what I called it. Others would be more blunt, say I had some growing up to do.

And I wouldn't argue either.

Maybe I knew all this, even way back when. But I blocked it out with the bottle, put reality far out of reach. And it worked, for a while. But reality has a strange knack of catching up with those who try to outrun it. Reality will catch you, and slap you about, scream, 'Wake the fuck up!'

Well, I was awake now.

Jesus, there was no denying it.

CHAPTER 13

I took the longest shower. Dried blood between my toes, flaking off and being carried away in a dark, red stream.

I let the water do its work.

'It has healing properties, don't you know.'

I hear the words being repeated in my memory and the advice of a twenty-something auxiliary nurse come back to haunt me. She'd said this to my ex-wife, at the lowest point of her life. I can still see Debs, standing before me in her dressing gown, her arms gripping her stomach. Her shoulders rounded and weak. She looked so lost, like a traveller in uncharted territory. Her dark eyes seemed so swollen; was there enough tears inside her to ever reveal the pain and hurt?

I wanted to slap that nurse. After all I'd seen growing up, the times my father lifted hands to my poor mother, I wanted to lash out and strike her. I could still see her face, the half-grin on her lopsided mouth. She was only spouting a line from a textbook, a training manual or something. She was just another repeater, she didn't even know the weight of her words.

Later, I felt guilty. Just the thought, without the action, was enough. I fell into the deepest self-loathing. I was no better than him. Later still, I felt more wounds opening. I wanted to know why I was preoccupied with that bastard when I should have been mourning the death of my only child.

I turned off the shower and stepped out into the cold of the bathroom. There was an old wrought-iron radiator in the boxy little room but the whole time I'd stayed there I had never known it to emit any heat. Its purpose was as a towel rail. I dried off and hobbled on the walking stick I'd retrieved from beneath my bed.

The stick was a remnant of an incident from my past. It may have been drunken, it almost certainly was brutal. There were so many memories — falls, collisions, beatings — I could no longer count them. But the walking stick remained. A solid gunmetal grey job with a plastic grip that would look more at home on a bike. Standard NHS issue. It did the trick.

I was ambulant again, and that was something. There'd be no more skipping across London Road, or anywhere else for that matter.

I dressed my wound. Plenty of wadding and Elastoplast. A fresh bandage to finish the job. I reckoned I'd live without stitches, which meant I wasn't going out. Last night's experience, and the return of nightmares, made the world beyond my door an option best left unexplored.

Clothes came next. Black 501s. Converse All Stars. And a white T-shirt. I tried to top the lot off with a recent purchase, a new shirt from H&M, but despite saying *large* on the collar it wouldn't fasten across my chest.

'The fuck are they making these for — Lilliputians?'

I flung the shirt back on my unmade bed. Knew I'd be too lazy to take it back, and have even less chance of finding the receipt in the wreckage of my life.

Grabbed a grey hoodie, an Asda special, and an old faithful that I used for dossing in the flat. I liked the way the hood doubled for dress-up: I could pull it over my head and lie to myself that I was living a monk's existence.

As I passed the hall-stand I took my mobi from the pocket of my Crombie. A stack of messages had mounted up. The majority were from Hod, detailing the drop-off at Wally's. Everything seemed to go okay, passed Go and collected the cash. There was another text from Mac, something about stopping by this morning, but my full attention went to the message from Amy.

Gus, I found a missed call from you on my phone. Sorry I didn't pick-up, life is all over the place right now. Anyway, maybe you just pocket dialled me? But if you do want to talk, I'll hopefully be able to answer next time.

'Shit.'

I hadn't forgotten about Amy, but I had let the fact I called her slip my mind. Rooting out Lee Donald, random dog bites and trips to casualty had seen me with other things on my mind.

I resolved to call her. She needed to know I'd been kept in the dark about everything. I had to explain why Hod and Mac hadn't told me about her child. Christ, I just had to talk to her.

Said, 'Right I'll do it.' But it was just a message to self. I didn't fancy explaining away the leg and walking stick. Would give it a few days, let myself heal.

I was making coffee, despairing over the state of my kitchen's contents when Hod's easily recognisable pounding started on my front door. I limped through with my stick and opened up.

'Fucksake, you'd think the place was on fire,' I said.

It was Hod, he'd brought Mac along. 'Ah, the traditional Dury welcome: "Fuck you and the horse you rode in on."'

Mac grinned, 'Get the cunt a key, Gus. He's going to put that door in one of these days.'

'A key, now that's an idea,' Hod turned jovial at the thought, 'we could turn this place into that Jack Lemmon movie, *The Apartment*.'

I bit back, 'You've more chance turning Mac's Transit into a shaggin' waggon.' I punched Mac playfully, 'Don't be giving that clown any ideas, he comes up with enough on his own.'

The bants continued into the kitchen for coffees, and on into the living-room. The lads seemed to be in high spirits. I put it down to Wally settling up promptly.

'So, last night …' I said.

Hod grabbed a cushion, made to relive his headlock on Donnie. 'Went a treat, I thought, even though I scraped my inner elbow on his jacket's zip …' He showed me the plaster on the crook of his arm, 'But, a result all right.'

Nodded, but wasn't so sure. 'Not for the girl it wasn't.'

'Oh yeah, forgot about her,' said Hod.

'I wish I could say the same. I haven't been able to put her out of my mind. What the fuck did Sharky want with her?'

Mac retrieved his coffee from the floor, sipped slowly like he was considering his response with caution. 'Well, here's the thing, Gus. Whatever Sharky wanted with Donnie's girl, it isn't something we'll benefit from finding out.'

He saw where this was going. 'Define benefit?'

'Not getting your knees blown off by Jonny Ladd.'

'He's right, Gus. Sharky's just a bottom feeder. The Bad Ladd pulls his strings and I for one don't want to find out what it feels like to get on his wrong side,' said Hod.

I got the picture. It wasn't one I hadn't run through my thoughts already. I knew Jonny Ladd was not a man to be messed with in Edinburgh. His reputation was legendary, if only one of many in this town, the place did a good job of nurturing nut-cases.

Did I want to rumble with Sharky? Or, worse, his paymaster? The answer was no, in both instances, but my conscience was pushing me in that direction. An alky with a conscience is a terrible combination — mainly because the self-destruct switch tends to overrule all else.

Said, 'I can't imagine Donnie's overly chuffed with our result?'

'Chuffed isn't a word I'd use to describe Donnie, no,' said Mac. 'Let's say he was more like ropeable. A man more fit to be tied I have not seen in many a long day.'

Hod nodded agreement. 'He was pretty fucked off, Gus. You have to understand we'd just snatched him and handed him over to Wally. Depriving a man of his liberty is never pretty, but depriving a man of his liberty, a Jag and his girlfriend is quite a kick to the nuts.'

The point was made. I won't pretend it didn't trouble me, or to be more accurate, the girl Sharky dragged from Aldo's troubled me. I could see her teary desperation haunting me over the next few days. I commended myself for my thoughtfulness, but as I'd aged I'd realised there were only so many battles you could fight.

'Here,' yelled Mac, tossing over a padded envelope.

'Pennies from heaven.' I ripped in, took out the cash.

'Not quite, unless Wally's your idea of an angel.'

I toyed with a response, but held schtum. You see, this was the thing. There was something that unnerved me about Wally. Always had been. I never bought into his explanation for Donnie's disappearance. And I never bought any of his bullshit about why he hired us in the first place.

'Oh, Christ, the cogs are turning now,' said Mac.

'*Wha—?*'

'You're thinking of going off on one.'

'I don't know what you're talking about, Mac.'

Hod spoke, 'He means you've got unfinished business … either that or you're going on the sauce.'

'Get fucked. The pair of you. Now.'

I pointed to the door.

Mac drained the last of his coffee, 'I mean it, Gus. Behave yourself, don't go doing anything stupid.'

I trousered my money and spread out on the couch.

'Thanks for the advice. Now mind the door doesn't hit you on the arse on the way out.'

CHAPTER 14

I spent the rest of the morning surfing the web, news sites mainly. Don't know why but my Spidey senses were tingling. I was looking for something, a piece on a court case, a local crime story like the papers used to report. Nothing. I was trying to tie Donnie to Jonny Ladd, but the Fourth Estate was now such an abortion of a business that I truly was pissing in the wind.

The first five minutes of stories about the Royal family, their fucking weddings and how much their women's outfits cost, had me ready to heave. There were roads going untended in the city, kiddie's play-parks being closed and libraries getting merged with dole offices. They never tired of telling us on the BBC — the Biased Bullshitting Cunts — that we were living in Austerity Britain. It was like a badge of honour.

But I wasn't the only one spotting the trouble brewing.

The news sites' comments pages were full of angry readers who were sure there was a plan afoot to strip the country of its few remaining assets. Our traitorous MPs were complicit, making sure there were enough bank debts to keep our children's children occupied. These puppets were only there to max out the country's credit card, then they'd leg it before jumping on the private sector gravy train for a few years. Full civil service pension included, of course.

The rest of the country was suffering. I'd been watching the place go full Ragnarök for years now. We'd given up on our needy and our pensioners, literally starved them with funding cuts. People were desperate, the country was looking more like France circa 1789 every day. No wonder people were pissed. No wonder the likes of Lee Donald had to supplement their income with whatever dodgy dealings they could muster.

I couldn't judge Donnie too harshly. By the standard of the day he was just another mug punter. We all were. But there was a taste in the air that said the wind was about to change abruptly.

I was readying myself for another jaunt to the kitchen for caffeine when my mobi took off along the table on vibrate.

Grabbed it, 'Hello ...'

'Gus, is that you now? I wasn't sure you were still on this number.' The voice on the other end of the line tore into me worse than the dog's teeth. It was Fitz the Crime. I hadn't heard from him in months, years maybe. If he was calling me now, there was a dark cause at the root of it.

'Fitz.'

'It's you, grand. I need to, erm, have a word with you ... in person.'

I could tell he wasn't happy on an open line. 'Okay.'

'Is there somewhere that we could perhaps meet. In private, like.' His voice was cracking. Fitz seemed unnerved, not the over confident Irishman with the shoot first ask questions later attitude I remembered.

'I know a place.'

Fitz cut me up, 'Perhaps there's no need to give me the address, on the phone.'

I knew where he was coming from and it only unnerved me even more. My curiosity was sweating harder than some of the city's sauna staff.

Said, 'I'm in the old flat. Same one. And I'm here for the day.'

'Grand, so. I'll pay you a wee visit in a little while then.'

Hung up.

I stared at the phone for a few seconds, trying to find proof that the call had actually just occurred. The caller ID registered Fitz's number all right, but I was having difficulty letting the information sink in.

Fitz and I went way back. There were times when I had a real job, on a real newspaper, that I'd help him out. Not big time, just the kind of casual 'you scratch my back, I'll scratch yours' that goes on between journalists and plod.

There'd been motoring offences — speeding, drinking, you name it — that I'd kept out the paper. The kind of thing that could stall, if not halt a police career. In those days, when we still had real people, a good turn didn't go amiss. Fitz repaid the favours and, for a while anyway, we became friends.

It was a strange friendship, neither of us were fully committed to it. It was as if we were waiting for a slip up by one or the other to cash in. Perhaps it was paranoia, but it wasn't the stuff friendships thrive on. Could it be that I was the one with the hang-up? Fitz had, after all, helped me out when I'd had a family tragedy — a shock death that he woke me from sleep to break the news in person. I was grateful, and I'd shown it then and later.

I put down the mobi, grabbed up the stick from the side of the couch. I trundled through to the kitchen and made a start on another pot of coffee. I liked to think I did my best work with a head full of caffeine, but then again, I liked to fool myself about a lot of things.

I sparked up a red top and returned to the living-room. I watched the smoke start to hang around the lampshade.

It was a paper lantern, one of those round numbers with a bamboo skeleton. The base was yellowing with nicotine, and the inside — which the smoke seemed to favour — was the colour of butter.

'Christ, I wonder what you've done to my insides,' I spoke to the orange-embers burning on the tip of my tab. 'Doesn't bear thinking about.'

I lit another from the fading glow, dowped the dog-end in the ashtray. I had too much to think about, too many pieces of the puzzle to try and fit together. Nothing made sense. I hadn't wanted to take the case in the first instance, and now here I was, hostage to Hod's idiocy once again.

The outside buzzer went.

It gave me a start because the lock on the front door was bust since a debt collector decided to kick it in to get to one of my neighbours. Everyone I knew just shouldered the lock and walked up to the flat.

'Hello ...' I said into the intercom.

'Gus, it's me. Fitz.'

'You better come up.'

I went along with the role-play, buzzed him in.

Fitz reached the door, dishevelled, ashen, both hands in the pockets of his Markies raincoat. He looked like a man who had bet the world and won, only to discover the ticket-stump had turned into a turd. I got the feeling he was about to relive the experience, and I'd maybe even be handed a turd myself.

'It's been a while,' I said.

Fitz looked me up and down, clocked the walking stick. 'Longer than I imagined.'

I nodded to the living-room and followed in Fitz's slow wake. He seemed to be checking out the place, his gaze flitting up and down, left to right. Was I under suspicion here? It was hard to tell with plod, you were always suspect to them.

Said, 'Can I get you a coffee?'

'Fuck, Gus, dispense with the niceties,' he said, 'this isn't a social call.'

He sat down on the armchair and knuckled the side of his nose, snorted. He brought out an old grey handkerchief and trumpeted into it.

'So, to what do I owe the pleasure?'

'Does the name Robbie McEwan mean anything to you?' he said.

'No. Should it?'

'If I added the prefix, Detective Chief Inspector, it might.'

'I'd be getting in the ball-park of warm ... does this McEwan know me?'

Fitz shook his head. 'Oh, I'd say by later today he'll be a fucking expert on you, Dury.'

I was tired of the run around. 'Spit it out, man. What's this about?'

I got the stare, one that says, "I'm doing you the favour here".

Fitz got up and started to stroll around the flat. He seemed distracted, unsure how to approach the subject at hand. After pacing for a few minutes, he put an elbow on the fireplace and leaned there. His eyes were searching me as he spoke.

'Robbie McEwan is what they used to describe as fierce. He's a swag man who made his name on the burglary beat, running in house creepers and random, desperate junkies. He's wild, dirty and now he's a murder squad detective and he wants your guts for garters.'

I hadn't committed any murders that I was aware of, said, 'Why would a murder squad detective be gunning for me?'

Fitz returned to the armchair. His voice had softened now, 'We got a call, late last night, I was the duty DCI. I drove out to a field in East Lothian, out Dunbar way, around midnight.'

'Dunbar?' I didn't know a soul there.

'To an old steading, rotten old ruin it was.' Fitz's gaze shifted into the middle-distance, 'You know, it doesn't matter how many times you see them, those eight-ball eyes, they never leave you.'

'A body?'

'Oh yeah, I'm coming to that.'

'Do I know them?'

'I'm coming to that too ... so there's a lad hanging up on the roof beam, they've got him on butcher's hooks through the oxters, one's sticking out the top of his shoulder, and there's blood and ...' Fitz trailed off into silence.

'The lad was murdered?' I said.

'Beaten to death, I'd say. He's on the slab now so we'll know better soon but my money's on a proper hiding, professional job. His face was just a mass of pulpy flesh, like a pumpkin that they'd played a game of footy with. We had to identify him by his fingerprints.'

'So he was a scrote?'

'He had some form, but you'd know better than me what Lee Donald had been up to, given I hear you were turning the town upside down looking for him, right up until last night.'

And there it was, a sucker punch to the gut.

'Donnie? He's dead?' I said. My head was swimming, or trying to. I was in a whirlpool and kept going under. The only thing that stopped me was a vision of swapping places with that prick Wally.

I'd had this vision all along, right since Windae Willis put the bite on Hod. Nothing sat right. We'd been fed a line. Someone had either planned this to put my bollocks on the chopping block, or was too fucking stupid to foresee the consequences.

Said, 'I take it your lads have been chatting to a fucktard by the name of Andy Wallace?'

'I'd say he's been doing most of the talking.'

I dug my fists into the cushions of the couch. 'I only went in there for a bloody car. A shitty old Golf that pissed oil like an incontinent greyhound.'

Fitz put his gaze on me. 'Time for some straight talking, Gus.'

I couldn't focus. My head was filled with bubble gas. I was the hunted, now. Either it would be the filth who got to me, or the Bad Ladd. I didn't fancy the prospect of either.

I reached for the walking stick, pushed myself off the couch.

'And where are you going now?'

'Far-a-fucking-way.'

'What? You can't go on the run, have you any idea how suspicious that will look?'

Fitz rose, forced me back to the couch. 'I'm not finished with you yet, laddo, not by a long chalk.' He started to pace the floor again. 'You should have seen what I had to see last night. It's not an easy image to get out of your mind, let me tell you.'

'Well, tell me then!' I bit.

'Up on hooks he was, beat rawer than I like my steak sure.'

'You said.'

'I haven't got to the rest. Did I tell you about the guts? They'd slit him from neck to nuts and his guts were spilled out on the ground beneath him.'

I turned away, an involuntary action that Fitz objected to. He grabbed my face and turned my eyes front. 'Some manner of country animal, a fox or whatever, had been at the guts and trailed them around the steading and out the door. Fucking reams of them were strewn about like Christmas decorations. A man's guts, Dury ... think about that.'

I had the image burned into my imagination already. The victim, Donnie, had ceased to be a man I once knew and was now more like a mythological creature. A man raised higher than men through inhuman suffering.

'I don't want to think about it.'

'No, you won't want to. And you won't want to think about the rats either. They were all over the place, fleeing the scene as it were, because when we walked in they were inside your friend Donnie's corpse, eating their way through his flesh and getting their fill of his entrails.'

'Stop it.'

'Going to chuck are you?'

'Just pack it in.'

'Yeah, I'm sure you've heard enough. Think yourself lucky you didn't have to pay a midnight visit to the scene in person.'

I felt my shoulders sinking deeper into the couch. I was waning, could almost feel the energy draining out of me. No wonder Fitz looked so rough; I felt sure he hadn't even slept.

'Look, Fitz, so what now?' I said, 'I mean, you didn't come here just to share last night's experience.'

'No. I didn't come for that reason.'

'So you came to tell me Wally had fingered me to McEwan?'

'No. It wasn't that either. Lee Donald was strung up in the wilds for one reason: he was left there as a warning to someone. I'm pretty sure there's going to be more trouble brewing as a result of this. Donnie might have been a sprat, but he swam with some big fishes.'

'I swear to you, Fitz. It was a simple missing persons for me. I don't want this any more than you.'

'Yeah, well too bad, Gus. We've got it now and if you want to stop Robbie McEwan from banging you up, you better start thinking straight and get to the root of this bloody mess.'

CHAPTER 15

I sat alone for an hour trying to figure out just what the hell it was I'd got myself into this time. I only realised I was chain smoking when I went to my pack of Marlboros to light another and found it was empty. The ashtray was overflowing, dowps evacuating, making their escape onto the coffee table down a landslide of ash.

The whole place looked like an unattended student kip house. The thought gored me. I'd had an idea of myself reclining on a Chesterfield, maybe a cravat and carpet slippers, by the time I was forty. It wasn't happening. By Christ, it just so wasn't happening. The way things were going I'd be lucky not to end up sharing a cell with a lifer called Bubba and his collection of Linda Lusardi page threes.

Something bit, the badness inside me perhaps. I wasn't going to allow myself to wallow in self-pity for the fuck-up that amounted to my life. There was Hod and Mac to think about, Mac especially, with his record he definitely wouldn't be getting any favours from plod.

There was Donnie's girl too, whose image still hounded me. God knows what levels of torture they might be inflicting on that young girl. I could see Sharky filming Donnie's final moments on his phone and replaying it to her later, just for kicks. He'd get a belt out of that, the sadistic bastard.

These were deranged people, I knew the sort. There's almost a league of them in the city. The lower rungs are full of dafties, just low IQ, low achievers, who wind up in bad company. In time, most of them become jail fodder. Those places are full of them. But the ones that are wily enough to avoid that fate soon find themselves in likeminded company. These societal leftovers, sociopaths and trainee psychos, then get scooped up by the likes of Jonny Ladd. That's when their hardcore days begin. All that youth and enthusiasm funnelled into dealing junk and doing-over schemies who get behind on their payments.

The likes of Ladd knew he had to be brutal, and be well known for it, to wield power in Edinburgh. I'd met his type before, seen what it did to a man, and it wasn't pretty. Savagery becomes second nature. After a while it becomes no more than a daily routine, like changing your socks, brushing your teeth. They might try to hide it with bling and designer labels or a fuck-off motor, but it's just show. Inside they're animals, and they know it. Can't hide that behind a Thomas Pink shirt.

When I thought about Fitz's description of what had been done to Donnie in that steading near Dunbar, I seriously wondered whether the best option was calling this DCI McEwan and asking him to come and cuff me already. It was more than just an idea that had popped into my mind — it was a playable card. The thought was spiralling out of control when my mobi distracted me.

Ringing.

Hod: 'Gus, how goes it?'

'Where have you been, man? I've been calling you for the best part of an hour.'

'One of the flats had a faulty ball-cock, should have been a straightforward replacement but try telling that to the builders' yard that's supposed to stock them, I swear …'

I cut him off. 'Okay, spare me. We have something of a situation.'

'Sounds ominous.'

'Yeah, well, I'd say it's a whole lot worse that that.'

I could hear Hod over-revving the engine, the traffic starting to flare up. Some horns blasted.

'Look … I'm not far off your place, Foot of the Walk. If these lights change any time soon, I'll swing round.'

'What about your faulty ball-cock?'

'This sounds a bit more pressing than a shitter that won't flush.'

Hung up.

I tipped the ashtray into the kitchen bin. Was I becoming one of those men who turned fastidious after living alone for too long? Didn't think so. I was a long way from doing the Shake 'n' Vac in the front room. It dawned on me that I really wasn't that well suited to living alone. The long hours of introspection were beginning to take their toll. Overthinking was a thing.

Hod announced his arrival in his usual fashion. Loud enough this time to evacuate a cloud of dust from the lintel.

I held schtum. Nodded him in the door.

'No telling off?' said Hod.

'Why bother?'

'Do I detect a hint of nihilism?'

'No. You detect a whole fucking load of it.'

I hobbled through to the couch, crashed. Hod took the armchair, planting his builders' boots on the table, they were splattered with paint, looked worse than any decorator's radio.

I let him settle for a moment before I gave him the news, both barrels. Maybe it was my interpretation, minus Fitz's histrionics, but he seemed to take it better than I thought he would.

'I see,' said Hod.

'That's it? "I *fucking* see."'

'I'm processing.'

'At the speed of an Acorn Electron.'

'It's a lot to take in.' Hod hoiked in his boots, sat up in the armchair. He was balancing his elbows on the faded knees of his work jeans as he spoke, 'So, this Robbie McEwan, do you know him?'

'Not from Adam.'

'But you know Fitz, and he's giving you the inside run. That's more than a bit useful.'

'I wouldn't count Fitz as an ally, not yet anyway. He's still trying to figure out what went on in that ruined steading. If he gets an inkling that we're in any way involved, he'll drop us. No question.'

'You really think so?'

'He's filth, whichever way you look at it. We go back, but right now he's just sticking his nose in the wind and trying to test which way it's blowing.' I changed tack, tried to steer Hod away from fishing for positives. 'You know who fingered me with this McEwan character — Wally.'

Hod's jaw started to flare, he was gritting his teeth. 'I don't know what he's playing at.'

'Well, he's playing us, I can tell you that for starters.'

'I'll cut him a new crack if I get a hold of him.'

Flagged him down, 'You'll get in line, mate. Remember it's only my name being bandied about with plod at the moment. Yourself and Mac might yet be fingered as well, but it's my nuts in the vice just now.'

Hod stopped grinding his jaws and let out a long exhalation of breath. 'Of course, there's the other mob to consider. You don't think Wally could be connected to the Bad Ladd, do you?'

I gave his suggestion a moment's thought. 'It doesn't matter whether he is or he isn't. Wally's put us in a shit sandwich with plod on one side and Jonny Ladd on the other. I find it hard to see a dickless little weasel like Wally running with the big boys, but then I found it hard to see Donnie there either.'

Hod rubbed the stubble on his chin, I noticed it had started to turn flinty grey. 'I can't get my head around any of this. I still can't believe Donnie's dead. I was just messing with him in a headlock the other night ... still got the scars to prove it!'

I saw Hod was overheating, so tried to spell it out for him, 'You need to get your mind on the job. Not what we thought the job was — a simple missing persons — but what it's become. We're seriously up to our nuts in it, we're facing the clink or a midnight jaunt to East Lothian.'

'When you put it like that, we've not got the greatest odds.'

'When have we ever, mate?'

'Never, far as I remember.'

I nodded my agreement. 'Look, Donnie's murder changes everything. We're going to have to dig out some answers, rapid style, or we might not be far behind him in the stringing-up stakes.'

'God knows what Donnie was really working, or what that bell-end Wally was really on to.'

'That's what we need to find out.'

Hod took a deep breath and leapt to his feet. He was wearing his man of action face, which terrified me more than anything. 'Right, come on, Gus, let's get going.'

'I presume you're thinking of taking a trip to a car lot in Newhaven?'

'Unless you want to stop and get tooled up first.'

I snatched the walking stick from the side of the couch, used it to push myself to my feet. 'You're joking, I know that. But when I say we're making one stop for just that reason I've never been more serious in my life.'

'*Wha*—?'

'We're going to a barber's shop in Leith first. Mac is as much a part of this as we are and he needs to be warned. And we need him primed and prepped to take Wally's face off if we find it necessary.'

'That's what you meant by tooled up?'

'Mac only has one tool of the trade — a razor.'

CHAPTER 16

Hod was too agitated to sit and wait whilst I got my Docs and coat on. He paced up and down the hall, cracking knuckles, sighing heavily and blurting the occasional, 'Fuck!'

I intervened, calling out from my bedroom, 'Hod, mate, fancy nipping down to grab me some smokes?'

'Yeah, fine, what kind?' He hovered around my bedroom door whilst I dug in my pocket for some notes.

'Marlboro … No, actually, make that Regal. Unless they've got Camels, which I doubt, but if they have, go for the Camels.'

Hod took the cash and stared at me, 'Most people stick to the one brand, y'know.'

'I'm not most people.'

Hod turned up a sly grin, 'You got that right. But, c'mon, why do you chop and change your fags like that?'

'Because, a bit like my fortunes, my tastes fluctuate almost daily.'

'Fair enough.' He seemed to be buying it, went for the door.

'I'll get you downstairs in Manna Mia.'

He looked at the cash I'd just given him. 'There's not enough here for a coffee as well. Not the kind you drink, anyway.'

The door closed on him before I could make any reply. I returned to putting on my cherry Docs. The laces had hardened on the boot that collected the blood from my dog bite. They were stiff, but the dried blood started to crumble when I touched them, flaking on my fingers. I got the boots laced, tightened up, and reached out for my walking stick. I felt far from capable for the job ahead, the Docs stabilised me a little, but I knew I wouldn't be making use of their bouncing soles any time soon.

On the way out I glanced at the cupboard with my stash of alcohol. For a second I considered the prospect of tanning the lot. Doing a Nicholas Cage in *Leaving Las Vegas*. It seemed doable, just not desirable. Not right now anyway, there were other people to consider in this mess aside from myself.

I found the best way to get down the stairs was to hop on my one good leg. The sore leg was easing up a little, the stitches were holding now, but bit when I stretched the calf too much. A few more days going easy on the leg and I was in the clear; I just didn't see much prospect for that.

Manna Mia coffee shop was empty. No sign of Hod, either. I went to the counter and was greeted by a heavily tattooed neck-beard. I had a good few years on him. I could remember when the swallow tattoo on his hand used to be a sign of the die-hard old Ted who was still slapping on the Brylcream.

'Two coffees to take out.'

He went into a list, eyeballs peering to the top right as he ran off my options. I noticed a badge on his apron that read, *"I think, therefore I am … dangerous"*.

I stifled guffaws. 'Sorry, two lattes.'

He went about putting the coffees together and I eavesdropped on his chat with the girl on the bakery counter. She was almost as tatted as her co-worker, a string of hearts and crosses round her neck like she was aiming at the cam-whore look. Their conversation, shouted over the hissing of the coffee machine, sounded like a *Guardian* editorial with some preaching on wrong-think thrown in.

Who were they trying to impress by being so bloody bien-pensant? And just when did kids start to sound like church ladies? It was like we'd leapt straight from the Sex Pistols to a generation of Mary Whitehouse clones, all snooping and ready to pounce. If this was where the revolutionaries of the future were to come from, then we really were in the shit.

Hod appeared at my side. He handed me a packet of smokes and clocked the coffees being placed on the counter. I put down a ten-spot and waited for neck-beard to take it.

'Nice badge,' I said as he whisked the tenner away.

My change came with a sneer in place of a thank-you.

'By the way, it's utter bullshit.'

I got a stare. He was waiting for the pay-off. 'What was that?'

I put the hard bead on him. 'You only *think* you think. That's why you're really dangerous.'

Neckbeard looked at me, then glanced at the sniggering Hod. 'Whatever.'

It seemed as good a way to end to the conversation as any.

On the street Hod took his coffee. 'What was all that about?'

'You came late to the conversation. You were lucky, I had to listen to a party political broadcast by the Millennials Party.'

'So you thought you'd rattle his cage?'

'It's what I do best.'

Hod took the lid off his coffee. 'I try to not let Generation Wuss get to me.'

'I've given up trying. Call it a failing, if you like.'

'I just cut them some slack because I think they're more fucked than any of us.'

'That's because they've no idea their world is a propaganda programme that's been playing their entire life.'

'Exactly, it's not all their fault.'

I sipped my coffee and glanced at Hod, this was as close to profound as I think I'd seen him get. 'You'll be telling me you give Boomers a pass next.'

'I think we're all fucked, mate. Each and every one of us.'

I nodded to cross the road for his truck. 'Some of us are getting fucked, Hod, and some are doing the fucking.' I balanced the coffee and my stick in one hand as I negotiated the door of the truck. 'Either way, it's not a situation likely to bring about a stable future.'

Hod started up. 'I fear you're right.'

I flicked on the stereo, Johnny Cash was singing about falling into a burning ring of fire. I'd never noticed how appealing he made it sound before.

I finished the dregs of my coffee, it tasted bitter. Put back my head and reclined the chair a little. 'Wake me up when it's over.'

Hod bit, 'It's never over.'

'Okay, then wake me up when we get to Mac's shop.'

The truck stopped and started with the traffic flows down Easter Road. At Lorne Street, Hod chucked a left and we shuddered along the cobbles. A few more turns, some harsh braking for a suicidal cat, and we were close enough to start looking out for parking. This end of Leith, at this hour, the cars were stacked two-deep in the road. Even the Yodel drivers were cursing missed opportunities.

'Over there,' I pointed.

'Nice one.'

An old dear in an Aygo was backing out. Ordinarily, the space an Aygo took would be too small for the truck, but she had taken enough room for two cars.

On the pavement, Hod spoke. 'How do you think he'll take it?'

'You mean the bit about Wally dropping us in the shit with plod, who wants to bang us up, or the bit about Jonny Ladd offing Donnie and the prospect of us joining him?'

'Yeah, all right. I was just asking how you want to play this?'

'Carefully. If Mac starts to froth at the mouth, or in any way looks like he might might want to run into the street and carve folk at random, I think you should be the one to pin him down.'

Hod glowered at me. 'And what about you?'

I raised the walking stick, 'I'll provide support.'

'I'll let you do the talking.'

'I thought you might.'

We crossed the road into Mac's barbers shop. The closed sign was already up on the door and Mac was sweeping his handiwork into a loose pile of clippings in the centre of the room.

He spoke with a cig dangling from his lower lip, 'Oh, hello lads, dropping by to take me for a beer?'

I looked at Hod. He looked at the floor.

Mac sensed we weren't about to take him for a casual pint. 'What's up?'

'You finish what you're doing,' I said. 'And we'll wait for you out the back.'

Mac took the cigarette from his mouth and leaned on the handle of the sweeping brush. 'I'm not liking the look of this.'

'Wait till you hear what he has to say,' said Hod. 'You'll be liking it a whole lot less.'

CHAPTER 17

Mac listened carefully, lighting a succession of cigarettes by laying each lit tip on the end of the next. He looked pensive, drawn. Like a man who was thinking deeply about something but only finding more and more gloomy solutions to his shitty situation. Hod and I stared at each other across the smokey little room and exchanged grimaces. There was fear and apprehension in those looks but something worse: a dread of consequences yet to be calculated.

I turned to Mac. 'You seem to be taking this well.'

'Is that supposed to be funny?' he said.

'A bit …'

Mac flicked ash on the floor and started to brush the top of his thigh with the flat of his hand. More stray ash evacuated on the floor. 'If Wally's sold us to the filth, I'll rip off his head and shit down his neck.'

Hod spoke. 'Be good for the lolz.'

'Well, what are we waiting for.' Mac rose, walked for the door. He had a leather coat hanging there and he grabbed it off the hook, wrestling himself into the sleeves with jerky movements.

Hod and I followed. In the shop front, Mac rummaged in a drawer behind the till. He seemed to have found what he was looking for, tipping the contents of a small box into his open hand. He plucked up the item with two fingers acting as tweezers. As we gathered at the till, Mac tested the hinge on the cut-throat razor, opening and closing, exposing the shining steel of the blade to the light.

'Wouldn't like to be in Wally's boots,' I said.

Mac closed the blade, dropped it in his inside pocket. 'Wally should have thought things through properly. What he's got coming, he brought on himself.'

I raised hands. 'You'll get no argument here, mate.'

We headed for Hod's truck. The road to the car lot in Newhaven was almost bumper to bumper with traffic. We'd hit the busy spell, but workies tearing up most of the road didn't help. Everyone was alone with their thoughts, no one spoke. The air was thick with the deathly silence.

When we reached the car lot the gates were still open. I'd expected Wally to shut up early, perhaps take a few days holiday, somewhere far away. But, there he was, middle of the lot. The space-hopper guttage was held in check by a thin blue T-shirt with sweat pooling at the pits. As he clocked the truck, Wally froze. It was as if the prospect of such a visit was only now entering his mind. He scanned our faces and spotted something lurking there he didn't like. It brought him out in terrors.

As Wally ran for the portacabin, Hod parked up the truck and we got out. It was a ridiculous scene, like some old Benny Hill sketch. Wally's skanky arse hanging over the top of his baggy Wranglers as he chanked it — dear life calling him — for what looked like safety.

He locked himself inside the portacabin. As we got closer, the sound of a table being dragged towards the back of the door was unmistakeable. I peered in the filthy window and saw Wally barricading himself in. He was now trying to get a handle on the filing cabinet, walking it towards the door, inch by inch.

Hod hauled up behind me. 'Is this guy for fucking real?' He slapped the wall, 'You could shoot peas through this!'

'I thought about smoking him out, y'know putting a fire under his arse.'

Hod shook his head. 'Much as I'd like to see the panic on his face as the flames rose, I think we could do without the fire brigade dropping by.'

'So, what are you thinking?'

He turned back to the truck. 'Leave it with me.'

I watched Hod lever open the back tray and reach inside. When he turned back for the cabin he had a sledge hammer over his shoulder and a shit-eating grin on his face.

'You have some style, bruv,' I said.

Hod eased past Mac and myself and motioned us to take a few steps back. He weighed the hammer in his hands a few times then took a swing at the door. The handle bucked and fell to the ground but the lock stayed intact. The second slam put the door in, knocking out the hinges. Hod decided the lock wasn't budging and concentrated on a demolition job instead.

From my position at the corner of the cabin I could see Wally spreading himself against the back wall. If Wally wasn't already shitting bricks, Hod made sure: ramming his face through a gap in the door and yelling: 'Here's Johnny!'

'Go away. Leave me.' Wally yelped.

Hod dropped the grin. 'Not fucking likely, mate.' He put his shoulder to the door and eased the table and filing cabinet back the way they'd came.

'What do you want from me?' said Wally.

Hod cleared enough room for Mac and me to push our way in behind him. The confined space seemed even smaller than I remembered it, but that could have been the recent rearrangement of the furniture. I kicked a pile of mouldy Auto Traders out of the way as I made for the cowering sack of shit in the back of the cabin. He looked like a snared rodent, there was no fight in him. I grabbed his collar and threw him towards the others.

'Get his arse on a seat,' I said, 'if he's lucky, we might let him get off it when we're done.'

Hod pushed Wally into a boxy, plastic chair. He sat gasping, searching us from face to face. He was looking for an out but found nothing.

'What ... What do you want with me?' he said.

I watched Mac pace towards Wally. He walked slowly, revealing the shiny blade of the razor as he went.

'No ... no,' said Wally.

'Shut the fuck up!' Mac put out a hand and grabbed Wally by the shoulder, wedging him in the chair. Wally squirmed, but Mac blocked him, jamming a forearm across Wally's neck. All Mac's weight held Wally flat to the chair; in a few seconds he realised struggling was useless.

'There's a way to give a Chelsea smile,' said Mac, raising the razor up to Wally's eye level. 'Some will tell you it's best to just put the blade in the mouth and push — one blow.' He gestured with the razor.

'No ... please.'

'Well, I disagree,' continued Mac. 'See, I take pride in my work and when someone asks me to inflict pain, I want to make sure they get their money's worth.'

'Please ...'

Mac waved the razor, left to right. It was a loose movement, a well-practiced flick of the wrist. 'So, I always do one side at a time — twice the pain, and it draws out the fun a little longer. Now, the scars either side of the mouth rarely match up, but for me that's just a wee bonus: it makes them look worse.'

Mac put the cold steel on Wally's face and played with the blunt side of the blade, tracing lines of potential scars.

'Look, what do you want?' said Wally. 'I'll tell you anything you want to know, I've nothing to hide.'

I tapped Mac on the shoulder. 'Let me at him.'

Wally seemed to try and curl away from us in the seat. He trembled. It was almost an instinct on my part to slap him round. I caught him a sore one, bursting his nose. The sight of the blood brought real terrors to Wally's mind. His lower lip quivered as he searched for words but found none.

'Okay, Wally, talk,' I said. 'I know you've been to the filth.'

'They came to me! I swear it, they showed up after they found Donnie's body. What was I supposed to do?'

Mac spoke. 'Not drop us in it for a fucking start.'

'He's right, Wally.'

'I didn't. I didn't, I promise.'

'I hear differently.'

'The cop, McEwan, he said he knew you were there on the night. He said you were seen in Aldo's.'

I looked at Hod and Mac. They both stayed still, impassive.

'Seen by who?'

'I don't know.'

'It could have been Sharky,' said Hod.

I stepped away from Wally towards the others. 'Talk sense, why's Sharky going to drop himself in it?'

'He could have done it anonymously.'

I didn't buy it. 'Bullshit.'

'You heard what Fitz said, this McEwan character was going apeshit, if he rounded up some boyos with a bit of form then maybe Sharky threw him a bone.'

I wasn't convinced, but if Hod was right then things were definitely worse than we thought. Jonny Ladd would soon be measuring us all for cement overcoats.

'Okay, Wally, say Hod's right and you never fingered us to plod — but you've still been feeding us a line about why you were looking for Donnie.'

He moved uncomfortably in the chair, his head bobbed a little, like he was almost ready to agree. 'Look, I had my reasons, I was worried you might not take the job if I told you everything.'

'He's fucking right there,' said Mac.

'You've got no choice but to tell us now,' I said. 'Unless you class with or without a face as a choice.'

Mac started to open and close the razor.

'Okay, look. Donnie was in trouble. I don't know what happened but he'd got mixed up with some bad people.'

'Go on.'

'I tried to get him to sort himself out for months because … he was with Stella.'

'Stella?'

'My daughter.'

I had a flashback to Aldo's on the night we snatched Donnie. That girl was still out there, with only Sharky and Johnnie Ladd for company. My stomach lurched at the realisation that she was Wally's daughter. I couldn't shake the look on her face, those pleading eyes. Jesus, she didn't know what she was dealing with.

'Wally, you stupid bastard, you've made this a hundred times worse.'

'Really?'

'Yes, fucking really.'

He slumped, his head dropping into open hands. 'Oh, Stella. I only wanted too see my daughter again. I thought if you found Donnie, you'd find her too. I'm sorry, Stella. I'm so sorry.'

Wally started to weep.

'What happened on the night Donnie died, did they come for him?' I said.

'No, nobody. When I was alone with him, I got a bit testy,' said Wally. 'Donnie clubbed me one and took off, said he was going to find Stella. I never saw him after that.'

Mac closed the razor and began to shake his head.

'I could have told him how knocking on Jonny Ladd's door would end.'

When Wally started the weeping once more, Mac walked for the gap where the door had been. Hod followed him.

I leaned over and eased Wally up in the chair. He slumped again the second I let him go, his tired red face now streaked with tears. He was in bits. 'Okay, I hope to Christ you're telling me the truth.'

'I swear, on my Stella's life.'

'You better swear it, Wally. Because I still have my doubts about you.'

'Gus, I swear to you. I only want my daughter back. That's all I ever wanted. I'm worried sick about her.'

I left Wally, a pathetic heap bubbling in the portacabin, and followed the others through the gaping doorway. Mac was leaning on the back of the truck, chugging deep on a cig. Hod stood with his fists in his pockets — he looked primed for a serious bag session.

'Well,' said Mac.

'We have to find the girl.'

'I was worried you might say that.'

CHAPTER 18

I wandered around the streets of Meadowbank for the best part of the early evening. It was a rare night, folk out burning up the recently mowed grass in Holyrood Park with their tinfoil barbecues. A couple of quid to eat alfresco. There was nothing like the smell of Lorne Sausage from Iceland — made me nostalgic for Kerry Katona's brief spell as an advertising icon. Like fuck it did, my mind was freewheeling, I clocked the symptoms easily enough.

There'd been a time, not too far in the past, when I could summon the powers of concentration. It wasn't a normal state for me, say I'm a dreamer, but I'm not the only one. I trained myself out of it, well, that's what I liked to tell myself. Truth was, the world had beaten the dreams out of me. At first with a razor strop, gripped in my father's fist, and later with a whisky bottle.

This neighbourhood was my home, even the brutalist stadium they flung up for the Commonwealth Games felt comfy. What did that tell me about myself? That I identified with steel I-bars and quick-set concrete? On the outside, maybe. Because inside I was fucking jelly.

I stood on the doorstep of the flat where Mac had told me Amy was staying and quietly quivered. What the hell was I doing? I'd never had an answer to that. I was forever a victim to the vagaries of deeper currents, unseen hands and invisible strings. If there were big questions in this life, and undoubtedly there were, I had some pathetically small answers.

I depressed the buzzer.

Silence.

Became aware of birdsong. I shit you not.

'Hello ...' It was Amy, a child was crying in the background. She sounded stressed.

'Have I called at a bad time?' Jesus, did I know a good time?

'Gus?'

'I'm afraid so.' I felt utter joy she had identified my voice, it made me feel like someone else.

Amy never replied, just buzzed me in. I felt my heart-rate ramping as I ascended the stairs but I was being pushed; this needed to be done. My damaged leg started to cramp up as I went on but I forced myself through it.

I heard the chain rattling on the other side of the door and then spotted a thin chink of yellow light escaping beyond the door's jamb. The first face I spotted wasn't Amy's, however, it was the nipper's. She was fair, a little girl, with the bluest of eyes I'd ever seen. Her cheeks were flushed, wet with tears, but she'd stopped crying and was smiling at me, wide and wonderful.

'Hi ...'

I turned to Amy, 'God, she has your looks anyway.' Was this an appropriate opener? Here I was, right at the kick-off, making the kind of inferences I should have been steering a mile wide of.

'Gus, is something wrong?' She was staring at the walking stick.

'This? Oh, no … it's nothing. Bit of a tussle with a couple of Bull Terriers.'

She didn't look convinced, her eyes rolling upwards in that way she had a habit of doing. 'Still living the dream, then?'

I smirked, 'Oh, yeah, only it's the stuff of nightmares.'

She ushered me through the door. 'Well, welcome to my world.'

Amy had the place done-up nicely. I'd only ever known her in student digs or shitty bedsits before. Now she had a whole flat to herself, well, nearly to herself, she'd made a lot of effort. The walls were apple white, she told me, she liked the crisp freshness. I nodded. There was something said about the wallpaper, a feature wall, or was that a statement wall. I dunno. I registered very little about interior furnishings. I had a couch and an ashtray and that did me fine.

'I wanted teal, but I thought it would overpower the room,' said Amy. 'If it was bigger I'd have got away with it, so I just used it as an accent.'

'Come again?'

She pointed to the cushion on the couch, a strange furry job that looked like it was made with the pelt of a dead Muppet. 'I'm boring the arse off you already, Gus … Sit down and I'll get you a coffee.'

Amy put the baby in its playpen and left the room. I sat staring at the kid, she was still smiling, but trying to cram her fingers in her mouth now too. I didn't get around so many kids these days, certainly not babies. It had been a long time since my nieces and nephews were that wee. The only reference I had to draw on was when Debs fell pregnant. My ex-wife had a problem going the full term, though, and my most prominent memories were painful ones. I could still see the crib and the baby bath, flung in a corner of the garage, never used.

'Gold Blend okay?'

'Shit yeah, the good stuff ...' I looked at the playpen, 'Sorry, my mouth running away. I'll avoid any F-bombs, promise.'

Amy grinned. 'I can't believe you're here.'

'I should be saying that to you, how long's it been?'

'What, since I popped sprog or last saw you?'

I supped my coffee, tried to hide my shame behind the cup. 'I meant, when did you move in?'

'Not long, nearly three months now.'

'I never get up this end.'

'You don't need to make excuses.'

I desperately wanted to smoke but knew it was a non starter. 'I drove past you on the Walk, I was with Hod.'

'Oh ...'

'I had to twist his arm to get the story.'

'And did you ... get it?'

I balanced the cup on my knee, it was a nervous gesture and we both knew it. 'Look, I'm sorry Amy.'

'For what?' She scratched her head and let out a long sigh. 'Look, Gus, you've nothing to be sorry for. I don't blame you for steering clear of me.' The kid squealed and Amy made a placating face. 'It's amazing how a pram scares the men off.'

'No, Amy, I didn't mean that. I didn't know. I'm sorry I never looked out for you, that's what I mean.'

'Gus, Jesus Christ, I'm a big girl! I don't need looking after.'

I was getting tongue tied. 'I didn't mean ...'

'Look, I'm perfectly content with my situation. Can't say it was always that way, it takes some getting used to, but that's life. I accept it, I'm not living a delusion like all those silly cows on Farcebook posting pictures of themselves out every night, or grinning next to every new present from their latest boyfriend. I know what's real.'

Amy had changed, she'd done a lot of growing up. It seemed like a lot more time had passed since I last spoke to her.

'Most people are lost, Amy, they swallow the prole-feed. I'm glad you have got yourself together. I just wish that I'd been a better friend to you, I could have been there for you, that's all I'm saying. It wasn't a choice of mine, to stay away, I just didn't know.'

She jerked her gaze from the kid. 'But, this was my choice, Gus. It always was my choice, I never ever considered getting rid of her. I never once bought all that crap about it just being a bunch of cells, or that because I'm a woman I had the right to murder because it was my body. That's all bullshit.'

I didn't know what to say. I flapped about looking for the right response. 'You always had your head screwed on.'

'I'm not claiming to be holier than thou, or clambering for some moral high ground. I just think that equating murder with "oh but I won't be able to go clubbing" or with "I won't be able to afford a new handbag" is shocking. It's evil … it's murder and I've seen more than enough of the kind of damage that does.'

She wasn't kidding. If I'd had any doubts about calling on Amy, they were evaporating. Motherhood hadn't softened her one bit, she was still as hard as brass knuckles and twice as dangerous.

'I'm glad we cleared things up,' I said. 'I don't care what most people think of me, but you're one of the very few I care a great deal about.'

She reached forward, bumping her cup of mine. 'Cheers, mate.'

If she had any ill will towards me for having been the worst of friends, then she was kind enough to let it go. It was difficult, verging on the painful, to have to be the one to make the first move but I fessed up to my wrongs. Shit, there'd been so many of them that it was almost a personality trait of mine now.

There was a moment of stilled silence in the room. I started craving a cigarette again but the place smelled too much like a scented candle store for me to even consider the prospect.

Amy looked at me, curling her hair behind her ear as she spoke. 'So, enough about me. What have you been up to of late, Mr Dury? Not living quietly, I presume.'

I nearly spat out my coffee. The prospect of a quiet life in my current situation was as close to hilarity as I was likely to get.

'Eh, no. Apart from the dog attack there was a bad scuffle in Aldo's.'

'The chippy?'

I nodded. 'Then there was an early visit from plod this morning.'

'The police!' She put down her cup and tucked her feet beneath her as she turned to face me on the couch. 'Are you working a case?'

'Well, yes and no. Let's just say, it's not the case I thought I was working.'

'Tell me more.' She sounded too interested.

'Really? Are you sure you want to hear all the gory details? I mean, they are very, very gory.'

'Of course. I mean, if I'm going to be any use to you, I'll have to.'

'*Wha—?*'

'C'mon, Gus, that's the real reason you're here — you need my help. You might not know it, but you obviously do.'

'Jesus, you're serious.' I looked over at the kid, she was sleeping now.

'Don't worry about Evie, she's at my mum's most of the time, I was about to start looking for a job anyway. This'll suit me perfectly, and it'll be just like old times, the A-Team back together, and all that.'

It was my turn to roll my eyes.

Amy was off the couch, running back to the kitchen. 'Hold that thought, I'll top up the coffees!'

'Amy, I didn't mean ... I mean, I was just ...'

She couldn't hear me over the noise of the kettle, and her do-de-do-doing the A-Team theme tune.

CHAPTER 19

It was well against my better judgement. But then, I was well beyond the realms of sane decisions. There was a point that every alky knew that I called "letting go of the wheel". It was a variation on the AA pledge of putting it all in the man upstairs' lap. I knew all about abnegating responsibility, so the whole theory appealed to me. I'd even looked into it in scholarly fashion, constructed my own philosophical reasoning.

Carl Jung called it enantiodromia. Heraclitus said something about the road up also being the road down. Nietzsche may have remarked about having to hit rock bottom before bouncing back. It all came down to the same singular point: when you went too far to one extreme, the elastic snapped and fired you over to the very opposite.

I'd been running around for months now playing the pillar of society, well, as much as I ever could. I'd had a job. I kept a car on the road. The sauce was something from my past. Who the fuck was I kidding? I could almost hear the elastic creaking, the sound of that one monumental whack on the arse when it snapped. Can't say the territory I found myself in was that enlightening, mind you. But, it sure was very familiar.

Hod grunted from the driver's side of the truck. I turned to catch him drumming fingers on the dash.

'What the fuck's up with you now?' said Mac.

Hod's nostrils flared. 'I don't do couch potato, this is far too long for anyone to be sitting on their arse.'

Mac tutted, turned to me.

'There's no point busting in there like a goon squad,' I said. 'There's only old bluenoses and dole moles who wouldn't even bat an eyelid. We need to wait for the big biffers.'

We were parked outside The Buck, the drinker where I'd attracted the attention of the pugs with dugs. It was a long-shot, expecting them to turn up again, just because it was the same time and place, but I was desperate enough to start leaning on pattern recognition.

'What makes you think they'll tell us anything?' said Mac.

'I'm pretty sure they won't tell us a damn thing, even if we ask nicely,' I said.

'Who said we were going to ask nicely?' said Hod. 'We're already being fingered for Donnie's death by plod and it's only a matter of time before Sharky's banging on our shins with an iron-bar.'

'Talking of iron-bars,' said Mac, nodding to the back of the truck, 'did you load up?'

'I brought the appropriate hardware, of course.'

I got the distinct impression that Hod and Mac weren't really connecting with me on the seriousness of our situation. Fitz the Crime had put the shits right up me: Barlinnie didn't have a members' bar, last I looked. Perhaps I needed to stress the point.

'Look, lads, we're really up against the clock. According to Fitz, this McEwan boyo isn't messing about, I fully expect to be hoiked in before the end of the day, and introduced to the rubber hose.'

'But he's got fuck all on you, Gus,' said Mac, 'apart from a possible statement from Sharky, and who's going to take that scrote seriously?'

'You're forgetting about Wally,' I said. 'If the filth squeeze that little fucker too hard he'll be squealing like a guinea pig. Can you imagine it: "Here's your statement, Mr Wallace ... sign here".'

Mac pushed his back further into the seat and groaned. 'And by the sounds of it this McEwan one doesn't mind cutting a few corners.'

We went further, some grumbling about the grey areas of Wally's story. Why hadn't he come clean with us from the start? Of course, we'd have ran a mile if he had come clean, but did Wally really have the marbles to foresee that? What was Wally's connection to Donnie, apart from employer and employee, with that bit of boss's daughter thing going on? The Bad Ladd was no idiot, though, and he certainly wasn't about to have someone wasted in dramatic fashion if there wasn't a definite need.

'Oh, hold up,' said Hod.

Mac and I broke off our discussion. 'That's the biffers,' I said.

Hod took the keys from the ignition and made for the door handle. 'Party time.'

'No. Wait. Let them get settled in first.' I was delighted to see they'd came without their trap-jawed back-up.

'*Wha*—?' Hod was clearly disappointed.

'Just cool the beans, Hod,' said Mac. 'What's the plan, Gus?'

All eyes turned on me. 'Plan? Oh, hang on, I'll do a wee PowerPoint presentation for the pair of you ... I've no plan for fucksake. Jesus, if I had any sort of a plan whatsoever, it wouldn't involve walking into a hardy drinker and squaring up to a couple of roided-up skinheads with "Fighting's Fun" tattooed on their knuckles!'

'I dunno, sounds the game to me,' said Hod.

I turned to Mac. 'You see what we're dealing with?' I pushed Hod out the door. 'Right, get going. Let's get this over with.'

He smiled. 'Nice one.'

'Hold up,' said Mac. 'You got some chibs for us?'

'Oh, yeah,' Hod walked to the back of the vehicle, opened up the truck-bed toolbox. He started to pull out a fresh brace of pick-axe handles.

Mac took a tight hold. 'I love a bit of hickory, smells like victory.'

'Yeah, well, they were all out of napalm,' said Hod. He chucked me a lump of wood and nodded towards the bar. 'Right, let's do some damage.'

'Not too much, please. I mean, it would be great if at least one of them still had the power of speech afterwards, that being the whole point and everything,' I said.

We made for the entrance, looking like Thugs 'R' Us. If a police car was to pass us in the next sixty-seconds we were done.

I let Hod and Mac go in first, to set the scene.

The biffers were at the bar, pints already propped in front of them. The barman was pouring a wee goldie for the heavier of the two — he placed the glass in front of his mate and nodded towards us at the door.

The biffers turned to face us.

I had expected Hod to be the first to break ranks, but it was Mac. The mad bastard was on. Mac lunged for the nearest of the two and pelted his kidneys with the pick handle. It was like a cue for Hod, a dog whistle sounding in his ears. He wielded the hickory in two hands smashing the butt in the other biffer's nose. An explosion of claret flushed the white shirt-front beneath the black leather. The contrast of colours was like a volcanic eruption.

As I strolled over towards the bar I was a little surprised by the lack of commotion. The punters seemed to be quite used to gang warfare in their midst. The dole moles looked on as if the evening's entertainment had just arrived. A gummy old git in a turquoise shell-suit got up and started to clap, revving us on. The only other obvious movement was the barman reaching for the telephone receiver. I let him get as far as dialling the first digit and then brought my pick-handle down on his arm.

The crack of wood to bone was triumphant for only a second or two before it was drowned out by the barman's wails.

'You fucking cunt!' He yelled. 'You've broken my arm!'

'You have another one,' I bit. 'And I'd keep that away from the phone as well, unless you want to try pouring pints with two stookies.'

Hod and Mac were on top of their opponents now, quite literally. Elbows were being flung back and fists planted deep in the fleshy mess of bloodied faces.

I called time, bashed the bell on the end of the bar.

Hod and Mac looked up like a pair of hyenas on a recent kill.

'What the fuck?' said Hod. 'I was just getting started.'

'Get them in the truck.'

He grabbed his pug by the collar and started to march him across the floor.

'You're dead, you hear me ...' yelled the staggering skinhead. 'Don't you know who I am?'

Hod rabbit punched him. 'Save your breath, you'll need it.'

We cable-tied the daft lads and flung them, face down, on the floor of the truck's cab. It was all over in under ten minutes. I couldn't believe our luck.

'I expected more of a put up,' I said, as we headed out of Leith.

'Why? They're just a pair of fat bastards with sovvies and tats. I eat them for breakfast,' said Hod.

I turned towards the floor of the cab. 'You're not so impressive without the dogs, lads.'

'You don't know who you're dealing with.'

I laughed that up. 'Oh, I think I do. At least, I've a fair idea.'

'I swear to fuck, you're all dead for this.'

'Really. I feel fine, how do you feel, Mac? Hod?'

Mac: 'Exhilarated.'

Hod: 'Ready for round two.'

'Grand. You brought the blow-torch then?'

'Sure did.'

'Good stuff. I'm a big fan of the blow-torch. Some folk will say that the battery acid is the thing, but I like the contact of the open flame.'

'Where are you taking us?' yelled the daft lad.

'A nice little run in the country. A nice private spot we know, where no one will disturb us.'

'You're off your head. You'll die for this.'

'Oh, you mean like Donnie did out in that steading in Dunbar.'

Silence.

'Nothing to say about that, then? … No? … Didn't think so.'

132

'Watch the speed there, Hod,' said Mac. 'Don't want to be pulled over and all our fun spoiled.'

'Sure thing. I'll take it easy, can't have anything spoiling our fun.'

Hod started to laugh and Mac joined in. It was infectious, a release from the adrenaline rush back in the bar. We must have seemed hysterical, insane even. The noise filled the truck's cab and rattled all around us. Was it gallows humour? We knew we were fucked and digging in deeper but what choice did we have?

We were still laughing hard when the screaming started. Two grown men, supposed hard men, screaming and crying for their mothers. Call us a bunch of callous bastards but we found the sound of their sorrow only added to our hysterics. Hod near swerved off the road before he reined it in, still guffawing like a lunatic.

CHAPTER 20

There's some of us would have reservations about this sort of thing. Complained about the brutality, or bemoaned the lack of humanity. But, I'd seen far too many nights of the long knives to be bothered by that shite. My own father was the most brutal human being I'd ever encountered and there was no one to hold a match to the bastard. Being asked to slit an animal's throat by Daddy Dearest, and having the hide tanned clean off my arse night after night, developed in me a certain level of indifference to the suffering of my fellow man. Call me a cynic and you'll get no argument, I was at least that by now.

Hod and Mac had no such excuses, unless you counted the fact they were both born psychopaths. I watched them turf out the two biffers onto the scorched grass. We were deep into Midlothian, a whole region away from the city. The lack of concrete made me feel uneasy. I hadn't seen a Yodel van for nearly half-an-hour and felt like I'd fallen into a wormhole.

'You hear that?' said Mac.

'I don't hear anything.'

'Exactly! Eerie isn't it?' He simulated a shiver passing down his spine. 'I wonder if Donnie's with us in spirit?'

I was tempted to tell him to get a grip, but I figured his statement really wasn't for my benefit.

The lads from The Buck took the bait and started to slither on the grass, trying to slip their cable ties. 'What are you going to do to us?'

Hod arrived with the lit blow-torch just in time to answer their question. 'Can I go first? I'm desperate to roast me some nut-sack.'

Screams.

Yelling.

Threats.

We'd heard it all before, but it was nice to hear the fear building in their voices again.

Hod turned the pair of them over, sat them up, back-to-back. He put the blow torch down in front of the one facing us; the flame was burning about two inches away from the button-fly on his jeans. He started to tremble, sweat spooled from his red forehead.

'C'mon, please … *please.*'

'You're in no position to bargain with us,' I said. 'Can you feel the heat off that thing?'

'C'mon, I'm begging you … what do you want?'

I looked to Hod. 'Do we give him a break?'

He lunged towards the biffer. 'You want me to break something?'

'Well, let's see if he's going to play ball first. If he doesn't you can feel free to caramelise his tackle.' I moved towards the baldy hard man, who was melting before me, not so hard now. 'You only get one shot at this now, do you understand?'

Nods.

Rapid style.

'Yes. Yes.'

I knelt down, stuck fingers on his scalp and pushed back his head. I could see the fear burning in his bloodshot eyes.

'Now tell me: why did you set dogs on me when I was asking about Lee Donald?'

'Is he dead now? You said he was dead.'

'You hadn't heard?'

'No,' he shook his head from side to side. 'Did your crew do it?'

'What? Kill Donnie?'

'Yeah.'

I looked at Hod and Mac, neither gave an inch by way of indicating an answer. I went with the flow. 'How did you know Donnie?'

'He, eh, was part of the firm.'

'What firm?'

He didn't answer, I tried again on higher volume, 'What fucking firm?'

'Bunny's firm.'

'Who?

'Bunny Veitch. Mark Veitch.' I didn't know the name, Hod and Mac looked on blankly.

'Is this some fucking lightweight outfit? Little boys playing with sticks?'

The pug was sweating harder now, he looked down towards the blow-torch and as I followed his line of vision I noticed he'd pissed himself, the crotch of his jeans was soaking wet. 'Bunny ran with Jonny Ladd for years, he's a proper player.'

'Can't be that much of a name if I haven't heard of him.'

'He's on the up, Bunny's going to be big time.' He started to bite on his lower lip and push himself into his mate. The pair struggled together for a moment, butting heads.

'What was Donnie doing for Bunny — dealing?'

'A bit. He did lots, this and that. They were thick as thieves. C'mon let me go now, I've told you what you wanted.'

I eased myself up with the stick and walked over to Hod and Mac. The daft lads fought together on the grass, pushing themselves away from the blow-torch and screaming at each other.

'What do you think?' I said.

'I've never heard of him, this Bunny character,' said Mac.

Hod spoke: 'Me neither. Think it's legit?'

'I'd have had my doubts if the pug wasn't sitting in a pool of his own piss. It's easy enough to find out.'

'He pissed himself?'

'You sound surprised.'

'Disappointed really. I was hoping he might have shit himself.'

I turned back towards the pugs and the blow-torch.

'Are you gonna let them go?' said Mac.

'No. I'm leaving them where they are, I'm going to get Hod's torch.'

I left them in the grass, still tied to each other and wrestling like dogs in a sack. The big one, with the pissed pants, was trying to kick lumps out of his mate. Neither seemed to have realised that we were pulling out. How they would make it back to the city was their problem now, but I suspected it would come to serious blows before long.

As I got in the truck I sensed Hod's disappointment immediately. 'Jesus, if it'll make you feel any better go and break their fucking legs for them!'

Hod leapt for the door, grabbing a pick-axe handle from the truck-bed.

I looked at Mac. 'I was only joking.'

'Never make jokes about breaking bones with him.'

There was some yelping, which turned into screaming and shouting. Hod jumped back in the cab and slammed the door.

'Thanks, mate.'

'You are off your fucking dial.'

'Don't like leaving a job half-done, you know how it is.'

'You utter, utter nut-case.'

Hod was sufficiently hyped to put on some Public Enemy and start drumming his knuckles off the wheel as we headed back to the city.

'So, we were right about one thing,' he said.

Mac answered: 'That Donnie was dealing.'

'Well, we knew he didn't pick up that motor working for Wally,' I said.

'Who do you think this Veitch lad is?' said Mac.

'I'd have said some kind of bottom feeder but if he's been connected to Jonny Ladd then maybe not.'

'He *was* connected to the Bad Ladd, not now. There's a big difference.'

'If he's parted company with Ladd on bad terms it could play to our advantage. Maybe even give us an in with the man himself.'

'I'd doubt that,' said Mac. 'Ladd doesn't need any friends, and what if they didn't part on good terms and Veitch is anything but a friend? We could find ourselves in the middle of a very messy situation.'

I put my uninjured foot on the dash. 'Jesus, the angles keep coming don't they?'

Hod lowered the volume on the stereo, leaned over, 'I doubt this Veitch bloke can be a big enough name to front up to Ladd. If we haven't heard of him, he'd have to be either stupid or have balls the size of watermelons to test the Bad Ladd like that.'

We hit the by-pass in deep thought. So another name had been added to the list of ponderables. Bunny Veitch was new to me but I figured that wouldn't be the case for much longer. What his connection to Donnie was might have been as simple as his employer, but it could have been a lot deeper than that given the way things had played out. I didn't know why Sharky and Jonny Ladd were digging out Donnie at the same time as us, but they weren't doing it simply because there was nothing on the telly that night. Something was seriously wrong.

Whatever Donnie had been up to, the consequences hadn't been pretty. He'd paid a high price but I didn't think it was going to end there. We weren't at the beginning of the end, merely the end of the beginning.

Stella was still missing, and that stung. The next move sure as hell wasn't going to be a playful pat on the arse. I had a grim vision of Wally's daughter being strung up in an abandoned outbuilding somewhere.

'This is nuts,' I said.

'I can't figure it out,' said Mac. 'All I can say for sure is we're missing something.'

'I hope Amy strikes lucky.' Her name slipped out before I had managed to engage my brain.

'What was that?' said Mac.

'Have you got Amy on the job?' said Hod.

I had to play it straight, there was no other option. 'I took her on yesterday. We need all the help we can get and she knows her shit.'

'But she has a nipper to mind.'

'Her mam helps her out most days. Look, she wanted to get back in the saddle. She's a first-rate snooper and she's a chick — we're looking for a missing girl and, no offence lads, but none of us could score in a brothel.'

'Speak for yourself, Gus,' said Hod.

'Mate, if you fell into a bucket of tits you'd come out sucking your thumb. Now get real. We need Amy and she's good at what she does. She's sniffing around some of Stella's friends and acquaintances today, so with any luck she'll turn up something useful.'

'I hope so,' said Hod.

'Yeah, it'd be a start,' said Mac.

Hod pulled the truck up next to the lights on London Road. I dipped out the cab and waved them off. I knew by the time he'd delivered Mac home Hod would have had a million go-nowhere ideas and be itching to discuss them over a few of my beers. Just the thought alone exhausted me. I stuck my key in the door and headed for my flat. As I opened up I had a strange feeling that the place wasn't quite how I had left it.

Call it instinct, or paranoia, but my heart-rate ramped. As I opened the living-room door I caught a familiar smell, there was no mistaking it: a Cafe Creme cigarillo was underway in my front room.

I pushed open the door and stepped in.

A pair of black Loake Chelsea boots were balanced precariously on the back of my couch. The other end of the room was rank with the stench of cigarillo. For a second I felt like I'd stepped outside of myself, like I was watching a movie which I starred in, but had no idea of the plot.

'Ah, Gus Dury, good to see you.'

I limped into the middle of the room, 'Who the fuck are you?'

Two Loake boots swung onto the ground and were accompanied by the skirts of a dark overcoat. As he stood up, the man must have touched 6'4" — a little less without the heel. He shuffled the Caffe Creme into his other hand and extended an open palm in my direction.

141

'Detective Chief Inspector Robbie McEwan, I've been expecting you.'

The hinges of the door wheezed behind me once again, and the sound of flat-feet stomping the boards came quickly, as two uniformed plod grabbed my arms and shoved me against the wall.

'And on that note, Mr Dury, let me add — you're nicked!' said McEwan.

CHAPTER 21

For the second time in 24-hours I was forced to endure the stench of another man's pish. The cell had a toilet, but the bed had obviously proved too much of a temptation for the previous occupant, who had undertaken their own dirty protest there. It sent me back to my school days and a memory of the dirty protests in Ulster, and the hunger striker Bobby Sands. There was a song the kids from the Protestant school used to sing to us Catholic boys back then:

Could you go a chicken supper, Bobby Sands?
Could you go a chicken supper, Bobby Sands?
Could you go a chicken supper, you skinny fenian fucker?
Could you go a chicken supper, Bobby Sands?

I hated those little shits then and I hated them more now. I was starving, I'd have killed for a chicken supper. Detective McEwan had not brought me so much as a cup of tea. As for my supposed friend Fitz the Crime, he had steered clear too. There was a time when Fitz would drop by with a quarter-bottle of scoosh in the evening to settle my shakes if I'd been lifted, and another wee heart-starter in the morning. Those seemed like glory days to me now.

My bad leg was starting to ache, so I took to walking circles around the cell. My mind was full of incriminations, I wanted someone to blame for my latest diversion down Shit Street. It didn't seem to matter how close I got to the leafy environs of respectability, it were as if the neighbourhood of bruised emotions was where I felt most comfortable. I certainly seemed to return there often enough. Something seemed to draw me to the self-destruct switch, a bit like that insect on *A Bug's Life* that can't take its eyes off the big blue light.

"Don't look into the light!"

"Don't stick your hand in the fire!"

It didn't matter who was giving the advice, or even if it was bloody good advice, I was on the down escalator and that only led one way.

I heard keys rattling beyond my cell door. I made for the Judas hole and opened up. I had just enough time to catch sight of Mac being shoved into the cell opposite. There was a further commotion a little way up the corridor and I heard Hod's admonishing tones.

'Get fucked, filth!'

The uniforms locked Mac and Hod in their cells and headed back the way they'd come. I waited till the outside door was closed behind plod before calling out.

'Mac … Hod … it's Gus, can you hear me?'

'Gus, how you faring?' said Mac.

'Fair enough, I suppose,' I said. 'This is a fine situ for the lads, eh?'

'It's like *Escape from Alcatraz*, the three of us in here,' said Hod. 'Who's going to be the one that trains a pet mouse to run back and forth with secret messages?'

'The mice have more sense than to come in here, they get bullied by the rats,' said Mac. 'Mind you, I'm not going the one that cuts his fingers off in wood-shop either.'

The patter continued in the same vein, with a row over who was going to be Charley Butts, the inmate that got left behind on the night of the escape. I was beginning to look back longingly on the previous peace and quiet of my pish-smelling cell.

'So, where did they pick you pair up?' I said.

'Right outside Mac's shop,' said Hod. 'They were sneaky fuckers as well, not a panda car in sight, just a black Transit, fit to bursting with bacon.'

'Well, McEwan was lying sprawled out on my sofa, hanging off the end of a cigarillo when I got back.'

'Seriously? How did he get in?' said Hod.

'Well, I'm guessing the door you knocked fuck out of fifty times a day wasn't up to the job.'

'I'll have to take a look at that when I get out.'

'If you get out.'

'Yeah, well, after my session with Mr Nightstick. They've nothing on us, this is just a scare tactic. They want to put the shits up us.'

Mac spoke: 'He's right, Gus. It's a fishing expedition. If this McEwan lad is as clued on as we reckon then he's not going to have bought into any of Wally's nonsense.'

'It's not what Wally might have said, or Sharky for that matter. McEwan's after a collar, quick and easy, and it wouldn't be too hard for him to pin on any one of us with our track records. Christ on a cross, Mac, you've done time for GBH!'

'It wasn't like I got done for murder.'

'To be fair, though, it's just a kick in the arse off murder,' said Hod.

'Well, you'd know, wouldn't you?' said Mac. 'Being the man who has a thing for breaking legs. Oh, shit … No!'

'*What?*' said Hod.

Mac's voice trailed off. 'The pick-axe handles were in the back of the truck.'

I'd heard enough.

Closed up the Judas hole and slunk back to the piss-reeking mattress.

I could hear the pair of them, back and forth, blaming and shaming. It meant very little. I knew what the real score was. If McEwan wanted to fit us up, he wouldn't have to try too hard. I'd been in similar situations in the past but only ever had myself to worry about. It gored me deep to think of the fact that I'd put Mac and Hod in this situation — if I hadn't actually come up with the idea myself, then I hadn't done a thing to stop it.

I dropped into a bleak pit. Wanted to tell them, 'Fuck it, I'll go Charlie Butts, lads'.

The cell door scraped open. A uniform in a blue apron and matching elbow-length plastic gloves appeared. He had the widest, most shit-eating grin on his chops I'd ever seen.

'Get stripped. Get this on.'

He threw a white bundle at me. As I unfurled it I clocked it was a paper jumpsuit. It had a hood attached.

'Don't you have them in green, that's more my colour,' I bit back.

'Move it!' he yelled, turning for the door.

I was asked to provide a swab from my gums. I say asked, but I got the distinct impression that I'd be giving it no matter what I said. Some other stuff, hair samples and fingernail scrapings, followed. I tried to be underwhelmed, after all I had nothing to hide. There was none of my DNA at Donnie's murder scene, was there?

After the forensic jaunt I was taken to an interview room. Cold grey walls, battleship grey I think they call it, and one formica-topped table with two chairs on one side and one on the other. I was sitting in my paper playsuit — it had feet attached for fucksake — trying to ignore the fact that I looked like a grown man dressed as Peter Rabbit.

No matter how hard I tried to put it out of my mind, there was an unconscious urge creeping up on me.

The Drink.

I wanted alcohol, in a way that I hadn't craved it in a very long time. Some instinctive part of me, that dark vault in my mind, was now unlocked. The beast was loose, and only one thing would subdue it now.

I was twitching worse than Angela Merkel in a 5G hotspot by the time the door-handle finally turned. The sound of expensive leather soles slapped on the hard floor. I looked up to see Detective Chief Inspector Robbie McEwan marching my way.

He'd loosened off his tie and managed to roll up the French cuffs on his shirt. The slicked back hair had more than a few strays, even a runaway kiss-curl; think it was safe to say the late shift didn't suit him.

'Right, Dury,' he said. 'It's time to pay the piper.'

'Is that what this is about? Marching kids out of Hamelin in the Middle Ages? You've so got the wrong dude for that gig.'

'Don't be fucking funny. I want your arse, Dury.'

'Well, thank you, but flattery will get you nowhere in this instance.'

He lunged over the table and grabbed me by the collars, yanked me out of the chair. I was waiting for a sledgehammer

147

right to the gut, for all the hair gell and aftershave, he looked a pretty useful player. But, he threw me back in the chair.

A finger pointed at my beak.

'Start talking sense, I want names and numbers. I want the real down-low on Donnie's death and not the rambling shite your mate Wally supplied us with.'

'You got rambling shite off Wally, I'm impressed — I just got shite.'

'What are you talking about, Dury?'

'Did Wally even mention to you that he hired us to find Lee Donald?'

'Hired? I thought you were done with all that bollocks.'

'I was, but I found myself a little financially embarrassed and Mr Wallace wanted to find his employee so it sounded like a no-brainer.'

He scratched his wrist, pulled the chair out. The uniform in the corner seemed to relax a little seeing McEwan's blood-pressure recede.

'Keep talking.'

'There's not much more to say. Wally came to me through an old friend, asked if I'd look into the sudden disappearance of Donnie? I said no to begin with, then I got the boot from my job and had a rethink.'

McEwan took down the details of my former employers. I had a dry chuckle to myself to think of Terry getting a call from the police later on. I hoped the call came in the middle of the night.

'So Wally hired you and the Chuckle Brothers out there? I thought he was fucking stupid right enough, but that defies belief.'

'I have a rep for getting things done.'

'Really?'

I grinned back, 'Check it out, when you're doing your police work stuff.'

McEwan put down his pen and leaned towards me, balancing on his elbows. 'Dury, I know all I need to know about you by looking at the sight before me. You're a washed-up, cocky little cunt. I don't know what wild ideas you have about yourself, but I keep hearing your name mentioned in some bloody dodgy company and that unsettles me.'

I presumed he wasn't talking about my visits to Easter Road to watch Hibs; though I did have him down as a Jambo, said, 'I think what unsettles you the most is that you had the fucking horn for me from the off. You went looking for an easy solution to a complicated problem and your forensic tests have turned up nowt.'

'Forensics are ongoing, there's no saying what that steading in Dunbar will yield. We haven't even looked over the half of it yet. Let me assure you, Dury, I turn up one useable cast of your Doc Martens or a stray hair of your head, and I'm going to put you down like a mangy dog.'

'I've never been there in my life.'

'Oh really, well why are you shaking?'

'That's unrelated.'

'Oh, that's right. I'd heard you liked a drop.'

I didn't reply, just tried to stare through him, but didn't have the bottle to pull it off.

McEwan brought a packet of cigarettes from his pocket, Embassy, and put them in front of me. A yellow Bic lighter followed. I took them and sparked up — wasn't what I was really after, but the nicotine settled my nerves.

'Thanks,' I said.

'Consider it the last kindness you'll get from me.'

I shrugged. 'Fair play.'

The finger came out again, 'You're holding out on me, Dury. I know it and you know I fuckingwell know it. Now, I haven't sussed what your role in all of this is, but I can see what you and your crazies are capable of and I'd put nothing by any of you.'

I resisted a reply, held schtum.

He pushed out his chair and stood up. He looked like he might walk for the door but he turned and planted his hands on the table, loomed over me. 'Andy Wallace has got you into a lot of trouble, we're talking murder here, I'm not fucking around. Now, Wally might be too stupid to do the right thing but you don't have to follow his lead. You wouldn't last five minutes inside, Dury, some big toe-rag would have you wiping his arse day and night. Now Mac and Hod are hefty boyos, but you're not in their league, you wouldn't stand a chance.'

He was trying to needle me. 'Get fucked.'

'You're the one that'll get fucked, Dury. Good and proper, I shouldn't wonder.'

He pushed himself off the table and turned for the door; the hem of his trousers had gathered on his Loake boots.

'Hey, am I free to go now?'

A laugh. 'God no.'

'Well, when?'

'That's up to you.'

I shot out my seat. 'Don't give me that shite, you can't hold me if you've got nothing on me!'

The door was opened for him. He stepped through, saying nothing.

150

CHAPTER 22

I couldn't even be arsed to put the laces back in my Docs. I gathered up my stuff and headed for the door. The bastards had broken my tabs: there were only three Rothmans left in the pack and they'd all been snapped off at the filter. I wondered what kind of petty mindedness compelled someone to do that? The same kind of sub-90 IQ that fancies a job in the filth.

Outside the station, I sparked up. Wasn't so bad, like smoking a rollie or basically any French fag. I coughed a little, spat out some stray spiders' legs of snout that found their way onto my tongue. In lieu of a drink, the tobacco seemed to settle some cravings.

I had an instinct to call Hod — something gnawing on my conscience — but his mobi went straight to voicemail. Fair put the shits up me, let me tell you. I didn't think it looked good for the bold Hod. I worried about that bloodied hickory he was holding, could see plod making improper use of it. Not as improper as Hod's use, mind you, but you never know. I certainly wouldn't have put anything past this McEwan character, he was a Robocop of the first rank.

I bashed in a new number, tried Mac.

Ringing.

'… Gus, you out?' He sounded breathless, anxious.

'Just this minute.' I drew on my filterless Rothmans, 'Where's Hod?'

'Dunno. I've been trying his phone but by the looks of it they must have kept him in.'

'It'll be those fucking pick-axe handles, the filth'll be planting them out at the steading in Dunbar next.'

Mac cut me off. 'No dice, buddy. I've got Hod's truck here. The sticks are already smoking in the grate.'

Relief washed over me, but it didn't last long. 'They never found them?'

'Never looked, the truck's not been touched. Still where he left it, right outside my shop.'

'Are you back there now, Mac?'

'Yeah, not opening up today — I'm still shaking worse than a jakey with a tin cup.'

I gave a grin. 'Don't want to lob off some poor bastard's earlobe.'

'Again …' Mac thawed some. 'Although last time was intentional. And I didn't stop at the lobe.'

'All right, *Chopper*, when you get out of memory lane, any chance of a lift?'

'Yeah, sure. I'll come and pick you up now if you like.'

'Thanks, mate. My bloody leg isn't up to the schlepp home.'

'I'm on my way.'

Hung up.

I sat down on the kerb, feet in the gutter. A Cornetto wrapper stuck itself to my Docs; thought about removing it but realised I really didn't care anymore. I was pondering what I'd got Hod into — tried to put it on him, say it was all his doing really. Didn't work. I knew Hod was a nut-job, going along with his radge ideas was something only I could feel guilty for. And I did. How did I let everything get so out of control? The thought to give Terry a call and beg for my job back flashed, but thankfully, it was only a thought, and easily batted aside. I'd got myself into this, I could get myself out of it.

I dowped my tab and ferreted in the pocket of my Crombie for the laces of my Docs. They were still crunchy with the dried blood from the dog bites. I was feeding the aglet through the little metal hoops when a big car flicked on the blinkers and started to slow. It stopped right next to me, a foot shy of the kerb.

An electric window went down, slowly.

It was Fitz, fleeing the station for the day, no doubt. He had one arm out the window, and was trying to look carefree, but fooling nobody.

'I heard you'd been released,' he said. 'How's things?'

I was still sore that he hadn't brought me a wee heart-starter. 'Well, my mouth's drier than a nun's muff, but apart from that I suppose I could be worse.'

The dig might not have hit home, he looked nervy now, fidgeting and glancing in the mirror. 'Look, I can't be seen here.'

'We really do need to talk, mate.'

He bridled, like I'd put too much emphasis on the last word. 'What's that supposed to mean?'

'It means, you weren't kidding about this McEwan character.'

'I said he was serious, Gus.'

'Yeah, well so am I now. He's kept Hod in.'

'I know.'

'You do?' Don't know why I was surprised he knew, but I was.

'There was a match.' That mirror again.

'What are you on about?'

'I don't know the details but the boffins turned up something on Hod.'

I couldn't believe what I was hearing. Had a rapid need to make a sharp intake of breath. I got up and leaned over the car. 'Jesus, you mean McEwan's got what he was after?'

'Gus, I have to go.' Fitz started to put up the window. 'I'll be in touch.'

He almost spun wheels out of there, leaving me only a grimace at the badge on the boot of his new Audi S4. Was the entire world driving a better car than me these days?

'Fitz, for fucksake.'

He was gone.

I felt a wound opening up in me for what had happened to Hod. I'd managed to drop him in the mincer several times before, but this was beyond the beyonds. This made my previous mistakes look shit-tier by comparison, like I really hadn't been trying hard enough.

A tic started in the side of my temple. My palms were sweating. In an hour I'd be a wholly pathetic wreck. If I didn't get a drink in me, that was. If I did get a drink in me, I wouldn't care what I became.

Tried to spark up another tab, the tobacco trailing from the tip wouldn't ignite. Had to turn up the flame on the zippo and near took the eyebrows off me. I was gasping deep, fighting off the tics that were dog-piling me now, when Mac showed. He pulled up, misjudging the kerb but the Hilux didn't even notice.

'All right, mate?' he said.

'They've got something on Hod. I just spoke to Fitz.'

'Are you for real?'

I dropped the slow nod.

'*Jesus.*'

I got in the cab and closed the door. I chucked the tab before going in, after all that trouble getting it lit, it felt a proper waste. But, what wasn't these days?

'Where to?' said Mac.

'Home, James. And don't spare the horses.'

The ride back to Easter Road was like a funeral procession. The thought of young Donnie going in the ground soon wasn't lost on me either. The Black Dog was well and truly with me now. Donnie murdered, in Biblical fashion. Stella, still missing. And now Hod in the firing line. The bad vibes kept coming, mashed up all my thoughts.

'There's one silver lining,' said Mac.

'Every one of my silver linings has a cloud.'

'Well, consider this: the cops never asked either of us about Bunny Veitch.'

I could see Mac was trying to throw me a life-preserver, but it wasn't working. I was in there, in the drink, with all my sorrows. Could see us drowning together.

'Maybe they're keeping that in reserve,' I said.

'I don't know so much. This McEwan sounds eager to wrap it up — why would he hold anything back?'

'I don't know, I just find it hard to believe we've done anything to get ahead of the posse.'

We'd reached the front door of my flat. A junkie was using the doorstep as a night-stand, a pile of random possessions put out; only reason I knew he was alive was the involuntary retching.

Mac eyed the puking derro. 'Gus, are you going to be okay?'

'What're you on about?'

'I mean, you've got it together right now …' he stopped flat.

'Oh, you mean the sauce.' I tried to sound dismissive.

He looked away, started to play with the button for the wipers.

I got out the truck, said, 'I'll call you tomorrow, mate. I need to get some rest.'

'Okay, Gus. You get some rest.'

The junkie had stopped chucking up and wrapped himself in a blankie. I turned and waved to Mac, knowing full-well I'd fed him a crock of shit. I wondered why he hadn't just spat it out, that he knew I was going to go on the piss. It couldn't have been fear of my reaction, because he'd seen every shade of those. Were we all so terrified of causing offence now, even Mac? The thought depressed me more: we were living in such a politically correct panopticon that friends policed each other.

I walked up the stairs in a trance, each twinge in my leg a vague reminder that I was still capable of feeling, despite my mindset. I wanted that hallowed ground: oblivion. I knew it was a cop out, a weakness, but simultaneously told myself that true strength came only from the realisation of one's weaknesses. I even bought it. Of course I did, I'm an alkie. Whatever the price-tag is on the bottle, I'll buy it; even if it means convincing myself of the worst kind of bullshitter's pop psychology.

The door didn't require a key, just wheezed open with my hand on the knob. McEwan's chimps had been handy with the jemmy, not even a shard of paintwork. It did cross my mind to try and repair the lock but that thought drifted out as quickly as it had appeared. I went for my room.

I knew at once what I was doing.

This was what it had all been about. I'd been stockpiling nuclear weapons and was about to launch World War 3.

I opened the door to the press and stared. I felt serene, my mind floating into the alpha state. Every brainwave was on a go slow. It didn't matter what I was doing because nothing mattered. This was the true power of now: an alkie facing a life-threatening skite is at one with the universe. Neither past, present nor future matter. All that counts is the first kiss of alcohol on the lips.

I took down the bottle of Dalwhinnie. No reason, really. It was just nearest. The first drop felt like a flame in my mouth. A strangely familiar sensation, the burn of comfort. An old port in a new storm.

I stepped back, staring and knowing full well what I'd done. But it didn't matter.

"If you don't have the first drink, you can't have the second!"

A pious voice chimed in my ear. It made me slug deeper on the bottle of Dalwhinnie. It lit my taste. I reached in for a bottle of Baileys Irish Cream. Then the Smirnoff Blue, with 100% proof on the label.

I clattered down on the bed, my fingers working the bottle tops. There may well have been some spillage, but I didn't give two fucks. I'd been waiting a long time for this — why deny it?

You always own the option of having no opinion. There is never any need to get worked up or to trouble your soul about things you can't control. These things are not asking to be judged by you. Leave them alone.

—Marcus Aurelius

CHAPTER 23

I awoke in the shower, with no idea how I'd arrived there. It was my shower, I recognised the lack of grouting and the black mould around the cracked tiles. The water wasn't hot, but nor was it cold. Lukewarm. Tepid. That indistinct place just short of body temperature. Though, I had the funny feeling my body temperature was through the roof.

Someone had told me the rise in body temperature after a skite was the liver heating up, trying to process the unduly heavy workload. It might have been right, or it might have been complete bollocks but either way, I didn't feel too clever.

I flicked the taps to cold, let the jets rush me. My face took the first hit — full force. It came like a slap, and by Christ did I need that. I took the punishment as long as I could, even managed some nauseating mint shower gel that reminded me of After Eights, and had me on the verge of throwing my guts.

Was still too fragile, too physically drained, to feel the pangs of regret and the killer — brute guilt. But they were in the post. I could sense it. This was the drill and I knew it well.

I dried myself off with a towel I couldn't ever recall setting out for myself and started to look about for my clothes. They weren't where I usually left them, the floor. The bed didn't look slept in but it was daylight beyond the shuttered blinds. I tried to piece together some semblance of a memory but there was nothing. I could have lost hours, or days.

I went to the wardrobe and got dressed. A clean pair of black Wranglers and a crisp white T-shirt, cotton from Fruit of the Loom — could pass the Daz doorstep challenge — it hurt my eyes but would have to do because it was all I had. I put a trembling comb through my hair and sat on the edge of the bed trying to regain my energy; even the simplest task was a chore. I was too old for this whack now — would I ever learn?

Some drinkers will bemoan the loss of untrammelled days of yore when the hangover was over the second you left the shower. The worst of these days were easily coped with by Anadin Extra. I'd heard that he of the cast-iron Welsh liver, Richard Burton, had one hell of a recovery rate as a young man. At Oxford, some envious wag had spiked his pint with wood alcohol, which dropped him down a flight of stairs. The resulting back injury, decades later, still required surgery. In his later years one such operation on his spine required surgeons to spend 24-hours scraping crystallised alcohol from his backbone. There's always a dear price to pay, but knowing it didn't stop me.

My old bones ached — thankfully not as bad as Richie Boy's — as I dragged myself without the stick all the way to the living-room. I knew at once the place had experienced a cosmic shift but still managed a double-take when I saw Amy sitting there. She had the big seat to herself, curled up and staring into the ether, a mug of coffee warming her hands.

'Oh, it's you,' my opener was as ridiculous as I felt.

'The very same,' she had her feet tucked underneath her but swung out her legs and started to rise. 'You fancy a coffee?'

'Er, no. Nothing, thanks.'

We sat facing each other, weighing the moment, and then Amy broke the silence, 'Head hurtie?'

'You being funny?'

'That would be you, last night ... Lolz, what a state.'

A sinking feeling settled on the centre of my chest. I ran a bunch of shaky fingers through my wet hair, 'How did I get in the shower?'

'I put you there.'

'And my clothes?'

'I wasn't going to let you lie in a pool of your own piss, Gus.'

I looked away. 'I'm sorry.'

'Don't be. I've seen it all before.'

Worst was, she didn't mean my tackle. 'That's not the point. You shouldn't have to, y'know, clean up my mess.'

'I just put your clothes in the machine and your skanky arse in the shower, Gus. It's really no biggie.'

I looked away, I couldn't fashion a sentence worth uttering and the thought of catching Amy's direct gaze terrified me. That phrase about wanting a hole to open up and swallow you was massively insufficient — I wanted a rollercoaster straight to the gates of Hell.

Amy got up, put down her coffee and threw me a packet of cigarettes. 'That's one of your brands, isn't it?'

'Yeah, red tops.'

'The woman in Asda called them Marlboro Classics.'

'They keep changing the names and packets but they're still red tops to me.' I wrestled off the cellophane and sparked up. 'Sorry, did you want one?'

'No, I quit when I was pregnant with Evie.'

'Of course ...'

Amy came and sat next to me, she seemed to have got over the novelty of her piss-taking. 'You were talking last night ...'

'Oh, really?'

'About your child.'

'I don't have a child.'

'I know. I mean the one you lost. Look, Gus, I'm so sorry ... I didn't know it hurt you so deeply. I mean, I know it must have been horrible losing your child, but you never spoke about it before.'

I stared at the floor, figured neither of us were ready for eye contact. 'It was just the drink speaking.'

'No, Gus. It was you, the words came out of your mouth.'

'Can we just leave it?'

'But ...'

'Please. For now.' I tried to steer the conversation in another direction. 'How did you get over here anyway?'

'On the night bus. Don't worry, Evie's at my mum's.'

Now the shame settled on me. I was like a child myself, relying on my friends to keep it together for me because I was completely incapable. I told Amy I was sorry again and then I blurted out the bad news about Hod. It had to happen sooner or later, it was all over my thoughts, and the cause of my fall from grace.

'Oh, God,' she said. 'Are they for real? I mean, is it even possible?'

'Well, Hod did the heavy lifting with Donnie, had to man handle him into the car. He'd cut his arm a bit, so it's not inconcieceable that he left some trace of himself on Donnie's clobber or something. Either way, the whole thing's fucked beyond words.'

'You're not kidding.'

'And neither's this McEwan bloke. He's just the type to throw the book at Hod if he thinks he can, or if he has no better options.'

'Are there any other options?' She seemed to almost plead for an answer.

I drew on my tab. 'There's a name, Mark "Bunny" Vietch.'

'Means nothing to me,' she shrugged.

'You do surprise me, we've all been drawing blanks on Bunny. Looks like your typical Edinburgh low-life though. He seemed to have been supplying Donnie with enough drugs to deal to the Leith dafties.'

'Well, there's no shortage of them in Leith.'

'Drugs or dafties?'

'Both.'

Amy's expression changed, she was toying with an idea. It unsettled me. Said, 'Don't get any crazy notions, by the way.'

'Meaning?'

'Meaning, leave Bunny to me and Mac. If you want to make yourself useful, get onto Stella Wallace's associates, known and unknown.'

'I already have been,' she put on the headlamp smile, like she was pleased with herself. 'You wouldn't believe what you can find out these days with a little bit of snooping on someone's social media.'

'Go on …'

'Well, our Stella was working for a temping agency — secretarial work, that kind of thing. They just put her in an estate agents a few weeks ago. Gladstone's in the west end. And she hasn't been in for a while, obviously.'

'Do I see where this is going?'

'I hope so.' That smile again, full-beam now. 'I put my exceptional shorthand and typing skills on the agency's website and they have a few jobs for me to try out for today.'

Amy flicked her wrist, checked the face of her watch. 'I'm interviewing for Gladstone's at 10.45, so I better get my arse into gear.'

She got up and pulled a carrier bag from the side of the couch. Inside was a navy business suit — the skirt was so short I doubted it would cover the whole of her backside.

'Holy crap!' I said.

'Like it?'

'Isn't it a bit …?'

'Tarty? Oh, fuck yeah.' She dug in the pocket of the jacket and removed something. 'But the tartiness is mitigated by these.'

'Glasses?' I watched her put them on, scrunching up her hair. I had to give it to the girl, she had some fucking style all right.

'Specs, say it right, Gus, and it sounds a bit like sex.'

'God, Amy, you've thought of everything.'

'And … a French plait.'

'Of course.'

She gathered up the navy suit and headed for the back room. 'I'll have to get dressed. I'll give you a shout if I need a hand getting into the push-up bra.'

I wanted to say, give me a shout either way, but let it slide. There were some paths best left in the past. And I needed Amy's help more than ever now with Hod inside and my own mind failing to spark.

I lit another tab and trailed Amy, as far as the hall. Outside the door I called to her.

'This Gladstone's place, what have you heard about it?'

Amy yelled back, 'Just that Stella was working there, right up until she went missing.'

'Nothing else, no tip-offs?'

164

'Nothing. I figured I'd play it by ear, maybe we'll get a bite, maybe we won't. But somebody there is bound to talk about Stella, maybe it'll be useful.'

I was hoping for a little more from Amy. A lead, at least. It sounded like a wild goose chase, but that's where we were.

Tried to sound encouraging, 'Knock yourself out, girl. You might be lucky.'

She stuck her head round the door, her hair pinned up, her shoulders bare. 'Lucky? There's no luck involved, mate.'

I realised how trite I'd sounded, said, 'Just trying to be, y'know, positive.'

'Well, don't be, it doesn't suit you.' She ducked back inside the bedroom. 'So, what's your plan of attack, Gus?'

'You mean beyond sobering up?'

'Obviously. And I don't recommend a heart-starter at the Safari Bar by the way.'

The thought appealed, but I had other plans. 'I'm going to grab Mac and see if we can't pay a little visit to a certain slippery customer by the name of Sharky.'

'Sounds like fun.'

'It won't be for him. Mac will make sure of that.'

'Meaning?'

'Expect shark steaks on the menu tonight.'

She appeared at the door. Her face was made up now, bright red lipstick and Spanish eyes. She rarely wore that much make up, didn't need to, it looked over the top but that was the aim. And she wasn't joking about the push-up bra. With the hint of cleavage, the cinched waist and 90% her leg displayed she'd transformed herself into a Weird Science wet-dream for middle-aged men.

'Holy smokes,' I said.

'Like it?'

I wanted to say, "You are not setting foot beyond the door looking like that, young lady". But went with, 'Stay off the main roads, you'll cause a fucking pile-up.'

'Perfect. Just the tone I was after.'

CHAPTER 24

We were well and truly through the looking glass. Up was down, left was right, and taking offence seemed to be a national obsession. This was my little considered opinion after five minutes scanning the Current Bun. Someone had left behind the paper as I sat outside Manna Mia waiting on a coffee. The hipster had sent out the tatted-up chick to take my order but from where I was seated I could see he'd dumped the badge I'd taken the piss out of.

Half of the population hated the other half of the population. We couldn't even agree on the meaning of words any more. Everyone anyone disagreed with was Hitler and no-one could keep it together. The paper told me feminists were now rounding on trannies for not being real women. Lefties were rounding on Muslims for not having their five-year-olds taught about anal sex. Drag Queen Story Hour in nurseries was a thing.

None of this ended well. Everyday it seemed people's mouths were writing new cheques that their brains couldn't cash. The world was an insane asylum and somebody, surely, was about to start rounding up those of us who needed corrective electro-therapy. I knew I'd be front of the queue. Would stick out a mile.

A coffee cup clattered down in front of me. Got the look, one that says, 'Drink up and fuck off, dickhead.'

I ventured, 'Thank you, now.'

Thought I might get the finger in return but was slipped the sarcastic smile instead. I made a note to start scoping for a new coffee shop. It would have to be one that hadn't quite caught up with modernity yet, think I could live without my avocado on toasted artisan cobbler anyway.

Was on my third red top when Mac appeared.

'You look like a man who lost a pound and found a penny,' he said.

Like I'd argue that. The artist Wyndham Lewis had once been described as being like a man who was relentlessly pursued by the Furies — I knew the feeling.

'Let's just say now the drugs don't work.'

Mac pulled out the chair in front of me and sat down. He was stealing one of my tabs when he spoke again, 'No they don't. They just make things worse — find that out last night did you?'

'Woke up this morning with the mother of all hangovers and worse, Amy playing at Our Lady in the living-room.'

'No way.'

'Way. Seems like I'd ran away at the mouth all night. Fair put a scare on the girl. I have to sort myself out, Mac. There's no way I can go on like this.'

He was courteous enough not to say I told you so. If he were playing hardball he'd have listed the times and places where he'd seen the worst himself. Maybe I'm being too kind, maybe he'd just given up on me — fuck knows I wouldn't blame him.

I told Mac about Amy's jaunt to Gladstone's. About the fact Stella had been temping there and how Amy hoped to feed back what she found out.

'It's as good a plan as we've got,' he said.

'Actually, when you hear what I've got in mind, you might say it's better.'

'Oh, yeah. And what have you got in mind, Gus?'

I leaned in, just in case there were any unwanted ears around. 'I was thinking of going shark fishing.'

'Y'wha—?'

'Shark fish ... fuck it, we hunt out Sharky.'

Mac drew on his fag, squinted through the smoke. 'I like your thinking.'

'Calm it. Remember who he's working for, any scare we put on him we can expect to be reciprocated in kind.'

'I wouldn't doubt it, but have you forgotten we have Hod being sent down for Jonny Ladd's caper?'

'Meaning?'

'What I mean is, if doing over Sharky brings Jonny Ladd into the daylight then I'm more than happy to put the bastard into the ground, right now.'

I got the picture, even sympathised with the reasoning a little, but Ladd was radge enough without us giving him an excuse to pump himself full of steroids.

'Just cool the beans, Mac. I'd sooner not see fucking Robocop McEwen put you in the cell next to Hod. Fancy hot and cold running beatings do you?'

Mac stubbed his fag, rattled another out the pack. 'You think I give a fuck, mate? If I'm going down it'll be guns blazing.'

This. The very reason I had Hod's liberty to worry about. I surrounded myself with utter mentallers.

'Let's not get carried away, eh. Leave the shit-for-brains thought to Sharky. If he steps out of line, though, then you can feed him his own balls.'

'Agreed.'

I got up and dropped some coins on the table. Mac followed, cramming the cigarette in the corner of his mouth as he started to button up his jacket. He looked like a perfectly-formed mass of anger. Take a man with no real family to speak of, no friends as such, and only a couple of fellow losers who had stuck around and formed a dodgy appreciation society with him because no-one else would, and you have the image. Mac was fired up. There's a phrase: "The man was ropeable", but he was beyond that. There was no chance anyone would get near him with a rope — he'd fuckingwell tear it apart.

As we got in the Hilux and drove past the cafe the hipster was out, pocketing my coin. He clocked me staring and gave a sly wink.

'Oh yeah,' said Mac. 'Ned Kelly has a thing for you.'

'I've got to get a new caf, the gentrification round here's getting right up my beak.'

Mac conceded a half smile. 'What is it with these fucking hipsters everywhere now?'

'They're trying to emulate something meaningful from the past, to compensate for the emptiness of the present.'

'Jesus, I can't believe you've actually given this some thought.'

Unfortunately, he was right. 'It's entirely false, as much a corporate prescription as the five hot-hatches or ten pairs of trainers they offer you to fit your off-the-peg personality.'

'Sounds sinister.'

'More than you believe, mate. Orwell got it all wrong. Communism was top down authoritarianism — but we do it all to ourselves, we've made it our culture.'

He put down the window and yelled at a jakey who was nearing the bonnet of the car. 'Get any closer to this motor, pal, and you'll be wearing your arse as a hat.'

The jakey sobered up pretty sharpish, weaved a new line in front of the traffic. Obviously it seemed the safest option.

'You want to hear my hot take on society's ills?' said Mac.

'Go for your life.'

'Well, I don't give this shit a lot of thought,' he shot me a look, 'it's not an obsession with me.'

'Go on.'

'It's this throw-away culture that's to blame. Nothing's built to last. Not houses, not cars, not washing machines, not ...'

I cut in, 'I get the picture.'

'Okay, so we're a throw-away mindset now. That applies to more than what we buy, though. Everything's throw-away. If you don't like your marriage or your partner, throw it away, get a new one. That's the biggest one, and it's totally fucked us all because I'll tell you this, Gus boy, we all need our families, we're all still sucking our mother's tits.'

I didn't know how to take Mac's observation. It wasn't what I was expecting to hear from the man who seriously rates Rambo 5 a work of art.

'Mac, you're a revelation to me, mate.'

'What's that supposed to mean?'

'It's a compliment. I mean, in spite of the amount of high-fructose corn syrup you consume on a daily basis, there's a battle going on in that brain of yours to beat hyper consumerism.'

'Cheeky prick!'

'No, I'm serious. I'm fucking blown away.'

That look again, said he'd keep his opinions to himself in future.

We hit the top of the Walk, took the deadwood roundabout that looked like it had been scraped in the road by waggon-wheels. There'd once been street furniture up here, nice monuments and sculptures but since the tram project the lot had been taken up and chucked in a corporation warehouse.

It was mid-morning and the lemmings looking at phones were dropping themselves in front of cars. Mac took a turn to the right, 'There it is, the Alabama.'

'It's a Hibbee's pub.'

'Of course it is, it's painted green and it's in the middle of Leith.'

I bit. 'No, I mean, so Sharky's not all bad.'

'He's not a Jambo, if that's what you mean.'

Mac parked up and got out of the truck. I noticed he was flexing fists as he made his way towards me. 'Mind you, as the Lawman once said: There's no friends on the park.'

'Jesus God … if you've started quoting Man-U players now can you at least make it George Best!'

Mac nodded, inclined his head, 'This pub do?'

'Now that's better.'

We were a little too relaxed when we went in, still laughing in unison, and it put the shits up Sharky. He was sitting at our end of the bar keeping an untouched pint of Guinness company and leering over the *Racing Post*. He made a move to get up but Mac put a hand on his shoulder.

'Sit yourself down, son,' he said. 'You won't be needing this, mind, think you'll want to keep a clear head.' Mac took up the Guinness and drained the top two inches, he was wiping the froth from his lips as he sat down beside Sharky.

I took the barstool on the other side of Ladd's pug.

'Mac the Knife, eh?' said Sharky. 'Jonny speaks highly of your work.'

'Jonny Ladd, now there's a name,' I said. 'He's been very busy of late, or so I hear.'

'Wouldn't know anything about that.'

A barmaid with an inch of pan-stick on her coupon appeared. Her chest was so wrinkled I thought she'd stuffed her blouse with a couple of scrunched up paper bags.

'What can I get you?' she said, in a 60-Berkley-a-day voice.

'Two pints, my love. Guinness.'

I turned back to Sharky, leaned close, so close I could count the blackheads on his nose. 'Oh, I'm guessing that you'd know a lot more than you're letting on, Sharky. Maybe even enough to get someone put away for Donnie's very nasty death.'

'Now, wait a minute. If you think you can stroll in here and expect me to cough up Jonny Ladd you're mental.'

Mac grabbed Sharky by the chops, turned to face him. 'I'm the fucking mental one, pal. And I'll put your missus on a widow's pension right away if you fuck me around.'

He yanked his face away from Mac's hand. 'You've no idea what you're doing, either of you. Did you see the state of Donnie?'

'No, we didn't,' I said. 'But you've just told us you did.'

Sharky, Leith as the Walk, spoke, 'Look, Dury, you are nothing in this town. Where do you think you get the fucking balls to front me?'

I nodded to Mac. 'I rest my case.'

Mac went into his pocket and removed a cut-throat razor. He played with the hinge a little then tapped the back of the blade on his open palm.

'Just say the word, Gus. I'll cut his tongue out and send it to Jonny Ladd, see if he's more talkative.'

Sharky tapped his hands on the top of his thighs. 'Okay, just calm down, and tell me what you want.'

The barmaid returned with our pints, placed them in front of us. Mac closed the razor and returned it to his pocket.

I spoke quietly, 'Tell us why Donnie was taken out?'

'I don't know. Some row or other, some disagreement. I don't know the ins and outs.'

'But you do know Bunny Veitch.'

An eyebrow was raised at that name. 'Bunny might have had something to do with it, but I don't know any more than that. I'm a grunt, I just do the leg work.'

We'd got him to talk, or start to. The pressure went down a few notches. I put the pint in front of him and indicated he could drink up.

'You put us in a very bad situation back there in Aldo's.'

'I was just there to get Donnie for Christsake.'

'But you took Stella instead.'

'What was I supposed to do?'

'Leave her the fuck out of it,' I said. 'What have you done with her?'

'Nothing. Jonny has taken care of her.'

'Y'wha—?'

'No, not like that. Has her in a nice place, he's looking after her. I don't know what any of this is about. I just do what I'm told, when I'm told. I don't go around asking questions or sticking my neck out.'

I got off my barstool. 'You don't need to stick your neck out, Sharky.'

Mac rose beside him. 'No, there's no need. It's already on the fucking chopping block.'

I drained the last of my pint, turned back to the pug. 'Where's Stella?'

'Who?'

'The girl. Donnie's girlfriend that you picked off the street for Jonny.'

'I've no idea.' His jaw drooped, he squinted to Mac,

seemed preoccupied with the fact that his hands were back in his pockets. 'I swear to you, I've no idea where she is.'

'What about Bunny?'

'The Vietch lad. He has a place in Newhaven, lock-up just off the main drag there's a couple of big white caravans, portacabin things, parked in the yard.'

I went for the door. Mac put the bead on Sharky, said, 'You mind yourself now.'

We walked in silence back to the truck. Mac opened up, the blinkers flashed and we went inside. We waited for five minutes and saw Sharky jinxing through the door of the Alabama and onto the Walk.

'And there he goes,' I said.

'You let him go,' said Mac. 'Why exactly?'

'Did you see how quickly he gave up Bunny? I thought it was all very suss. And then there's the fact that we caught the little bastard with our first cast, he didn't even put up a fight. There's something not right there.'

'You think Jonny's got to him?'

'No. But he knew right away to drop Bunny in it, that tells me that Jonny's got another enemy. I don't quite know what to make of it but after seeing Sharky's eyes I know one thing ...'

'What's that?'

'We're going to need a bigger boat.'

CHAPTER 25

The drive to Bunny's lock-up was as depressing as the scenery.

Off licence.

Betting shop.

Stand and tan.

Rinse and repeat.

The only break in the monotony came when a shopfront was boarded over. Even the charity shops had upped sticks.

The theme seemed to have penetrated through to the populace as well. Massive land whales pushing brat-carts, trailed by girlie men who compensated for their status reversal by inking up.

'These sleeve tatts don't work on pencil necks,' I said.

'Ah, the David Beckham job you mean,' said Mac. 'Kind of defeats the purpose, copying one of the most famous men on the planet to make yourself look individual.'

'You got that right.'

'It's the skinny jeans that do me in.' Mac made a face — close to the dictionary definition of derision. 'They look just like women's leggings, what's going on there?'

'It'll be a part of this new trannie agenda, get the men looking like women and the women looking like men.'

'Not just looking like, bud, actually acting like too. Go down the Grassmarket on a Saturday night, you'll see plenty of scrubbers pishing in the gutter.'

I didn't doubt him for a moment. The permanent revolution had moved well beyond kicking at the pillars of society — now it was kicking at each and every one of us. Daily. I couldn't wait for the collapse into the *Mad Max* apocalypse, would be a blessed relief.

I used to think the decay I was dealing with was all my own. And all my own fault. But I'd started to see decay everywhere; the house I was living in was coming down, once I'd blamed the tenant but now I blamed the builder. Everywhere the mouth-breathers carried on regardless, kept casting their votes and hoping for change. I was with Billy Connolly on that one: "Don't vote, it only encourages them!"

I clocked the two white portacabins that Sharky had mentioned and Mac started to pull over. Wheels on the kerb was an invitation to be hit with a parking fine; the mind boggled that the Council had the balls to charge for parking in this shithole in the first place.

'Looks quiet,' said Mac.

'As the grave.' I walked round beside him and we stood staring at the building, checking for any irregular features that we might be better knowing about before going inside. All I spotted was a pigeon with a mangled claw hobbling up and down the window ledge.

'It's a bit of a bloody tip,' said Mac.

'Even by the standards of the neighbourhood, and that's saying something.'

'Do you think there's anyone inside?'

'I doubt it. But let's check anyway. It's not like we have much else to go on.'

We headed for the back of the lock-up. A little brick-lined lane with a crumbling tar-surface. Looked like there'd been some serious glue huffing by the number of tins of Evostick on the deck. The usual graffiti was everywhere, a 69-er, some swastikas, but the most prevalent was the initials YG.

Said to Mac, 'YG..?'

'Young Group.'

'Ah, the lad crew.'

'Every postcode has one.'

'Maybe they should coordinate, like the EH7 or the EH9.'

He didn't respond, was wondering if I was serious or just being my usual radge.

The back lot was accessed by a wooden gate, there was a bolt on the door but the jamb had long since rotted away, leaving the lock useless. The door was lacking a few screws in the top hinge and had to be pushed; I felt my leg twinging as I eased in. Was minor though, I was glad to be able to ditch the stick now and simply hop when the need occurred.

'Over there,' said Mac. He pointed to the back of the lock-up. A window and door, barred over, and painted white at some point in the period 19-canteen.

'Well, isn't this just a lovely spot,' said Mac.

'Tea on the lawn, anyone?'

'What fucking lawn?'

The door was locked. Peered into the window and the interior was in darkness. 'I think Sharky's been feeding us a line.'

Mac was checking out our surrounds, alighted on a quarter of crumbling brick. He gave it a good pelt, and the glass behind the bars shattered. He stuck a mitt in and rattled the Yale. The door wheezed like every Scooby Doo cartoon ever.

'We're in,' said Mac. 'Come on.'

The place was in darkness but I could make out a rough looking kitchenette. A sink, some cups and a bag of PG Tips — half expected a couple of chimps to come sliding through on a piano saying, *'You sing it and I'll play along.'*

I said, 'Jesus wept, I'm presuming the cleaner's on holiday.'

'Looks like everyone's on holiday,' said Mac. 'The kip of this place tells me it was a fairly rushed exit as well.'

He walked over to the sink and held up a cup, poured out a half-inch of tea. 'I leave an unfinished brew lying about in my gaff and it's capable of growing penicillin spores in a week or so. This place was abandoned recently, Gus.'

I found the light switch.

'Don't know if I prefer it with the light out.'

We moved through to the storage area — a large floor space with a mechanic's trough in the middle. Half of the dugout had been boarded over and the other half looked like it had been lifted by the fucking Queensland Yowie.

'Oh, I love what they've done in here,' I said.

'Look, a desk, and that's a rug.'

'Y'think that sat over there?' I pointed to the trough. 'Under usual conditions like.'

'Nice spot for a stash, if you ask me.'

'Fuck of a big stash, mate.'

Mac frowned. 'I don't think it was for personal usage.'

We walked around a bit more, found some antique-looking tools that had been left to rust. A sweeping brush, with more brush-head than bristles on the end. And a couple of boxes of hardcore Dutch porn. I could tell it was Dutch because one of the stories was titled, *Two-Lips from Amsterdam*.

'Funny they left their jazz mags behind,' said Mac.

'They were obviously in a hurry, and cracking one off probably wasn't on their mind.'

'Suppose, nobody buys this shit anymore since the advent of PornHub.'

'You'd know better than me, mate.'

He thrust out his fingers. 'Do I look like I've got an overdeveloped right hand?'

'No,' I said, 'but your left one does get a lot of action working that mouse.'

'Fuck off!'

The sound of a paint tin tumbling behind us broke off the chat.

'What was that?' I said.

'Cat maybe, or a rat.'

I was buying into his hypothesis when a bundle of black rags started to move on the floor. Mac sprinted over; I bounded behind him.

He had the rags pulled back before I arrived.

'What in the name of fuck?'

There was a young boy, streak-thin and filthy, lying on the floor. He couldn't have been more than 14.

'Please, mister ...' He held up his hands, put them over his ears.

'Okay, okay ... nobody's going to hurt you.'

The lad sat up, curled his knees towards his chest and hugged his legs. He looked terrified, but Jesus, he had worse things to worry about.

'What are you doing here?' I said.

'Nothing. I didn't touch anything, it was raining, that's all.'

'How long have you been here?'

He shrugged his coat-hanger shoulders.

'Aren't you cold, son?'

Nods. 'Suppose.'

I spotted he was trembling.

'When did you last have something to eat?'

More shrugs.

'Right, on your feet, laddo. Let's get some scran into you.'

Rory had been living in Bunny's lock-up for the best part of a week and hadn't seen a soul. He wasn't very talkative at first but a couple of rolls on slice, lashed with brown sauce, and a stream of tea, thawed him a bit. He said he was sixteen — Christ, I had T-shirts older than him — a runaway, and didn't want to have anything to do with social services or any kind of authority. I got the impression extracting more information than that would have to involve waterboarding.

'We're not interested in your story, lad,' I said. 'You can keep your secrets to yourself, but if you've got anything to tell us about folk coming and going at the lock-up, we'd like to know.'

'I've already told you. It's been empty, you're the first folk I've seen.'

'But we had to smash the door to get in,' said Mac. 'How did you get in if you haven't got a key?'

'The garage up the side, you can get on the roof from there. You only need to take a few tiles off and then you're in.'

Mac looked at me, shaking his head.

I said, 'How long have you been living like this?'

'Dunno. Months. Maybe longer.'

I wanted to ask what he'd seen. I wanted to know what drove a bright young boy to pitch up in the shitiest part of the shitiest city in the country and just hope for the best. But, then I thought about my own childhood and the bold Cannis

Dury and knew there was very little I'd want to reveal about that saga at Rory's age. When you're a kid, you don't know anything, so you think everything must be your own fault.

'Is there anything we can do for you?'

'You've done heaps ... thanks for the feed.'

He was stubborn. He didn't want any help. He didn't want looking after by adults — that's clearly what he was running away from.

I took out my wallet and separated a few sheets, 'Here, try and put some meat on those bones.'

Rory looked at the money, but didn't move. I dropped it on the table in front of him.

'That's not charity, I want you to do something for me.'

'Like what?'

'Like pick up a phone when or if you see anybody back at the lock-up.'

He snatched up the cash, pocketed it. 'I can do that.'

I wrote down my mobi number. 'Call me here. And remember, anything at all, a car pulling up, blokes looking about. Pick up the phone.'

He nodded, 'I will do.'

'Try and clock as much info as you can, descriptions, number plates, accents. You get me?'

'I get you.'

I stood up, said, 'And, Rory, anything else, use the number for that too.'

Mac and I trailed the streets back to the truck in silence. The sky was blacker than a dog's guts and the threat of rain was ominous. When he started up the engine Mac turned to stare at me, 'We'll never see that little bugger again, he'll have that bundle blown on fucking Panini stickers in a day.'

'Yeah, well, whatever.'

'This has been a waste of time, Gus. And I'll tell you another thing, this Bunny character has shot the crow.'

'He's done a runner, that's for sure. We just don't know how far he's actually got.'

'The Costa Del Crime is my guess.'

'Not with a stash that size. Unless he's offloaded that in a hurry too, and the only person with the base to shift it is Jonny Ladd.'

'Why would the Bad Ladd pay him when he could just do him over like Donnie and take it?'

'Exactly. And there's been no body ... yet.'

Mac chucked on the blinkers, looked in the mirror. 'Well, when you put it like that. We very well might still be in business, Gussie boy.'

CHAPTER 26

Managed to grab a few hours in the company of the everyman. What did they call them these days: blue collar? Workies? Gammon? No matter, they were my people, they might not read *The Guardian* but they had a closer grasp of reality than any fucker I'd seen with a four-inch byline photo.

The chat varied from how that cunt Cameron had fucked us all over, to how that cunt Blair had fucked us even harder. My argument that they were two cheeks of the same arse didn't gain much traction. If ever I needed a reason to drink, I had it now, in malt shovels.

My thoughts kept flitting back to the young lad I'd met earlier, Rory. There was a time he might have had a chance — not because the powers that be were looking out for him, but his own people surely would have been. I got the impression that nobody was looking out for anybody anymore. We were all elbows out, heads butting together. Not a soul had any spirit. Transcendence was a new perfume by Victoria Beckham, or some such nonentity.

I poured down pint after pint. It was in the contract. One that says, the only way out of this nightmare is down your neck. Half a dozen Guinneys and a shit-ton of wee goldies later and my head started to feel normal. That's by today's standards, of course. Aldous Huxley had it right: life had become a vice and living was merely subsidising the vice. Soma was the answer, only I didn't take mine in tablet form.

I staggered down London Road on my way back to the flat. I put the collar up on my Crombie and tried not to sway too much in the slipstream of all the scoosh I'd swallowed. I figured, the kip of me, I stuck out worse than a donkey's cock anyway. But, if Jonny Ladd was looking for me, he'd have given me a rattle by now.

The thought set off a warning buzzer: maybe the Bad Ladd had me where he wanted me. Was I doing his leg work? Here I was turning the town upside down, noising up known faces and generally sticking my mitts in the mincer — for what? For who? My answer was Wally's girl and poor old Hod, but maybe Ladd wanted me to run amok for other reasons.

I got the key in the door and shouldered my way in. Managed about half-way up the first flight of stairs before I started to look over my shoulder. I was in no shape to defend myself if the answer to Hod's pick-axe handles appeared. The lack of caution shocked me, I'd become completely immune to my own safety. Gave less than two shits about yours truly.

I stumbled into the back room and managed to prise open the press. There was a bottle of Grouse sitting close to the front — the infamous Wee Flying Burdie. I twisted the cap and settled down on the bed. The first two swallows had a familiar burn, but I think it was just the burdie reacquainting itself with my thrapple. I supped ever downwards, watching the tideline slip below the bottle's halfway mark. By the time I'd downed the last drop my legs wouldn't respond to my request to negotiate the way back to the press.

The kilts never came out. There was a tartan blazer that I wore until I was about four as a sort of nod to tradition. But I was nearer ten now, well old enough to take on the kilt.

I couldn't say it was a rite of passage. We weren't one of those middle class families who went to church every Sunday and had regular visits to restaurants and holiday parks. We never, and I mean never, did anything as a family. This is the only time I can remember a proper family gathering … like normal people had.

It's a wedding of some sort. Not relations, but an associate of my father's. He's something in the club, a coach or a manager. All the players are there and their wives and even some of their children. My mam gets all dressed up, she looks like a movie star. I never see her in lipstick; the closest I get is when she puts the big sunglasses on to hide her shiners. She looks happy, sipping on a Babycham and taking the occasional puff from her Regal Smalls.

'Can I go and play, Mam?' I say.

'Of course. But behave yourself, mind.'

Her bare shoulders sway with the music from the band. I want to take a picture of her so I'll always remember the way she looks right now. I tell myself that I'll look at the picture whenever he causes her any grief, whenever there's tears.

Soon, I meet a boy called Gerald. He's from another place, not Leith, and he speaks funny. He uses different words, calls a dick a bobby.

'That's a policeman,' I tell him.

'What — a bobby?'

'Yeah.'

Gerald laughs hard at that and sets off about the hotel. We find a trolley with little yellow cartons of milk. They're tiny, only about the size of a thimble. There's hardly any milk in them but we drink millions, until we get tired of the taste. Then we fill our pockets and set off again. In the corridor outside the lounge I have the idea to put the little cartons on the floor and watch people stand on them as they come off the dance-floor. It's hilarious, watching all the men cursing as the milk splatters up their trousers and onto their shoes.

I lose count of the hours I play with Gerald, I want to go to weddings every weekend now because they're such great craic, but then Gerald's uncle comes looking for him and he's whisked away. I say goodbye and go back to my mam's table.

'Where have you been, Angus?' She's changed, the smiles have all gone now.

'Just playing. I made a friend.' I want to tell her more, but can tell she's in no mood to listen.

Then I notice my father on the other side of the table. I hadn't seen him crashed out on a row of three chairs. He's snoring, completely out of it.

My little brother Michael starts to cry and it wakens my father — he pushes himself up straight, and slouches over the table.

'Oh, the little bugger's back is he? Right, let's get in this taxi.'

I feel like the best night of my life has just come crashing to a close. I want to complain, to say, 'No, let's stay,' but the thought's overruled by something else: fear.

I've seen the look on my father's face before. The look has no name but it always means the same thing. There'll be trouble for anyone who steps out of line now. I look at my mother and can tell she knows this too. She holds my hand tight all the way to the taxi.

I'm told to carry a box of wedding cake in the taxi. I ask if I can eat some but I'm told not until we get home. There's a piece of cake for every one of us. But, I'm hungry now and I wonder why we're not staying for our dinner.

'We were supposed to get dinner, Mam.'

'Shut up, Angus.'

Mam never says shut up. She never says shut up and she never swears, or raises her voice even.

He falls asleep in the taxi and has to be wakened up when we arrive at our house. Mam pays the driver and he slithers out of the back door. Inside he heads for the kitchen and starts to light the gas on the hob.

'Where's the fucking fryer?' he bellows at my mam.

'There's no chip-fat,' she says, 'it's all done.'

'Shite!'

He starts pulling the cupboard doors open and finds the fryer, full of fat, under the sink.

'Cannis, you're not fit to cook chips,' she says.

He bangs down the fryer and lights the gas. 'I'm fit enough to mind you, another word and …' He shows her a fist.

I want to smash that chip-pan over his head, to crush his skull and watch the blood pour out of him. I want to kill him for making my mother's lips tremble and for wiping the happy smile from her face so completely. I want to do all of this but I do nothing and he heaves out the bag of spuds and shoves them at my mam.

'Oh, Cannis!' The dirty potato sack leaves a smear of mud down the front of mam's dress. She starts to cry and he belts her. She falls and the back of her dress splits at the shoulders, she runs away crying.

'You ... cut up them spuds.'

I do as I'm told. As he takes up the wedding cake — the portions of cake all cut nicely for each of us — and starts to cram every slice into his face. He sways before me and plants his back against the bare plaster of the wall. As he slides down the cake goes with him and rolls over the floor, trailing crumbs and icing and little raisins that roll away.

I keep looking, watching, as I peel the spuds.

I cut the chips up and don't know what to do and then everything starts to go black.

I cough and cough.

There's flames, leaping up from the chip-pan and they go right the way to the ceiling. Soon the room's full. I make it to the door and yell, 'Mam!'

I hear her footfalls on the stairs above. Quickly, like the danger is sensed.

'Holy, God,' she says.

My mother wets a towel and throws it on the pan. The flames subside immediately but the smoke remains.

'Get out, Angus. Get your brother and sister.'

I do as I'm told but Michael and Catherine are already outside, crying and shaking in the garden with the cold. I watch my mam start to drag out my father and I run back in.

'Help me, Angus.'

I want to say, 'No.' I want to say, 'No. Leave him.'

'Angus,' she calls out, 'take an arm.'

I know she'll not stop asking. I know it could be the answer to all our problems if we just leave him. But she won't.

'Gus ...'

'Gus ...'

I feel a cold slap across my face.

'Jesus, it's yourself.'

* * *

Fitz the Crime looms over me like a gargoyle. I notice how much he's aged, the greyness of his hair matched by the greyness of his pallor. He keeps an eye on me as he grabs my collars and sits me up in bed.

'By the holy,' he says. 'I thought you were done with the drink.'

'So did I.'

'Turns out it wasn't done with you though.'

'I guess not.'

I'm confused. My head hurts and my mouth is caked in cement. I try to turn away, to avoid his gaze but it doesn't seem possible.

'You were away with the fucking pixies there, lad,' says Fitz. 'Had the fists flying and everything ... thought you were going to do yourself an injury.'

I swung my legs off the bed and put my head in my hands.

'Just a wee trip down memory lane,' I said.

'Holy Christ, Gus, I wouldn't like to spend a minute inside that head of yours.'

'No you wouldn't. Trust me on that.'

Fitz loomed, moved round the bed and made towards the window. As he pulled the curtains I let out a yelp.

'C'mon, man, shut them back up.'

He turned towards me. 'Sorry, Gus, I need you back in the land of the living.'

Fitz opened the window and the air breezed in, along with some blaring horns and the sound of street chatter.

'I'll make you a coffee,' said Fitz. 'And after that, you and I have some serious talking to do.'

CHAPTER 27

I ran the cold water tap. The stream blasted off the porcelain sink and kicked off a throbbing in my head. I tried to negotiate the plug, but locating the hole was an impossibility. Eventually I just dangled my face under the tap and tried to take the pain as long as I could.

The cold jets seemed to do me some good. As I stood back up I felt a little more lucid, awake even. My mouth still felt like the inside of a rotten corpse, though, as I contemplated the toothbrush. Opted instead for a dod of Colgate on my finger. The whole rigmarole was like a three-act drama and made no difference to my teeth, gums, or mouth in general, except for making me want to puke.

Heard amplified clanging from the kitchen where Fitz was making coffee and headed towards the noise on autopilot. I was a ghost of myself, so worn out that I could be knocked over by a stray feather.

'Jesus, Gus, you look like shite,' said Fitz, greeting me with a mug of coffee. 'Why the hell do you do it to yourself?'

'Why do we do anything?'

'Always with the riddles, eh? I'll never understand the likes of ye.'

I took a seat, it felt soft, like the rest of the world around me, as if I were floating in space. This is the way it always gets me. It's easy enough to unplug from the Matrix, but re-establishing a connection is misery.

I caught Fitz staring at me from the corner of my eye.

'*Wha—?*'

'Do you know how many men I've seen do this to themselves?' he said.

'Are you interested in an actual number?'

'No. Look, I'm being serious. My own father drank himself into an early grave.'

'I'm sorry to hear it.'

'Don't be. Sure, wasn't he a bollocks.'

I smiled. 'You too?'

'Ah, sure there's a club for us somewhere.' He seemed to relax more, sank back into his chair. 'Gus, I heard you yelling … at your father.'

'In my sleep?'

Fitz nodded.

'Doesn't even give me peace there.'

'I don't want to know, I mean, I wouldn't ask you for his form. But, I'll say this, by your age you should have let it go.'

I couldn't face the coffee, put it down. 'The guilt. How do you let that go?'

'What do you mean?'

'I couldn't give two fucks what my father did to me. The beatings, the complete annihilation of my self. But how does a man, one of us, Fitz, ever reconcile the fact that he didn't save his own mother from the same fate?'

'You were a child, Gus.'

'I was old enough.'

'He was a grown man, though. He could have done you over without thinking.'

I turned to face Fitz. 'You've seen people that have killed, looked them in the eye. Look at my eyes now. I swear to you, Fitz. I wish I'd killed that man.'

Silence.

I heard the tick of the kitchen clock.

'Gus, I've felt the same way about many a man, but it's not the answer.'

'How isn't it?'

'Because I know it never brings the relief you think it will, only another kind of shame altogether. Jesus Christ, a moment ago you were telling me that you had guilt for not minding your own mother ... what kind of guilt do you think you'd have for killing your own father?'

I hadn't contemplated Fitz's reasoning. I still wanted to have killed my father but I was at an age where I questioned every decision I'd ever made. I always, always found my reasoning wanting.

'Maybe you're right.'

'Trust me, I know I am.'

He had the authority of a man who had committed murder himself and faced the guilt. I wouldn't have put it past him, but nor would I have ever asked him to confirm or deny it.

'Fitz, you know me as well as anyone ...'

'I guess I know you pretty well by now.'

'And you know I'm a fucking train wreck of a human being.'

'You're pretty far from beatification.'

'Let me ask you ... so what do I do with this?' I tapped the side of my head, the real source of my misery.

Fitz took a deep breath and sighed out. 'Now, Gus, I'm in no position to be giving advice out to anyone. But I've seen men who're clinging to the past before. Men who've lost wives, they think they can go back, re-live their mistakes and better themselves. Men who've lost everything, money, family, health. Jesus Christ on a cross, Dury, that's you. Living in the past ye are. Let it go, man.'

'And what — embrace this future? Get tatted up, become a fucking prepper? What?'

'No. I don't say that. Sure, this place is beyond the beyonds. But even in our darkest days we have to find the strength to live.'

'I don't understand.'

'It's staring you in the face, son.'

I hated being called *son*. 'What?'

'Ask her? Ask your mam if there's anything you could have done differently. I bet what you discover is that she feels exactly the same way.'

Fitz rose, took the cups away to the kitchen and left me to think. I tried, I tried really hard to picture me doing what he'd suggested but I couldn't even face the image. I went into the back room and retrieved my ciggies. I was two draws into a Lucky when I stepped back into the living-room.

'I made you another coffee,' said Fitz.

'I didn't want the last one.'

'Well, I'm sorry, but I need you some way closer to sober.'

I remembered. 'You wanted to talk about Hod.'

He started to get twitchy, put down his cup and loosened his tie. His neck was crimson. 'You any more of those fags?'

I lit him up and we sat facing each other; it felt like a wake. Maybe we were practicing one for Hod.

'Before I go any further, Gus, you know this is a sensitive situation.'

'Fitz, for fuck's sake, I'm not about to broadcast anything you tell me. I think you can trust me on that, perhaps more so since my besto is inside.'

He looked uncomfortable with the cigarette, like he was new to them. 'I had a check on Hod last night and ...'

He stalled.

'Yes, and ...'

Fitz's voice dropped, 'They've been at him.'

'What is that, some Irish speak?'

'He's been worked over. Pretty badly, I'd say.'

'Did you talk to him?'

'Erm, no. I didn't. I don't know if he was ... communicable.'

'He's that bad?'

Fitz looked around for an ashtray, somewhere to flick his ash. It was a stalling manoeuvre. The moment after I slid over the ashtray he started to stare at the palm of his hands.

'This McEwan I told you about, he's part of a new breed you might say. They don't play by the rules.'

'And you always did?'

'There were lines even I never crossed. Everything's changed now, Gus. McEwan is protected.'

'Protected ... by who?'

'Upstairs, but it goes beyond them. Secret services are in and out like flared jeans. There's a political agenda now, the police are politicised. It's like a private army, I swear to you, I'd never have predicted it.'

I was having trouble getting my still-aching head around what he was saying, said, 'Let me get this right. The police force has turned into the Gestapo and McEwan is Himmler?'

'Not quite, but you're in the ball-park. It started with these paedo scandals, they touched too many of the top brass, it had to be covered up. Now there's a paranoia in the Force that someone will get found out, someone will get the finger pointed at them and nobody wants to be that man. Now, Gus, I may not be the purest of the pure, but I'm no way sticking my neck out for kiddie fiddlers.'

'What do you mean by that?'

'I mean, I'm leaving the Force.'

'What?'

'You heard me. I'm done with it. I can't deal with this any longer so I'm off. It's not the job it used to be, we spend more time policing wrong think on Twitter than policing the actual streets.'

'You're going to leave Hod to rot?' I got out of my chair, I couldn't believe what I was hearing.

'I have another job. I'm going to head up security at the Parliament.'

I laughed in his face. 'And you think those cunts aren't going to be twice as corrupt?'

'I won't have anything to do with that, now. I'm only looking after the security of the building and those inside it. Nice simple gig altogether.'

I flopped back into my chair, I felt my heart ramping. I envisioned Hod being lined-up for daily beatings and slowly, but surely, the life ebbing out of him.

I scratched my scalp. 'Walk me through this … I mean, when are you off?'

'I have a few cases to clear up before I empty by desk, and I assure you I will keep an eye on Hod during this time, but I want you to know he's not in good shape and I'm not going to be able to protect him. McEwan wants someone to go down for Donnie's murder and there's nobody else on the cards right now, apart from Hod, so things are not looking good for the lad.'

Now I put my head in my hands. 'Why Hod? Why didn't McEwan put me in the frame? Just what the fuck does McEwan have on him?'

A grey cylinder of ash had sprouted from the butt of Fitz's cigarette, he looked at it and then cupped his hand underneath as he took it towards the ashtray.

'McEwan's playing the odds. He's making use of what he has. He couldn't find anything on you, even after the forensics sweep, but he got something on Hod.'

'What? What did he have on him?'

'I haven't been able to look at the case files. I don't have access, it's not my case, I'm not involved in any way and I'm not exactly pally enough with McEwan to ask for a shuftie.'

'You must have some hint, there must be a whisper going around the station.'

'Well, there's this: I heard that forensics found some of Hod's DNA on Donnie's clothing. Not much, maybe even not enough to be useful to them, but it's something. Why the fuck does a murder victim have Hod's DNA on him? It's something I can't answer — can you?'

I couldn't believe what I was hearing.

I got up and started to walk around the room.

Said, 'There was a scuffle ... getting Donnie in the car.'

'What scuffle?'

I pulled a bunch of my hair. 'The night, the night Donnie went missing ...'

'I need more than that to go on, I need a proper explanation if it's to make any sort of a difference at all.'

'Hod grabbed him, he had him in a head-lock ... Jesus, I don't know, he had a choke-hold on him and Donnie was struggling. Hod scraped his arm, he must have drawn blood because the next day he had a plaster there.'

'It's not good enough. It's not an explanation.'

'It fuckingwell is, Fitz. It's the truth and you have to make it heard in that station or Hod's going down and the real killer's going to walk.'

'I can't do anything with what you've given me, Gus. It's useless!'

Fitz got up and collected his blazer from the back of the chair.

'Where are you going?' I said.

'I've been here too long.'

'Whoa-whoa,' I flagged hands, 'wait a minute now, you can't just drop that bombshell and split.'

'Gus there's nothing I can do for you … or Hod, now.'

'Wait a minute, what if I give a statement? And Mac? We can verify Hod was with us.'

'You are about as popular as a fart, no a full-blown shite, in a spacesuit down at that station and Mac has a conviction for GBH or is it worse, I don't even know?'

'Are you saying we're unreliable?'

'No. I mean, yes. In the eyes of the court you're likely to do more harm to Hod — think about it — a good prosecutor could make a three ring circus out of the pair of ye. Hod would be better pleading silence and denying he even fucking knew you, Gus … Now, that's the hard truth.'

CHAPTER 28

I took a wander down London Road. Was aimless, shiftless. Whatever you wanted to call it, I wasn't myself. I had thoughts bashing up against each other in my mind that had never occupied the same space before. I felt tired. Worn out.

Somehow I found myself in a pub on Leith Walk. Not a drinker's place, it was quite trendy. I took in a few shots of JD for no other reason than it was prominent on the wall behind the bar. It tasted rough, harsh. It worked.

I tried a pint after the shots. Guinness. The head-of-cream came like cold comfort, a familiar friend with bad news. I didn't know where to look, or turn. After only a few sips I found myself back on the street wandering towards Edinburgh Cathedral.

Inside, I was stunned by how busy it was. There was a time when, as a schoolboy, I'd visit with my class and the teacher. There'd been confession then, too. I recalled being silent, scared rigid by the priest's voice on the other side of the box. There was no way I was revealing what was on my mind to him, but the fear came from not being able to summon up a sufficiently plausible list of offences.

One time, the priest gave me an out. Maybe the old boy sensed my discomfort.

'And have you cursed at your mammy?' he said.

'I have.'

'Okay, and what else?'

'I don't know.' My mind was a blank.

'Have you been near that orchard, robbing apples?'

'I have, Father.'

'You are a bold child. Now go out and say ten Hail Marys and four Our Fathers.'

'Thank you.'

In those days, you prayed on your knees. The stone floor was cold on my bare knees but I'd survived another confession. I hadn't been found out. I don't know what I thought might have happened if I confessed my true sins but it doesn't say much about my faith in God. Or perhaps it did, just that he was a vengeful Old Testament type.

An old woman in a bobble hat leaned over from the front pew, 'It's very busy now, isn't it?'

'It is, yes. We must have picked the rush hour.'

She smiled, a pearly row of dentures on display. 'Oh, every hour's rush hour now. It's the Poles, y'see.'

I didn't know what she meant at first and then the penny dropped. 'Oh, the Polish immigrants.'

'They do a Polish mass now, in their language.'

'Is that so?' She was a dear old soul, it kicked my heart to make me think I was probably the only person she'd spoken to all week. The world seemed too harsh a place for the elderly now.

'I just love them, the Poles, y'know,' she said. 'I think it's just fabulous what they've done for the city and the church of course.' She stalled, seemed to be thinking, looking back with a nostalgic gleam in her eye, 'It's like they've resurrected the place. Yes, it is so.'

She smiled, got up to leave and grasped my hand with hers. The skin on her fingers felt so soft that I thought she was wearing silk gloves.

'Goodbye,' I said.

I watched the old lady leave. She nodded and smiled to everyone. I felt an uncontrollable urge to get her home safe and sound — like the city wasn't safe for her, wasn't fit to lace her shoes.

I sat for a few more moments and wondered just why I had come into the cathedral. I didn't know. It was as if I was summoned by unseen forces. It had happened before. When my child died I came here and prayed to God that I found the strength to accept His will.

I never did.

I was weak and I was pathetic and I knew I always had been. There was no point pretending. At 20 you can tell yourself the world will be yours. At 30, with some luck, you might believe a small portion of the place had actually fallen into your lap. But past the big 40, there was no deceit big enough to fool you anymore.

The atrophy had begun. The results were on show. And the road ahead was far shorter than the one leading the other way.

I rose.

Lit a candle of mercy for Hod and made a weak plea to Our Lady. It had come to that. It was all I had.

What was that saying the old soldiers used to have?

"There are no atheists in foxholes."

I believe they were right. For no reason I had felt a change sweeping over me. A surrendering. Did I throw up my hands or did I stumble on?

Outside the sun had appeared. Splitting the clouds and making the sky above look wholly foreign; we didn't do nice days in Edinburgh. I tested my leg on the pavement, there was no pain, the walking must have done me some good. I set off for the bus stop, knowing full well that I had no choice but to confront the demons that had descended on me.

My mam's house in Restalrig was a squalid affair. I pictured it as the bus pulled up. It seemed to me the whole city was sliding off the face of a cliff but Restalrig seemed to be taking the brunt. Junkies and derros wandering the streets like we were already post-Apocalypse. After all she'd been through, my mam, it didn't seem fair to put her in a pathetic little shoebox and leave her to see out her days, fearing for her life. She deserved better; we all did.

Even on the top deck with all the windows open it was too hot for me. As I folded my Crombie, shoved it down on the seat next to me, my mobi started.

Ringing.

'Hello?'

'Gus, how goes it?' It was Amy.

'Is that a trick question?'

Laughter. 'Jesus, lighten up. I almost have some good news for you.'

'You do? I've had precious little of that lately, I'll have you know.'

'Well, it is kinda, I think.'

'Backtracking already?'

'No, I'm just a bit pressed for time. I'm on my lunch break.'

The image of her dressed to impress for her first day at Gladstone's Estate Agency in the West End flashed before me.

'Tell me more,' I said.

'I can't, I'm in Costa, Mandy's just gone to the loo.'

'Who the fuck is Mandy?'

'I think you mean "Who the fuck is Alice!"'

'Right. Of course I do. Look, is there a point to this call or what?'

Amy's chatter speeded up. 'I'm done at five, can I meet you somewhere in the city? I have some interesting developments to lay on you.'

I resisted the obvious answer. 'Sure, I'm on my way to Restalrig just now, but I can be back in the city about that time. Grab me in the Cafe Nero under Blackwell's.'

'Done. See you then, Gus.'

Hung up.

It was a short call, even by Amy's blunt standards but it had started me thinking.

I was all out of luck, and the precious few ideas I was batting around in my bonce were as much use as tits on a bull. There came a point when, as Jim Morrison said: *'You can always whip the horse's eyes.'*

This fucking nag was well due a lashing. I hoped it didn't come to that, because the image of an already tooled-up Mac resorting to all-out violence was far from pretty.

The bus pulled up and I made my way to the front behind a line of stumbling, coughing junkies. I imagined they'd all been for their dose of methadone. All the chemists had little cubicles for them now, so they could go in and down their hit in private. I guess, even in this deranged day and age, it just didn't do to put that kind of thing on display. There was also the fact that there'd been reports of some smack-heads holding onto their methadone — keeping it in their mouths — and selling it on. It had become so common it had picked-up a tag: the Barlinnie Spit.

The sun was high in the sky, bleaching out all the colour. I kept my Crombie under my arm and set off into the glare.

No matter how many Indian summers came to Scotland — and lately, there'd been a few — the natives never got used to the sight of the big yellow fella up there. Battling harsh climes was locked in our DNA, made us who we are: moaning bastards when it comes to the weather.

When I hit my Mam's street, it took a bit of a pelt on the senses. Her house was in the middle of a long row, that had once been filled with old geezers who spent the nice weather planting flowers. They were good old boyos, old soldiers with war stories, but they'd been dying off at a fair clip now.

The replacement mob, my own generation and below, hadn't kept up the tradition. Now the gardens were strewn with junk — old tyres and washing machines, engine parts and bust prams. There was a collection of shopping trolleys rusting in the street and an absolute shit-ton of scratch cards blowing with the breeze.

I made it to my mam's gate, the only tidy, painted gate on her side of the road, and I saw her down on her knees, weeding the border. I wanted to ask what she was doing, it seemed utterly pointless planting flowers amidst the ruins. But I stopped and watched her, a little trowel attacking the soil, and realised there was nothing else she could do. It was ingrained in her, a host of standards and lost merits that seemed wholly out of place in the modern world. They had currency once, I'm sure of it, but this display was all for her own benefit.

I stood over the gate and spoke, 'Hello, Mam.'

She turned, looked lost. 'Angus?'

'The very same.'

'What are you doing here, son?'

The question, and the use of the word *son* put the heart crossways in me. It had been a while right enough, but there were reasons for that.

I opened the gate and walked in.

'Any chance of a cup of tea?'

CHAPTER 29

In my usual fashion, by the time we got inside, I'd changed my mind.

'Actually, Mam, do you have any coffee?' I said. It was always the way, when I picked up the drink, in any organised fashion, I hit the caffeine big time as well.

'I don't think so, I never touch the stuff. But hang on, Catherine sometimes leaves those sachets around, she likes a coffee, so she does.'

I watched my mam potter about the kitchen. She chattered endlessly the entire time. Trips out to the big Markies with Catherine, and a garden centre visit where she'd smuggled out some Nescafe freebies.

'I didn't take them, I never could, but your sister popped a few in her bag. Felt like stealing to me but she said they were free.'

As her chat continued I could feel myself shedding IQ points at a rapid rate. The size of the strawberries they grew in the garden centre was a topic of choice that she managed to stretch out to a full five minutes.

'And there was a man dressed as a lady!' She sounded genuinely shocked now. 'And one of the kids in the cafe stood up and pointed it out.'

'Is that right?' A lengthy response by my standards.

'A little boy, he stood on his chair and yelled it out, "Why's that man wearing lipstick?" … It's the kids I feel sorry for, he got a right row, but how could he know at that age?'

I collected my coffee cup, it tasted just how I imagined a freebie sachet would, but the caffeine kicked in. I let my mother prattle on, it seemed to be good for her — like therapy — I tried to change tack, move the conversation over but she was running on rails now, I truly wondered if she could breathe through her ears.

'Mam, I wanted to talk to you … about Dad.'

The conversation stopper, as always. Her mouth shut like a zipper.

'Sorry, I kind of dropped that on you there.'

'Yes, you did.' Her tone had altered, she had lost the hell-for-leather velocity in her speech. She sounded like a different person entirely.

I looked out the window, a thought flashed to simply change the conversation again, talk about the weather. But, something else was steering this course.

'I'm sorry, Mam, but it's on my mind … back on my mind, Christ, I can never get away from it.'

She took a sip of tea and stared into the cup, like there was some form of answer to be found there. 'That's twice you've said *sorry* now.'

'Is it?'

'It is.'

I nearly made it three times. The truth was, I didn't really know what to say. How do you confront your mother about things that happened thirty-odd years ago? It was past, and probably should be left buried there.

'You're drinking again, aren't you?' she said. 'Oh, no, I'm not going to criticise you for that, Angus, it's your life.'

'You can tell?'

'I can smell it on you. I never have drink in the house now. You know that.'

'You're still sensitive to it, then?'

'I am. And many other things besides.' She put down her cup and saucer on the floor beside her, a little grey liquid evacuated onto the carpet. 'What is it you want to know?'

I felt my eyes widening, searching my mother for some sort of an explanation for her being so forthcoming. In all these years, she'd never once talked openly about what we all went through. She was so stoic. She was the one who held us all together. I didn't know how she did it.

For the first time since I'd heard Fitz's suggestion that I approach my mother and ask her what caused my guilt, it seemed like a bad idea. It was just that, though, an idea. This was real life, the here and now. I felt like I was a boy again, getting ready to run, or trembling in the cupboard under the stairs, terrified that I'd be found out.

I got up to go.

'It doesn't matter, Mam.'

A cold hand was placed on mine. 'Sit down, Angus.'

'No. I shouldn't have come.' For all the years between those events, it still seemed too soon, too raw, to even contemplate such a discussion.

'Angus, go back and sit down, *please* …'

I did as I was told.

She saw I was haunted by this; perhaps she was too. We'd seen things, been through the same experiences, Christ on a cross, she'd have to be made of granite not to be haunted.

'I understand, y'know. When the memories come back it's like it was yesterday, but don't think I hold them off any better than you,' she said.

'You don't?'

Mam shook her head and removed a tiny hankie from the sleeve of her blouse. 'That little boy, the one at the garden centre, he set me off for the first time in a while. It can be anything.'

'The kid you just told me about?'

'He was only young, maybe four or five. I remember you at that age, I can still see your face, how your hair sat, the colour of your knees in those shorts … always filthy dirty.'

She dabbed at her eyes with the hankie.

'You changed so much. Every few months you were a different person then, your whole face changed sometimes and it shocked me, it made me wonder what was happening inside you.'

I walked over to the couch and put my arm around her, 'Don't do this to yourself, Mam. It's not why I came here.'

'You should have come much sooner.'

'It wasn't my way.'

'I know.'

We held each other for a moment. I smelled the lavender she powdered herself with and I knew I only smelled of drink. I pulled away again.

'I always wondered, could I have done more?' I said.

That stare. Deep dissatisfaction. I recognised it immediately. 'You were a child.'

'If it weren't for me, for the rest of us, maybe you could have escaped. I kept you there, trapped.'

'No, Angus. It wasn't like that.'

'I wonder.'

'Don't do it to yourself. There is nothing you could have done. It was the time and it was your father's father's time that caused it all, there's nothing, not one thing a little boy like yourself could have done.'

She'd lit something in me. She didn't even know it, but there was a hint, an inference, in her words that I latched onto. What did she mean by it?

'My father's *father*?' The words sounded hostile, accusatory. I wanted to rope them back in.

Mam turned to face me. A stray white curl unfurled itself from above her blank forehead. 'I shouldn't have said that.'

'I think you should say more. If there's something you know, that can help me ... I think you should.'

She shifted uncomfortably in her seat. 'Well, it was The War, really.'

'The War?'

'Yes, Cannis was born when his father, well his mother's husband, was away at The War.' She crossed her legs and turned away from me.

'Are you saying what I think you are?'

She looked back. 'Cannis never knew his real father.'

This was all entirely new to me. 'What ... happened?'

'It's not something people ever talked about in those days.'

'Perhaps they should have.'

She looked out the window, clearly trying to compose herself, looking for the right words. 'Well, Sylvie wasn't the one to point the finger at if that's what you're thinking.'

'What are you saying? Grannie was assaulted?' My mind flushed with a million strange scenarios, sepia-tinted it seemed, from a time that occurred before I was born but determined the entire outcome of my life.

'It was during a blackout, no one was ever caught. Your grandfather never accepted the boy, he was another man's child. There was a lot of tension, he was shell-shocked when he was demobbed. The marriage was never the same, I mean, I think they tried to pretend for years and years but your father suffered then.'

I couldn't take it all in. It was too much. It had been my natural instinct to want to kill this man for what he had done to us and now, here my mother was, confounding that assumption. Anger rose up inside me, I didn't want Cannis Dury to have an excuse for his actions. It was far easier if he were just a monster, plain and simple.

My mother spoke again, slowly, coldly. 'He was beaten, everyone knew it. And he was beaten horrendously, there was bones broken; unimaginable in a child. But George was drinking heavily then. And Sylvie was taking the brunt of it too.' She dropped her head in her hands, 'Oh, sweet Jesus, it's all too much to consider. Can you believe we saw the same all those years later?'

I couldn't speak. My throat was frozen. My mind was somewhere else, all I had was a new reality to conceive of, and to find my place in it.

'Angus, your father was tortured blind by that man. George came back from the war a basket case and he took it all out on the boy. He knew his wife had drifted away from him too, and that's why he battered the boy — to hurt her.'

It all sounded so depressingly familiar that I thought I might weep. But I didn't. Somehow, I found the strength to stand.

'Your father was sent to an approved school and that was the end of them as a family. George and Sylvie couldn't live under the same roof — he left her. A couple of years later Cannis came home and things settled down, but the damage was done.'

'It was indeed.'

'What?'

'The damage was done.' The words came out like arrows.

'No, son, you don't understand. I tried to explain why he was like that, how he didn't have a choice.'

'If you don't have a good father, you have to invent one.'

'What does that mean?'

'Nothing. Just something someone said, once.'

'I-I don't understand, Angus.'

'Neither do I, Mam.' I headed back towards the door, 'You see, I never copied my own father, I went the opposite direction.'

I turned away.

'Angus, come back.'

I couldn't face her anymore.

I walked.

CHAPTER 30

I took the bus to the end of South Clerk Street. Had my beak glued to the window the whole time so I don't know how I managed to miss Blackwell's. There were precious few real bookstores left in the city — the dumbed down didn't read — so the corner building was a bit of a landmark these days.

The street was packed. This end of town was becoming beyond cramped thanks to student gaffs and the attendant takeaways and shops selling nothing but fucking cereal. I felt uncomfortably old among them, or maybe it was the extra layers of history that had been revealed to me by my mother.

By Surgeon's Hall my injured leg was taking another turn — I'd been overdoing it but was glad not to be trailing the walking-stick in to meet Amy; the wind-ups from her would have been severe.

I slipped past the main entrance to the bookstore and there she was, sitting in the window seat, power dressed to the absolute nines.

'Don't tell me you're getting to like this new look,' I said.

She pecked me on the cheek. 'Fuck off, would you?'

It was a sort of greeting, very Amy.

She trotted off to the counter and ordered some more coffees. I was getting settled in my seat, watching the world walk by, when she returned with the full-beam smile on.

'So, have I got news for you,' she said.

I thought of my own recent discovery, about being the descendent of a rape baby, and decided to let her lead.

'Go on.'

'Gladstone's has proven a mine of information. Before I kick off, I assume you've found no hide nor hair of Bunny.'

'Not a carrot.'

'Funny.' She sat upright, enthusiasm brimming. 'Well, I think I found the next best thing.'

'Stella?'

'Okay, so the *next* next best thing.'

I was done guessing. 'You're going to have to tell me.'

Nods. 'Right, well, Stella had a best mate in the estate agents, Mandy Baird, I've connected with her. Big time.'

'I should know this name, I take it?'

Head shakes. 'No. Let me explain, Mandy is what you might call a spurter!'

'I'd never use such misogynistic language.'

'Yeah, right. Well, she looks the part and the boss, Stevie Fergusson, fancies himself a bit of a player. They had a thing a while back and because of Stella's position, well, let's just say Bunny got involved.'

I was confused. 'Swinging? Foursomes? I'm lost.'

Amy stood up and took our coffees from the waitress. She was sighing as she did so, knowing full-well she'd made a complete arse of explaining this great discovery to me.

'Let's try again. Mandy and Stevie were a thing, a couple.'

'Got that much.'

'But, and this is the interesting bit, Jonny Ladd was a business associate of Stevie's — something to do with flipping flats.'

I laughed. 'Got to do something with those proceeds of crime earnings I suppose.'

'Well, the story goes, according to Mandy, Jonny took a shine to her and there was a bit of a falling out between Stevie and the Bad Ladd.'

'Understandable, I suppose.' I tasted my coffee, the yarn was so good I wished I'd brought popcorn. 'Go on … '

'Yeah, well, that's nothing. Now it gets tasty. Ladd set up Stevie with a prossie, unbeknownst to Mandy, and gave strict instructions to Bunny and Lee Donald to record the event on film and put the threat on Stevie that if he didn't dump Mandy, she got an invitation to the picture show.'

I shook my head. Nothing I'd heard was in any way original, but I admired the balls of Jonny Ladd. If you're going to fuck over your business partner, completely and utterly was the way to go about it.

'Amy, how the hell did you get that out of this Mandy woman in one day?'

She smiled. 'Easy. I could tell you all my secrets, but then I'd have to kill you.'

I thought to tell her she'd have to join a long queue, but went with, 'So, to summarise, Bunny and Donnie had instructions from Ladd to put the threat on this Stevie Fergusson … *but* … I'm assuming there's one of those.'

'Oh, yes, there always is. *But*, Bunny and Donnie got the idea of bleeding Stevie for a few quid, instead of the original request to dump Mandy so Jonny could move in.'

'Oh …'

'It gets worse. Their plan didn't, er, go to plan.'

'What happened?'

Amy sat back in her chair and shrugged.

'*Wha*—?'

She picked up her coffee and sipped. I waited for her to return the cup to the saucer and prodded her again. 'Amy ... what happened?'

'Isn't that enough?'

'You've done very well, yes, but I need the bit where this blows up into Donnie being killed and Bunny going to ground.'

More shrugs. 'I don't know that bit.'

'So, I just fill that in with guesswork, I take it?'

'I don't really know, I'm still working on that. But, I can tell you this much — Mandy never got to see any pictures, and although she's still in a job, things have got very shaky for her.'

'In what way?'

'Well, for example, today she told me that a lot of her previous responsibilities have been revoked, like getting access to the safe.'

'Really? Are you saying what I think you are?'

'That maybe Stevie Fergusson has some glossies in there that he wants to keep away from prying eyes.'

I wasn't convinced. 'Surely he'd just destroy them.'

'Not if he was in the process of a beat down for them. He might want to hold onto the evidence, to show he'd been set-up ... Or, maybe he's just totally pervy and likes to look at them.'

I still wasn't sure. 'I don't know. But it would be interesting to get a poke about in that safe.'

'Which is why I've stuck my hand up for some banking training tomorrow,' she raised her coffee in a salute, 'Great minds and all that.'

*　*　*

I schlepped down the Mile and past Holyrood Palace, that glorious monument to rubbing the proles' noses in it. Across the way, on the other side of the road, stood the later-day, concrete version, known as the Scottish Parliament. Was still carrying my Crombie as I headed onto Holyrood Drive, passing Arthur's Seat. There was a trickle of ants — or were they tourists? — making their way to the top of the hill. In this heat, I wondered, why bother? Were I in possession of my youth, I'd be spending my energy more wisely.

Got to the first copse of trees that sheltered the road and felt relieved to be in the shade. It was cooler, but also darker, walking under the speckled light. I caught sight of a white van slowing down, a V-dub, and the thought of giving directions to campsites in North Berwick fair bust my hump.

The window went down, just about the same time as the side-door opened up and I cottoned pretty sharpish that this was no camper-van.

'Get the fuck in, Dury,' yelled Sharky. He had a plaster on his nose and a lovely looking shiner bursting onto his right temple that told me he'd been done over lately.

Said, 'I haven't heard a ... please.'

The whack to my gut fair toppled me. There's a phrase, hear it all the time: *Knocked the wind out me.* I got that part, but the coffee I'd drunk half-an-hour ago was also evacuated in a flash.

'You filthy piece of shite!' I didn't recognise this voice, but the shoes I'd just barfed over looked very expensive. Black brogues, in beautiful leather, even if they were full of holes.

Jonny Ladd stepped out and grabbed me by the collars, threw me inside. 'Look what you've done to my shoes, I'd heard you were a pisshead but you're worse than I thought.'

'It's only coffee.' Where I got the balls to dig out the Bad Ladd, I've no clue.

'Shut the fuck up.'

He kicked me in the guts, then started to wipe his shoes on my back as I curled over, retching.

Ladd was broad but had the physique of a wasp, or a boxer. He was the type of man who had thrived on his presence and wasn't about to let the years take that away from him. I imagined him breaking away from the desk every now and again to 'squat and give me ten.' Maybe he feared back-chat? Worse, maybe he feared the Big House.

'Where are you taking me?' I said.

'I'll ask the questions, Dury, and you'll give the answers. If they're not the ones I want to hear then you'll not give two fucks about where you're going because one hole in the ground looks much like the next.'

We drove for about twenty minutes, as I massaged my aching guts and eventually managed to start breathing normally again. My insides settled and I discovered I was still suicidal, not enough to tackle Ladd again, but, enough to take the piss out of Sharky.

'What happened to your face, Sharky?' I said. 'You're not still chasing parked cars, are you?'

He looked at me in disbelief, then turned to Jonny Ladd, as if seeking approval to batter me.

'You want to see the other guy,' said Sharky.

I managed a laugh, my guts strained but it seemed worth it. 'I bet. His knuckles will be a bloody mess.'

Sharky lunged for me but was held back by Ladd. The van was screeching to a halt. I heard the traffic whizzing by the open door. I was yanked out and pinned against the side of the van. A main road stood to the front of me, dual carriageway, and open fields either side. I tried to clock the location and put a guess at somewhere along the A1.

Ladd approached. He walked slowly, as if letting his composure speak for him. I imagined this was a well-practiced stance. He stood before me with a needle-point gaze, then grabbed my face, pushing me towards the burning-hot metal of the door. 'Right, wide man, speak.'

'It's kinda hard with your hand on my mouth.'

'Don't get fucking lippy, Dury. I hear you've been making not so discreet enquiries about me.'

'I'm not the only one.'

He let my face go and stepped away. 'Are you talking about DCI McEwan? I'm not worried about him, not in the least.'

I felt my blood rise. 'Is that because McEwan has Hod taking the rap for you?'

Ladd showed me his palms. 'What do you mean? I'm utterly blameless.'

'Tell that to Donnie's people. You could tell his other-half, I hear you've got her under wraps.'

Ladd turned to his driver, a paid-up pug, with all the bulges to prove it. He seemed silent enough, though, so Ladd turned to Sharky for acknowledgement.

Sharky nodded. 'Dury's clueless, he doesn't know anything.'

'Don't I?' I figured I had one chance of keeping myself from being thrown in front of one of a speeding HGV, and that was playing a bluff. 'I know all about Donnie and Bunny, about their little scam to blackmail Stevie Fergusson for you. I know it backfired and I know one or two other things.'

Sharky looked ready to dribble on himself, his mouth opening and closing like a recently landed fish. Ladd barged past him and pointed a stubby finger at me. 'Where is he?'

'Who? Donnie? You should know he's in the morgue because you put him there.'

'Don't fuck me around, Dury, where's that cunt, Bunny?'

'Is that what this is all about? Is that why you've picked me up and taken me for a nice run in the country?'

Ladd lost it. 'Get him.'

The pug lunged at me — for a big lad, he was impressively agile. He had me in an arm lock, leaning over the road in seconds. Now I saw why they'd selected this particular lay-by, there was a bend on the road, and an awkward camber, that for a few moments rendered the oncoming vehicles subject to a blindspot. At upwards of 70mph, my head would be removed cleanly from my shoulders before any one of these drivers could say, 'Holy fu…'

'One chance, Dury, tell me where Bunny is or your face becomes road-kill.'

I felt the next car breeze past, close enough to part my hair.

'Get this fucking clown off me, Ladd.'

'Tell me where Bunny is.'

I knew that if I told him — told him anything, because I knew shit — there'd be seagulls picking bits of my brain out of the tarmac a second later. Ladd didn't have the marbles to look beyond the next five minutes.

'I can't, not right now.' I raised the volume to compete with a cattle mover, 'But, let me go, and I'll bring him to you.'

'Are you pulling my prick, Dury?' Ladd lunged forward, he bellowed in my ear, 'I'm not fucking about here. I want that cunt now.'

I freed my arm from the pug and stepped away from the road. There was some confusion, Sharky made his way for me with his fists up but got flagged down by his guv'nor.

'Stay the fuck away from me, I've got all the bargaining chips here, Jonny, don't you understand that?' My arm ached like it had been through a mangle, I rubbed at my stiff elbow. 'I've got Bunny, or at least can get him for you, but you knock me off like Donnie and you'll never see him again.'

For the first time since I'd met him, something like thought started behind Ladd's eyes. He motioned Sharky and the fat pug back to the van.

'Okay, Dury, now it's your turn to do some listening.'

'I'm all ears.'

He seemed strangely calm now, like I was dealing with another person. 'You give your friend Bunny a message from me. I know what he was planning, why he took that money from Stevie Fergusson, why he stiffed me, and why he's emptied out his lock-up.'

I played coy. 'And what, you think he doesn't know too?'

'Of course, why else would he be running scared?'

'Perhaps because he doesn't want to follow in Donnie's footsteps.'

Ladd took a deep breath, two sharp arrow-heads appeared either side of his mouth as he smirked out a response, 'Why are you concerning yourself with this, Dury? What's Bunny got on you?'

'Nothing. And that's exactly what Bunny is to me. It's what you have that concerns me.'

'And what might that be?'

'Stella Wallace.'

The name failed to register with him immediately, then from somewhere a lightbulb went on. 'Donnie's bit. I see.

Okay, Mr Dury, I'll do you a deal, you deliver Bunny to me and you can have the lovely Stella back.'

'In one piece?'

'Not a hair on her head, or anywhere else, will be harmed.' He put his hand on his heart, it was the most insincere reaction imaginable.

I said, 'When?'

'24-hours.'

It wasn't enough time, but I was bluffing. If I made a plea for more time he'd see through my bluster. 'Okay, you have a deal.'

'Not quite, Dury. I also want that money Bunny and Donnie scammed from Stevie Fergusson. Every fucking penny, and for every penny missing you will watch me take it out of that bint's arse.'

He turned back for the van. Nothing more was said. I waited to see if a lift would be offered but as they spun in the road and crossed the central reservation I got the impression that wasn't going to be an option.

I watched the van speeding back to the city and a window was opened. My Crombie was thrown out. Figured I'd have to risk my neck in traffic to retrieve it. After all, my tabs were in the pocket, and I was gasping for a smoke.

CHAPTER 31

Managed to thumb a lift from an old truckie. He was delivering a load of trainers to the sports outlet at Fort Kinnaird. Said he'd been shitting himself the entire time because in Scottish cities sportswear now had a higher black-market value than crystal meth, apparently. He'd been jumped, beaten, driven off the road and had to run for his life in the dark of night.

'Are you sure it's not the SAS you're in?' I said.

Laughter. Two rows of battle-scarred teeth on show, as if presenting evidence.

'The worst part of this job is finding dead bodies in the back of the trailer.'

'No way.'

'Oh, it happens. They jump on in Calais by the hundreds, you don't dare stop or you might get a machete through the windscreen, or fuck knows what else.'

'Where's the police?'

'The what? It's like *Mad Max* down there, did you see many speeding tickets handed out on the road to the Thunderdome?'

I took his point, but didn't want to pry. I had enough problems of my own to worry about. *Mad Max* was closer to home than I ever imagined it; it was possible I'd met him in a lay-by on the A1 already. I left the old boy at the Fort and dropped him a few sheets to buy a pint, then wished I hadn't bothered.

'No, you keep it, son,' he said. 'To be honest, you look like you need it more than me,' he said.

Wanted to say, "Don't call me son, not ever". But, went with, 'And they say manners are on the way out.'

It was late evening now but the shops were still doing a roaring trade. The land whales were all burned to a crisp, topping up their calories with Cornettos and Ben & Jerry's, straight from the tub. It was a joy to oversee this descent down the evolutionary ladder first hand, as fingers and faces got fired in directly.

'For fucksake,' I couldn't watch, reminded me too much of those nature documentaries where a pack of wolves tear into a deer carcass, just substitute blood for Caramel Chew Chew.

Took the first bus heading back to the city centre. The old Walkman was still in the inside pocket of my Crombie. It'd survived the impact with the asphalt — mind you, it was held together with so much Sellotape and Elastoplast now that there was very little of the original casing left.

Pressed play.

The Doors, 'The End.'

Turned the tape over.

The Smiths, 'Girlfriend in a Coma.'

It struck me that I had a particularly morbid taste in music. If I were hoping for something uplifting, perhaps setting the mood for me to channel some brainpower into getting myself out of the shit, then I was to be disappointed.

I sunk back in my chair and tried to become invisible, to block out the outside world. It was my daily modus operandi now, but nothing did the trick like the sauce. There was a dark well inside me crying out to be re-filled with scoosh, but it would have to wait — the nerdy part of me was making other plans.

The worst thing about having a mind that recognised patterns, and a wordy way about you, was having a head-full of quotations to reel out on demand. If there were an occasion, you could be guaranteed, I had just the wanky quote to hand. It annoyed the life out of some, myself included, but I had other things that annoyed me more, at least I did now.

History doesn't repeat, but it rhymes.

—Mark Twain

I had a vague notion of what Twain meant before visiting my mother, but now I feared I understood completely. Her reasoning, her excuse, for my father was that he'd only played the hand he'd been dealt. He'd watched his stepfather beat the living shite out of his mother and thought it was the only way.

Well, bullshit.

What happened to free will?

What happened to rejecting what you knew to be wrong?

Mam's understanding only seemed to go as far as finding a way to let the man she married off the hook. It wasn't the truth. Like most of us, she feared the truth.

I knew I would never have followed my father down that dark path. I'd been married, and never once felt the need to belt my wife. For fuck's sake, I was never shy with my fists either. But, my father, he made a habit of choke-holding and floor-slamming his own family. Jesus, the blood and gore was witnessed by all. How could Mam ever excuse that?

I had a new anger burning me up now: I had previously sought solace in my abject hatred for the man that was my father, now though, I had other ideas to consider. Whether or not I rejected them didn't matter, they were in my head, and would need to be explored.

The drink called to me like the most sweet-tongued of the sirens now. I knew in my heart it would never work. There was dark blood in my veins. It might be doing battle with a counterpart of sorts, but Gus Dury was the battlefield. And that was never going to change. Not as long as I lived.

The bus took me all the way to Meadowbank and I dinged the bell for the stop outside Amy's street. It was a long row of old Victorian tenements, the kind you find all over the city. The bay-windows and dressed stone still carried an air of faded grandeur but belied the fact that inside the flats had been sub-divided into rabbit hutches.

I sparked up a tab as I walked the street, trying to put the words together to explain to Amy why I was back hounding her after such a short interval of time. I never got past the initial idea, though, was stopped in the street right outside Amy's block.

Ringing.

Answered the mobi. 'Hello …'

'Gus, you won't recognise the number, or if you do, you shouldn't.' It was Fitz.

'What's up?'

'You mean you haven't heard?' His voice dipped into a reedy pessimism.

'Has something happened?'

'It's Mac, he's been picked up by our very own DCI Robbie McEwan. It's not looking good for him, they have him down in the cells now.'

My tab slipped from my fingers, watched the amber sparks fly in the street. 'Mac, but how? Don't tell me fucking Robocop's got some forensic shit on him now, too.'

He shuffled the phone from hand to hand. 'Gus, Mac got into a fight in a Leith drinker, the Alabama.'

Fitz didn't need to fill me in on any more. The name of the pub set the warning buzzer off. Then my mind's eye saw Sharky's bandaged face.

'He gave Sharky a rattle, then.'

'I thought you were in the dark?'

'I am. But, I'm also a fast learner. And I just saw Sharky looking like Frank Bruno after Tyson had finished with him.'

'Right, well, I know what you mean, *Harry*.' A moment of silence passed on the line. Fitz coughed, 'Sharky fingered Mac to McEwan, said he'd clocked him on the night that Donnie was murdered.'

'Why's nobody taken Sharky in? He knows more than Hod or Mac.'

Fitz exhaled. 'If you'd let me explain.'

'Go on.' I felt my sore leg start to ache, made my way over to sit on a garden wall with weeds poking over the top. Kept a close eye on the thistles.

'Sharky's been feeding McEwan some biccies on the case. He dropped Mac on our doorstep this morning and as soon as I heard I gave Mac the tip off to get out of town fast. Thing is, Mac never took the hint. He went round to Sharky's local and battered the living shite out of him instead. McEwan picked Mac up right on the spot about five minutes after the main event.'

231

Sharky's reaction to me winding him up about the state of his face started to make sense now. Nothing else did, mind. I wondered how I was going to bring this all together on my own. Who was next? And, Jesus, was Amy in any danger?

'Fitz, you need to tell me, if there's anything else on the go I need to know about. I mean it, you can't hold back on this … I've had Amy working this case too, she has a kid now.'

'I haven't heard anything about Amy. But, Gus, there is something else.'

'Go on …'

'McEwan has something on you, too. You can't go back to your flat because that's the first place he'll think to find you.'

'He's after me as well?'

Fitz's voice speeded up, 'There's a lot of stuff I can't figure out. It's as if McEwan has you pegged, but is waiting for the nod from up above to haul you in. If he finds you, he won't let you out of his sight, so take my advice and don't get caught, Gus.'

'I'll try not to.'

'Good.'

I had a million more questions for Fitz but he cut himself off. I noticed the number hadn't been retained in my phone either. If things were desperate before, they were a notch or two higher now.

I made my way into Amy's. My heart ramped. I kept a constant watch over my shoulder but spotted no one in pursuit. My mind flashed with images of Mac in a cold cell, battered and bloodied knuckles his only company. I scolded myself inwardly that I hadn't kept a closer watch on Mac. If anything, he was as bad as Hod when it came down to having a volatile temperament, maybe even worse.

If McEwan had done a job on Hod, then with Mac's reputation, and record, he certainly wouldn't have to try hard with Mac. It was beyond grim. Dismal. Barbed-wire twisted in my gut for what I'd do if I got hold of that bastard Jonny Ladd again. I'd do fucking serious time, just to wipe the smug grin off his puss.

All this because Ladd's ego was damaged.

I didn't have the whole picture, I was still missing bits and pieces. Bunny must have something Ladd wanted badly, because Ladd was ready to burn every boat he owned in this town, just to fuck over Bunny.

I smacked a fist into the wall. 'I swear, I'll fucking burst him.'

A sash-window groaned from above me.

'Gus, what are you doing?' Amy was hanging over the window-box.

'Get inside, Amy.' I went for the front door. 'We need to have a chat, right away.'

CHAPTER 32

Amy opened the door in a peach-coloured bathrobe, a matching towel tied around her head. Despite the garb, she still managed to drip water all over the polished floorboards.

'Come in, I'm dripping,' she said.

'I bet you say that to all the boys.'

'Funny. But, I don't actually.' She closed the door behind me and pointed through to the lounge. 'Evie's sleeping, give me five minutes to dry my hair and put some slap on.'

I thought to tell her she looked nice enough without the make up, she could give it a miss, but knew I'd change the current mood from friendly messing to something more serious.

Amy's living-room looked exactly as it had the last time: spotless. A couple of cushions might have been off point but that was it. The contrast with my own gaff was startling — I was living like I had for years now, the only difference between myself and a total jakey was that my arse didn't get wet when I sat down. Way things were travelling for me, that was coming in the post, though.

I chucked my Crombie on the couch and strolled over to watch the sleeping nipper. There was something soothing in the act, I didn't get it, though. After all my experiences with childhood and children the last thing I expected to feel was at ease.

Evie moved a little, opened and closed one of her little hands. I looked at the tiny fingers and couldn't resist placing my own on her palm. She gripped. It was a joy like no other to bond with a child, but something chilled my insides and I pulled away quickly.

I heard the hairdryer blowing from the back bedroom and hoped Amy would return soon. Christ above, what was she thinking, leaving me alone with a child? After all my history, and after my father's real truths were revealed, I was unsuited to child minding. It was bullshit, of course. Just that sick form of self-talk that comes when you feel the need to beat up on yourself. Did my discovery change anything? Did it change me? Supposed I'd find out.

I pulled one of the dining chairs from beneath the table and sat down beside Evie, just watching, observing. She had a thing for blowing bubbles on her lips, made her turn up an imperious nose. She got that from her mam.

'Now, Evie, let me give you some advice,' I leaned on the edge of her play-pen, if anyone had seen me they'd have laughed, but it felt the most natural thing in the world to me. 'Always, *always* now, go with the flow. Do you hear me, Evie? Don't ever question the rules, respect authority — even when you know for certain it doesn't deserve it — and never question the received orthodoxy.'

She didn't wake up, or start to cry, so I carried on.

'You see, girl, that's how you get on in life. Basically suck up all those rebellious thoughts — the ones that make you feel human. Uh-uh. Don't ever stray off the reservation, kid, or ever run for the fence. That's what I did … and I've been running ever since.'

When I was finished the room felt lighter, quieter and then I realised why. The hairdryer had stopped blowing in the other room. I turned and locked eyes with Amy. She was standing in the doorway, her arms clutching her waist and tears dragging black mascara down her face.

'Oh, I'm sorry, Amy.'

She shook her head, started walking towards me. 'Don't be stupid. It's beautiful.'

'Wha—?'

'What you said was lovely, Gus.'

I didn't know how to respond, my instinct was to be embarrassed, felt a beamer spread across my cheeks.

Amy sat down on the couch and I moved away from the play-pen to join her. 'Kids, they're the best, aren't they?'

Nods.

'You have a little corker there, Amy, you should be overjoyed.'

The sobs were still coming, she wiped a black smear on the sleeve of her dressing gown. 'What a mess.'

I couldn't see what had sparked all the upset, said, 'Is everything all right?'

'I know some people think I've fucked up, but I don't feel like that. Well, I didn't until just now. You don't know the pressure that's on us — my generation — not to do this, not to have kids, but to go and chase career ...'

I cut in, 'Don't pay attention to any of that shite.'

'I don't, usually. It's just, you can't get away from it. Everywhere I go, every TV show, every magazine article — it's all about women with degrees and PhDs and flashy careers and they're all saying how hard it is to find a decent man, so if they can't find one then what chance have I got now?'

She didn't strike me as all that needy. 'Are you sure you want one?'

'I have a child, Gus. I want to raise Evie in a proper family. I wouldn't change my choices, but how was I to know she'd change me inside?'

'You weren't to know. And, let me tell you something, those career women that can't find men that you read about, they're not scaring men off for the reasons you think they are.'

'They're not?' The tears receded.

'No way. Men aren't intimidated by hot-shot babes, they're irritated by them. Who wants to spend their days with an egotistical bore that expects you to worship at the altar of her degree in Media Studies?'

Amy laughed. I thought Tony Robbins would be shitting himself if he heard this coming out of me — I had the motivational speaker gig pegged.

'Amy, I'll tell you what men want — a nice smile and a big heart and everything else is up for negotiation. Trust me, you've got absolutely nothing to worry about.'

As if to prove me right, she put on that nice smile of hers. I smiled back and then Amy took my hand. The moment altered when we touched and I feared the next contact would have deeper consequences.

I yanked my hand away.

Amy spoke, 'Why didn't we work things out, Gus?'

She'd utterly T-boned me. Had absolutely no hope of a coherent answer.

'Well …'

'Don't dare say, "Is that the time?" …'

I took a look at my watch, made a show of changing tack. 'Shit. You do make a good point, though. Look, I've something to tell you, Amy.'

I filled her in on the conversation with Fitz. About Mac being lifted and about my earlier encounter with Jonny Ladd.

When I was finished, the poor girl looked like I'd buried her under a ton of bricks.

'God help us.'

'I've tried that, too.'

'What?'

'Nothing ... I need you to do something for me.'

She perked up a little, always the action junkie. 'Of course, name it.'

'This new boss of yours, Stevie Fergusson.'

'What about him?'

'I need you to arrange a meeting, like yesterday.'

Her eyes rolled a little, gazing upwards towards the ceiling, where she seemed to locate her inspiration without too much effort. She leapt from the couch and took her mobi from above the fireplace.

'I'll put this on speaker-phone, so you can hear ...'

Ringing.

'Hi, is that you, Stevie?'

'Yes, who's calling?'

'I'm sure you won't be expecting this call but I just can't help myself.'

'Who is this?'

'It's Amy. I just started working on you, I mean *for* you.'

'Oh, hello, Amy.' His voice tilted into a curious tone. 'And what can I do for you?'

She winked at me, a mischievous smirk creeping up her face. 'I'm a very direct sort of girl, Stevie, so I'm just going to come out with this ...'

He cleared his throat. 'Erm, okay then.'

'If I find myself attracted to a man I don't like to mess about with all the stupid preamble that it usually entails. You must know what I mean.'

'I-I think I do, Amy. Yes, I know what you mean.'

'Since I saw you behind that desk of yours today, in your tight, white shirt, I've been fixating on one thing. Do you know what that is, Stevie?'

Stevie grew cockier, 'Oh, maybe I can guess.'

'I'm sure you can. I'm sure an experienced man of the world like you has no shortage of imagination, especially involving women.'

'I've had no complaints, put it that way.'

'Stevie, I don't care where you put it. And I mean *where*. I just want it, right now, on that big desk of yours. Do you get me, Stevie? Do you want me, Stevie?'

'I'm sure it can be arranged, Amy.'

'One hour. I want you stripped and ready for action when I get to the office. I'll be in my overcoat and silk hold-ups. Nothing else.'

'One hour?' he said.

'If I can wait that long, Stevie.'

Hung up.

We laughed so hard that I thought I was in danger of doing myself some kind of injury. The girl had some moves. No question.

'Sh-sh … we'll wake the baby, Gus,' she said. 'Let me get dressed and I'll call my mum to mind Evie.'

I put the brakes on. 'No way.'

'How do you mean?'

'I mean, there's no way. I've put Hod and now Mac in the firing line already and there's no way I'm doing the same to you.'

She looked angry, disappointed. Then she turned the situation to her advantage, said, 'Aww, Gus, I didn't know you cared.'

'Really? I must be giving off all the wrong vibes.'

Amy put her hands behind her back, loped towards me, and placed a peck on my cheek. 'Not any more, you're not.'

I'd parked the Golf in Rossie Place, one of the side-streets off Easter Road. It was a bad spot to park, plenty of car windows getting spark-plugged for stereo removal, but it had one major advantage: access from the Abbeyhill colonies. The street was bumper to bumper, even a couple of DHL drivers doing deliveries whilst leaving the van running in the middle of the road. The jakies outside the mini-mart were looking curiously at the contents of the vans but were clearly too far gone to pose a threat.

I kept my head low. Was cool enough to put the Crombie on now — the collar went up on instinct. As I opened up the Golf I turned over the engine and prayed that Wally's once-over hadn't been another one of his fuck-ups. The engine purred to life, without even a splutter. I pinged the ciggie-lighter and pulled out.

I kept looking in the rearview, anticipating a couple of lardy plods to be in pursuit but nothing showed. I was in the clear, well, clear enough. I parked one street away from Mac's shop and took the dark close to the back green. He had a planter that he kept a key under for emergencies and those late-night, back from the pub lock-ins.

There it was. 'Bingo.'

I had as much chance of the filth being called now as I ever did. Looking rough as guts and sporting an edgy peering-over-my-shoulder-every-five-minutes twitch. In this part of Leith, break-ins were on the hour, two an hour on Saturdays, but thankfully I found my way into the backdoor without any interference and closed up behind me.

The light outside was fading and it was getting dark inside, but I didn't want to put on the lights. I couldn't risk being hauled in at this stage — I was the last shot for us all — before the buzzards descended. The thought that it had come to that didn't sit well with me.

Flicked my Zippo and followed the thin blue flame towards the kitchenette. I opened the cupboard under the sink and spotted a tool box. Inside was a roll of duct tape. Pocketed it. And searched out a steel rule — it was just the size to slot in the loose floorboard that I'd been shown once before.

The floorboard hid an item that Mac had said was a "necessary evil" these days, but one I'd never had cause to test. Lifting this board was my *break glass in case of emergency* moment. I reached in and felt a cold, plastic carrier bag.

As I held the bag up it was heavier than I imagined and it made my breath still to think of the consequences of what I was doing. This alone was a locking-up offence. I dug in and retrieved the dirty oil-cloth, inside was Mac's old Enfield revolver — fully loaded. It might have looked like a museum piece, but it could still tear you six new arseholes for suggesting it.

I tucked the shooter in my waistband and headed back to the car. There was a strange lightness in my step that might have been over-confidence or might have been my guts sensing a checkered flag.

Either way, there was no going back now.

I touched the handle of the shooter through my coat.

At least I had a fighting chance.

CHAPTER 33

I couldn't, realistically, say that his failure to install a proper security system on office premises in the west end of Edinburgh was Stevie Fergusson's first mistake. But it was one of them. A big one at that. Even a video-phone on the buzzer would have saved his randy old arse this time, but despite being blackmailed by Bunny and brushing shoulders with Jonny Ladd on a regular basis, the thought hadn't occurred to this moron.

I heard the key turning in the Yale lock, just after the mortise slid, and I waited for the chain to be removed. He was talking, yakking away from the tip of his dick, probably expecting Amy to be there with her raincoat open — the goods on full display — as he went. It was difficult not to laugh, give myself away.

The chain dropped. In the same second, I put my boot into the doorframe and felt that familiar sensation of wood on bone. It wasn't quite as sonorous as Hod's hickory, but I'll take whatever PVC-covered laminboard this was any day of the week.

The groan was uncomfortable to listen to. When I rushed the door, the sight of Stevie Fergusson's doughnut-sized male pattern baldness winking at me was enough of a target for

243

round two. I slapped the handle of the Enfield over his face and opened up a nice gash to match his bleeding nose.

'Is that fucking tears?' I said.

He was howling, worse than a bloody five-year-old that had come off his bike.

'What kind of a man are you?' I was ashamed to share the same gene-pool as this piece of shit. I grabbed his collar, kicked the door closed, and marched him through to the office.

He'd applied the same poor sense to his boudoir as he had his back entrance — though I'd want that sentence to be read carefully. A bottle of Talisker, an ice bucket, and a couple of nice glasses — the thick crystal jobs that I knew from experience went off like a ten-bob rocket when you threw them at the wall.

I threw one at the wall.

Hands shot to his head.

'What the hell is this? What's going on? I demand to know,' said Stevie.

It was my turn to laugh now.

I tipped the ice-bucket over his head. 'Polluting a good drop of malt with H2-fucking-O!'

He smarted, put out a hand to steady himself on a grey filing cabinet. Stevie Fergusson looked ready to keel already. I tucked the shooter back in my waistband and did my poor man's Rutger Hauer from *The Hitcher*.

Paced. Gave Stevie some more time to build up a proper head of panic. I sensed him watching me as I went.

'The night not working out quite how you planned it, Stevie boy?'

'Y-you, know my name?'

'I know quite a bit more than that, old son.'

He tensed, edged his backside onto the front of the desk. 'Like what?'

'Like, it wasn't your arse you were expecting to see planted on that desk tonight. Sorry to break it to you, Stevie, but the only action your bollocks will get tonight are if I decide to use them for target practice.'

I opened my coat and gave the revolver another showing. His gaze followed my intent.

'What do you want?' he said.

'Now, that's an interesting opening gambit. You see, were I in your boots, sunshine, I think I might have been asking what the mad bastard in my midst had done with my proposed little fuck toy?'

'Did you kill her?'

I nearly spewed my guffaw. 'Are you for real? No, Amy's fine, I'm sure you'd be glad to hear if you gave two shits for anyone other than yourself.'

He double blinked. His gaze shot to the door, eying his only escape route. But he decided against trying to outrun a bullet.

I walked in front of him, closed the door; it was more of a statement than a practical measure. When I got back to my side of the room I went over to the shitty John Bellany print that Amy had told me about — ripped it off the wall. In the absence of the print sat a beige-coloured safe, the whole works covered about the size of a sheet of A4.

'Open it,' I said.

'So, that's what this is about: money!' He seemed disgusted.

Said, 'Oh, you'll wish that's all it was.'

The grey features lost a few more shades. 'What do you mean?'

Tipped my head. 'Open it up. If you make me ask you again, you lose a kneecap, and gain a wheelchair for the rest of your days.'

'You can't get away with this, you know.' He started to punch in the combination on a row of buttons like a telephone.

'What makes you think I give two fucks about getting away? Do I look like someone who's making plans for early retirement in Switzerland? No, I'm more your "born to lose" kinda cunt.'

He opened the safe and stepped back.

I looked inside. Couple of folders, some money bags, some manila envelopes. Turned and wiped my hand over the desk, pushing the laptop and a pretty little Ikea light onto the floor.

'Empty it. Pile it up there.'

Stevie was sweating, a thin plumbline smeared down his back. His top-lip was so salty he couldn't stop himself dabbing it with his tongue. I watched him empty the safe and pile the lot on the desk in front of me.

'There's over thirty-thousand in cash,' he said. 'Take it.'

I rummaged in the bank bags, 'Oh, I think I will. Though, it's not for me, you understand. I need this to pay someone off for one of your mistakes, a quite egregious one I might add.'

'Pay who?'

'Well, it wouldn't be Bunny Veitch, because you've already paid him off, haven't you now?'

He didn't answer. I continued to rummage on the desk, found what I was looking for. I held up a black thumb-drive, 'Pick up that laptop, I want to see what's on this.'

He moved slowly, unsteadily. Stevie Fergusson was a man in a trance, watching the life he thought he had being flushed down the toilet as a fresh new hell opened up before him.

A silver apple appeared on the screen.

'Sign in …'

He did as I told him. But there were no words now. The building could have started to crumble around us, I doubted there would have been words even then.

'Give me it.' I took the laptop and stuck the drive in the USB slot. It took seconds to produce a screenful of picture icons. I clicked on the first of the jpegs.

There's a phrase, hear it all the time: *You can't unsee something.*

I knew right away that I'd have that image of Stevie Fergusson, balls-deep, in a skinny little arse the second it appeared. I knew what to expect. This was a beat down, a serious demand for serious money. I'd been informed about the prostitute and expected the worst. I expected gore. What I didn't expect was a girl of barely thirteen summers to be playing the lead role in this pathetic porn flick.

'You utterly sick bastard,' I said. I removed the pistol, pointed it to his head. None of this was planned, I was running on instinct from here and I was fired up to be capable of anything.

The hands went up again. As if that would make any difference.

I ran for him, pinned the snivelling bastard right against the wall.

'Give me a reason, just one, why I shouldn't put you down right here and now?'

I watched his eyes widen. I listened, but all I heard was the muffled sounds of a man choking on the business end of a revolver. I stepped back, but kept the sights between his eyes.

'Speak, Stevie, or forever hold your peace.'

My pulse was ramping, my heart pounding high in my chest. It wasn't easy to contemplate a killing, even killing a shit-stain like this.

'You work for Jonny Ladd, don't you?' he said.

'What in the name of Christ makes you think that?'

He licked his lips again, 'Well, you mentioned Bunny, and he's been paid.'

'I see that.' I tapped the screen of the laptop, 'You wouldn't have this otherwise.'

'Look, I-I know about the other one ...'

'Who? Do you mean Lee Donald? What do you know?'

'Yes, him. Lee Donald, that's him.'

'You know about Ladd and Donnie, then?'

He looked away, seemed to be struggling with his words. 'I was there, the night he was ... murdered.'

It made sense to me that Jonny would want to put the scare on Stevie, especially if he wanted his money back, and more so, if he wanted to find Bunny.

'You must have had something that Jonny wanted?'

A slow nod. 'Veitch, er, Bunny, as you call him.'

'Well, why doesn't Jonny have him, then? And how are you still walking the streets?'

'It's complicated. Bunny went awol after I paid him. Jonny let me pick up the debt.'

'How much?'

He shrugged. 'About sixty-grand.'

'You paid him?'

'Some. Not all. I was going to make another payment.'

I lowered the shooter, tucked it back in my waistband. My mind was doing loops. I had this fucker here, in front of me, spewing his guts up. But he was no use to me, I'd be as well wasting him and doing the world a favour.

I paced about, looked at the clock on the wall. I grabbed the cash-bags, bundled the lot together, and stuffed it in the poacher's pocket of my Crombie. 'Well, this might buy me some time. Unfortunately, Stevie pal, time's ran out for you.'

'No, wait. I can help you ...'

'Dream on, bud.'

'You're not with Jonny Ladd, are you? Then you must be looking out for that girl?'

'*Stella?*' My thoughts shifted.

'Yes. That's her. I can point you to her.'

'What the hell are you saying to me?'

His words came like a bust tap. 'The flat. The one in Pilrig. Jonny bought it just last month. He buys them all the time, he flips them. Look, I know where it is, I put the sale through, he buys them all the time … The girl, the girl Stella, she'll be there.'

I stopped still. My mind cleared. 'Well, I suppose Jonny needs to rinse his dirty money.'

'Pilrig. It's in Pilrig. I have the address in my diary … the top drawer, over there.'

'Sit down, Stevie, would you?' I kicked the back of his chair, it rolled towards him on its plastic castors. 'Now, just chill for a moment.'

I removed the diary and checked he wasn't lying about the address, then started looking about me. There was nothing I could make any use of. I opened the door, stared into the hall. There was another door in the corridor, with a key in the lock. I opened it up — a pretty sparse stationery cupboard. Shelves of paper and cheap Post-it notes, the odd highlighter and some pots of Tipex.

'You'll do.' I tested the door. It was heavy, one of the remnants of the old-school building materials they used in this end of the town. The lock was solid too — would take a 60-pounder to put it through.

I walked back to the office and took out the duct tape. Stevie was sitting where I left him, doing a pretty good impression of Whistler's mother. He spied the tape.

'What's that?'

I reeled off a wad and tore a strip, just enough to cover his moist mouth.

'I think I've heard all I want to hear from you. If the information you've given me turns out to be bogus, I'll be back, though. We can have a nice chat then.'

I took out my mobi and took a shot of the laptop's screen. Made sure it was a pic with Stevie Fergusson easily identifiable in the frame — which is exactly where I was going to put the bastard.

I removed the thumb-drive and slipped it in my pocket.

The sound of the duct tape spooling again seemed to put the shits right up, Stevie. He'd be even more worried if he knew what I had planned for him next.

CHAPTER 34

I left the door on the latch, but something told me the next visitor would be using a size 10, or a custom built battering-ram.

On the way to the car I called Fitz. The number rang out and went to voicemail. I thought about leaving a message but thought again. If he was locking horns with McEwan, it wouldn't be too hard for that prick to access his voicemail.

Got as far as the car when my mobi started.

Ringing.

'Hello ...'

'You called.' It was Fitz.

'I did yeah.' Tried to light a tab and talk at the same time. 'Look, that thing you were saying a while back about losing faith in the job.'

'What about it?'

'Were you for real?'

'As real as the hole in your arse, Dury.'

I got the tab lit. 'Well, I might just be able to do something about that. What if I were able to give you a nice tasty collar, and the potential for a sweet fuck-you to McEwan.'

'Go on.'

I detailed the latest turn my search had taken. Promised to send the picture of Stevie Fergusson, in flagrante, and drop the thumb-drive in Fitz's hand at the first chance I got.

'I don't recall detailing my suspicions to you, Dury, so just what makes you think this has got something to do with McEwan?' he said.

'What's that old *Police Squad* line? Just a little hunchback at the office.'

'Is this you with the riddles again, Dury.'

I started to cough, I was inhaling too deeply. 'I have to go, Fitz. Don't leave Stevie tied up for too long, he might chafe himself. I'll be in touch.'

'Dury ... *Dury* ...'

Hung up.

I got rolling.

I knew Fitz still had a million and one questions but they would have to wait. I'd given him enough to whet his appetite and, as I pinged over the photo, I sensed that would be plenty to get his blood up, too.

I couldn't call him one of the good guys, he was filth after all, but Fitz did have a sense of right and wrong. There were lines, and some of them you just didn't cross. If you did, you could wear the consequences, which weren't at all pretty. Stevie Fergusson was facing a long stretch, and longer nights shitting through the eye of a needle if I knew anything about the inmates of Peterhead.

I parked up in Pilrig. Took the street opposite the one where Stevie had directed me. Call me cautious, I was at least that by this stage. I put the thumb-drive in the glovebox of the Golf and made sure it was out of sight, the bulky cash-bag I couldn't be so cautious with, but got it stuffed in there.

I locked up the car and made my way onto the street. I checked the shooter in my waistband — more for confidence than anything — was I really doing this?

Seemed so.

Last I looked, I might be twelve-stone dripping wet. I was hardly any serious opposition to one of Ladd's pugs. It would be like a Chihuahua taking on a Rottweiler — the only chance the Chihuahua had was if it got stuck in the Rottie's throat.

Fuck it, I'd shoot first and ask questions later.

It looked like an ordinary Pilrig street. Tenements that could have been anywhere in the city, but just not wearing as well. The whole place was covered in what I jokingly referred to as street furniture — bust couches, old chests of drawers, and the ever present piss-stained mattress.

Little urchins with dirty faces patrolled the streets looking for patter.

'Hey, mister, you got two-pound-fifty for a scud mag?'

'Fuck off, before I tell your mother.'

'She sent me, she's in the scud mag this month, mister.'

I found the door, it was swinging on its hinges. Headed in.

'Hey mister, that's where I stay. My mum gives away free free seafood in there.'

'The fuck are you on about now?'

'They say my mammy's given crabs to every man on the street.'

In normal circumstances I might have laughed, but I'd lost my sense of humour somehow. I dug in my pocket and found a fiver.

'Here, take this,' I handed it to the urchin, his face lit. 'Now fuck off and play with the cat's eyes on the motorway.'

I tried to close the door behind me but the latch had been removed. I'd seen this once before, in Leith, when one of the flats' occupants lost their key. Their solution was to merely remove the entire lock, with a sledgehammer.

'Jesus wept.'

Four suspiciously placed little holes indicated where the lock had once been. I proceeded to the stairs, my gut tightening at the prospect of what awaited me. As I touched the banister I noticed my palms were sweating, a great wet handprint left there to signal my unease. I gulped down some air and tried to get a grip of myself.

The flat's door was relatively new looking. There was a slew of junk mail piled up on the mat outside and it made me think. Someone had superglued the letterbox shut — so they wanted their privacy. I listened at the door. Nothing. A faint hum from a distant radio. But it might have been the neighbours'.

I knocked the door.

Nothing.

Knocked again.

Footsteps.

My heart-rate increased rapidly as I took out the shooter. Figured I'd only get one chance at this. If I fucked up, then I was likely to be the one with holes in me.

A chain rattled.

A bolt slid.

Two inches of light appeared in the jamb.

I saw the chain before I heard the door stop on its links.

Docs have a great footprint, nice and wide. When placed in the correct spot, they can do some proper damage.

The jamb splintered.

Little shards of white wood fluttered to the floor.

I put a second boot in to stop the door from swinging shut. I surprised myself with my competence.

As I stepped in there was a figure lying supine on the grotty carpet. Blood was streaming out his nose like sewage from the Porty outflow. He seemed to be out cold.

I looked down the hall but the place appeared empty. No noise emanated from the interior of the flat. Eerie silence. I wondered if I'd made a terrible mistake.

The lad on the floor had a nice clean line down the middle of his forehead. I guessed it would jam perfectly with the door's edge. But, not for long. There'd be some swelling to halt that process.

I grabbed the biffer's belt and put him in the recovery position. Not so much as a groan. He lay limp as I stepped over him and set about searching the flat.

An old Sharp twin-deck was on the downlow in the living-room — the sight of it made me half expect to hear a Mark Goodier jingle at any moment. There was a small kitchen, occupying one wall, but that was it. Nothing else, no*body* else.

I ran back to the hall. The pug was groaning now. The first door I tried turned out to be the bathroom: turquoise ceramics and black and white floor tiles like a bloody Masonic lodge. Did Jonny buy this sight unseen?

There was only one bedroom. I had to step over the groaning pug to get to it. As I opened up I saw the back of a woman, she was sitting on the edge of a single bed. The room was spartan, not another item on show. Nothing on the bare walls. Not even a cup or a book on the floor.

I felt for Stella Wallace.

She got up. The last time I'd seen her, she was wearing a long cardigan. It all happened so quickly. But, I wondered, how the hell did I miss that?

'Stella …' I said.

She nodded. 'You. From the chippy.'

'That sounds better than "Aren't you a little short for a Stormtrooper?" I suppose.'

She scrunched her eyes. Looked confused. Who wouldn't?

My gaze fell back to her belly.

'What is it?' she said.

'You're pregnant ... '

'Yes.'

I couldn't think clearly. This changed things, complicated matters completely.

More groans came from the hallway. They were getting louder now.

I put out my hand. 'We'll figure this out later, Stella, let's get going.'

She walked with one hand on her belly, breathy and shambling. The look of her made me even more nervous.

'How far gone are you?' I said.

'That depends?'

'On what?'

'What day it is?'

We stepped over the groaning pug on the hall floor and went through the doorway.

'*What day is it?* Why do you ask that?'

She didn't look well in the full blaze of the stairwell, the glare from the skylight making her eyes smart. 'Well, if it's past the tenth of the month, then, I'm overdue.'

I looked at my Casio.

'Holy shit — it's the thirteenth.'

'The thirteenth!' she said.

'Never you mind the date, just don't drop sprog on me, got it?'

She seemed to find it all amusing. Was super-fucking sure I didn't.

'Don't make me laugh,' she said. 'A little pee got out there.'

I face-palmed myself.

'Right, no more funnies. I promise.'

I took Stella's arm and walked her slowly down the stairs and towards the street. Her breathing went up and down, didn't seem natural, but she kept asking about her dad and Donnie.

I didn't have the heart. 'Wally's all good and well, just the same as ever, what a character your old man is.'

'And Donnie?'

'What about him?'

'How is he?'

'Oh, well, I wouldn't know. Haven't seen him myself. He's a friend of a friend of mine. Do you know Windae Willis?'

'No.'

'Erm. Bruce. They call Windae, Bruce now.'

'Why's that then?'

'Like Bruce Willis, y'know, the *Moonlighting* guy.'

'What's *Moonlighting*?'

'*Die Hard*. You must know *Die Hard*, then.'

'Why are you getting agitated?'

'I'm not.'

'Why are you looking at me like that?' Stella stopped still in the street. I carried on a few paces and tried to call her on.

'I'm not looking at you like anything.'

'My bump. You're looking at my bump.'

'I'm not.' I was. 'Come on, we need to get going.'

'I feel funny out here.'

'You've been locked up for a good while, you're bound to feel a little strange. It'll wear off.' I pointed to the car. 'Stella, please, we really need to get going. That guy with the bust nose won't be lying down on the job for ever.'

Stella shook her head at me. She looked adamant. Like she wasn't moving. I tried to ascertain just what the expression she was wearing was, and then it clicked: fear.

I walked towards her, but she seemed to look clean through me.

'What, what is it?' I said.

'It's him.'

'Who?'

I followed the line of Stella's sight, right back down the street. Two heavy figures were sprinting towards us. Behind them, leaning on the bonnet of my car with his arms folded, was Jonny Ladd. He looked straight at me and offered a little wave, then he blew a kiss to Stella.

'How the in the name of Christ did he get here?'

'You know him?' said Stella. 'That's the one, the one that kept me locked up.'

'Yeah, well, he'll have to lock us both up now.'

I put my hand on the handle of the Enfield, as I did so, Ladd's aggro-merchants arrived next to us. I took a glance at Stella, the swell in her belly, and my thoughts stalled completely.

CHAPTER 35

I did the math. Was three against one. It might not have fazed Clint at the end of *The Good, the Bad and the Ugly*, but then he didn't have a pregnant woman by his side to think about.

I let the pugs put my arms up my back and march me down the street to Jonny Ladd. I stopped traffic, well, to be exact, the bunch of kids that were playing in the road. They watched me, wide-gobbed, like I'd just declared open freebies on the ice cream van.

Jonny looked riled as we were hauled up in front of him.

'Don't tell me, Dury, you just stumbled across her.' He made a nod towards the black Merc sitting with the engine running and Stella was shuffled into the back seat. Her wide eyes were on me, pleading for help, the whole way. Don't think I'd ever felt worse.

Said, 'What are you playing at?' I had some front left.

'Me? Has the drink damaged your brain, Dury?'

'Probably. But I can still count to 24. That's how many hours you gave me.'

Ladd's face creased, his heavy brows pushing his eyes into slits. He lifted a flat hand in a side-ways salute and pointed to the flat I'd just left.

'Our deal was a straight swap, Bunny for Stella. I don't see any Bunny.'

'You're forgetting something — the money.'

'What?'

'I was supposed to deliver Bunny, and the money he got from blackmailing Stevie Fergusson.' I tipped my head, motioning him out of the way of my car. As I opened the door he blocked my path.

'What are you doing?'

'Do you want your money, or don't you?' It was all I had. One last long shot. An attempt at betting the farm.

'No tricks, Dury.'

'Cop on, man. You have a pregnant woman over there, what kind of tricks do you think I've got left up my sleeve?'

He nodded me on.

I opened the glovebox and removed the cash-bag.

'There you go.'

Ladd looked inside and allowed a thin smile to grow on his face.

'I'll give you this, Dury, you're full of surprises.'

I pushed the boat out. 'Seems like surprises are springing up all over the place.' I closed the car door and stood facing him.

'Meaning?' he said.

'Well, it might not have been 24 hours since we last spoke, Jonny, but a lot's happened since then.'

He stuffed the cash bag inside his coat. 'Such as?'

'Such as Stevie Fergusson being picked up by the filth. There's an interesting little story going around about pictures of him and an underage girl, and I don't think they were just playing footsie under the table.'

Ladd looked defensive. 'Who told you this?'

'You're not the only one with some friends on the force.'

'What else did this friend of yours tell you?'

I rummaged in my pocket for my tabs, pulled one out and sparked up. I offered the pack to Ladd but he declined with a frown. 'He told me how Sharky's face ended up looking like a butcher's floor. Mac hits hard, but that's two of my friends in the frame now.'

'Such a shame.'

'Is it? There's no way it'll stick. Especially when Stevie starts to chirp like a budgie.' I looked down the road, 'I hear Stevie did the deal on the flat for you. Does he know anything else about your business? Like, where and how you get a hold of 13-year-old girls to turn tricks for you?'

Ladd eased himself off the wing of my car and made a show of wiping away any residue he may have left behind. 'Oh, Dury, you are a trier. I'll give you that.'

'Come on now, Jonny, it's called logic and even the police can put two and two together. I know Sharky's been feeding Detective Inspector McEwan quite a few biccies lately, how's that going to look when the truth about Donnie's murder finally comes out? It's not far off now, y'know, till they link Donnie with the blackmailing of Stevie and then you're well and truly fucked.'

Ladd walked towards me. When he stopped there was barely a hair's breadth between us. 'What makes you think I'm buying any of this shite, Dury?'

'Don't take my word for it,' I held firm, 'call your mate McEwan if you want clarification.'

Ladd placed it on my shoulder, gripped tightly. 'I'm warning you. Stay put and don't get any ideas. I'm not done with you yet, Dury.'

He looked frustrated, angry, as he turned away, removing his mobi. He walked out of earshot but I watched the conversation through his jittery actions: the fingers in hair, the grimacing at the sky.

As Ladd returned, I knew thoughts were spinning in his head. He hadn't heard what he'd expected to.

'Okay, Dury, talk.'

'I've told you everything.'

'No, you haven't. You haven't told me what you want.'

'Well, that depends — has McEwan called off the dogs or am I liable to be lifted by the first Edinburgh plod that clocks me?'

'I don't think there's anything to be gained by hauling you in now.'

'I suppose they must be running low on cells down there.'

He started to show his frustration. 'Stop the fucking about. What are you after?'

My tab was burnt to the filter. I flicked it on the street. 'You can start with handing over Stella, like we agreed.'

He laughed. 'No dice. Stella remains my ... insurance policy.'

'I thought we had a deal?'

'We did. But, like you say, a lot's happened since then.'

'You got the money.'

He tapped his jacket. 'I did ... but still no Bunny.'

'Give me Stella and I'll get you Bunny.' I was at it again. I had no hope of finding Bunny in a city this size, in such short order. He knew this, because if it could be done, he'd have done it already.

'That was the original deal, but now you've seen her, you'll see it's not a fair swap. Two for one, as it were.' He let his lips crease over his teeth in a wayward smile.

'What about, Donnie? That's one you're not adding into the total.'

'Unfortunately that muppet had no value. Can you believe he actually bought Bunny's bullshit about turning me over, mopping up my supply lines?' Jonny Ladd's eyes blackened when he spoke about Bunny's actions. 'That little fucker, Bunny, was all for moving in on my routes. He sounded out my supplier but got nowhere, so he decided to cut a slice off the top until he had enough stored up in that lock-up of his to start his own run.'

'Sounds pretty devious.'

Ladd brought a fist down on the roof of the Golf. 'Devious? That doesn't even come close, Dury. Bunny saw himself as a challenger, as fuckingwell taking over. And you were supposed to bring me the cunt, so where is he? Well, where is the rancid little cum-stain? I want him, Dury. I want him here ...' He opened his hands in front of me. 'I want Bunny here in my grip so I can see his fucking face when I throttle the life out of him.'

I left Ladd to savour the image for a moment longer. Made a show of lighting up another tab and offering him one.

'No. Fuck that,' he said. 'I don't fucking smoke.'

'You might want to start — snout trades well inside I hear.'

He grabbed my lapel and drew back a fist. 'Who do you think you're dealing with, Dury?'

I kept it together. Just. My mind was yelling otherwise. 'You're going down, Jonny, live with it.'

'What? Am I hearing right?' He clearly wasn't used to having facts served cold.

'It's over, everything. This is the end of days for you, mate. The only hope, the only solace you have is to find Bunny and make sure he swings for it instead of you.'

His hand slid off my lapel and onto my neck, he squeezed tightly. 'Bunny's gone. You've no chips left to place, Dury.'

I could barely get the words out. 'No he's not. I know where Bunny is.'

'*Where?*'

'No dice. And no fucking Bunny until you hand over Stella.'

When you drink as much as I do, punish your body as much as I do, your stomach becomes a sensitive spot.

I'm pretty confident that Ladd's fist touched my spine, soon after it connected with my gut.

Couldn't say I curled over, more like totally collapsed. My face touched the cold asphalt at some speed and I found the familiar salty taste of blood in my mouth. I hoped it was a tooth gone. Maybe a bite out of my tongue. I didn't want to contemplate the other possibility: that something had been ruptured inside me.

I lay on the ground, watching the flashing lights. Bright spots of white light and a woo-wooing noise that sounded like a siren. I moved a hand, put it out in front of me and I saw Jonny Ladd stamp on my fingers. He seemed discontent with his move, so repeated the process again, and again. The cracking of bone was the first thing I heard as my hearing returned to normal.

'Midnight, Dury. You bring him to me, to the steading in Dunbar by midnight. Or Stella swings. You get me, Dury?' Ladd's voice was a roar now.

He grabbed my hair, slapped my head.

'Midnight,' I said, followed by a mouthful of blood.

I watched him pace away from me. A round-shouldered bolus of hate. He was still making fists as he reached the car.

The black Merc spat exhaust fumes at me as it went.

I eased myself onto the side of the Golf. My hand was numb, I couldn't feel a thing. The only place registering pain was my gut. I tried to force myself onto my feet but my boots slipped.

'You okay, mister?' It was the little urchin from earlier.

'Yeah, fine.'

'Want to buy some photos of your sister?'

'Fuck off!' I aimed a kick at his arse but he was too quick for me.

Gradually, I felt the order of the universe returning to normal. The spinning slowed, then ceased, at least to a pace I couldn't track.

I needed a drink.

I needed lots of things.

A vague notion of an idea.

A plan, perhaps.

But more than anything, I needed a drink.

I walked into the Black Bull Tavern with half-an-instinct that I'd be pegged as a drunk and promptly pointed back to the door. My knees were knocking, my mouth trapped in an involuntary rictus, just to make the simple act of breathing less painful.

The good old days of my dog bites seemed like a holiday in the sun compared to how I felt.

'Pint,' I wrestled the money out my jeans and dropped it on the bar. 'Chaser, double goldie.'

The barmaid looked like a recent school leaver. Actual pigtails and a badge that read *Lisa*. She looked to be scared shitless of me, but brought the drinks without so much as a frown.

I necked the pint and asked for another. I'd tanned the two goldies by the time it arrived.

'Shall I fill up the shots again?' said Lisa.

I smiled, gave a nod. It might have been the Florence Nightingale effect, but I was warming to this girl.

'By the way, do you have such a thing as a first-aid box in here?' I held up my hand, it was bruising away nicely. Lied, 'Had a little accident changing a tyre on the car.'

'Shouldn't you go to the hospital?'

'I probably should. I'm in shock, though, just wanted to settle my nerves.'

She got the first-aid box and dropped it in front of me, retreated behind the bar. There was a crepe bandage, I wrapped it round my hand and tried to tighten it as best I could. Reckoned three of the four fingers were broken, but the fourth still had a nasty knuckle gash.

The barmaid came back to take away the first-aid box when I was finished and I asked for another pint. She fired me a look, as if to say, "Make it your last". I still felt someway grateful. If I had another drink, the temptation would be on me to wait until closing. And that could never happen. Time was running out and I had to find Bunny soon.

I supped up, then walked for the carpark with my bandaged hand, tucked inside my Crombie. I must have looked like a bad Napoleon portrait, not so much despot, as crackpot.

Driving with three broken fingers was easier than I thought, though I would have preferred an automatic. I remembered a story Wally had told me about his business being kept afloat by Americans in hire cars with manual grearboxes.

'They fly into the airport and say, "Sure I can drive a manual!"' he'd told me on the day I bought the Golf. 'Then they get to the outskirts of Corstorphine and wonder what the burning smell is. Doesn't take long to wear out a gearbox, couple of miles in first will do it.'

It was the last time I'd laughed at Wally's bullshit. I wanted to say I wished I'd never met the bastard, as I totted up the impact on Hod, on Mac, on my fucking fingers. The bitterest pill to swallow though, was Stella. That poor girl, and the baby growing inside her, I'd never be able to live with the consequences if anything happened to them.

I planted the foot. Trawled round and round. Went to Leith, all Donnie's old haunts.

The street where he was dealing.

The Buck.

Aldo's chippy.

And back down to Wally's lot.

Nothing.

Not a thing.

I wanted to scream out, to start accosting people in the street and asking them where the fuck Bunny was. My mind was awash with dark visions. Pictures of Stella in the steading, going the same way as Donnie.

'Man, get a hold of yourself, Gus.'

I spun the wheels and headed back for The Buck. They knew Bunny in there, it was my only hope. The fact that my last two visits had been shit-shows didn't seem to bother me.

I pulled up outside.

My heart was pumping, but I put it aside as I stamped my way through the snoutcasts at the front door.

'Out my way, for fucksake!' I yelled.

Inside, the place was busier than I remembered it. Perhaps word had got around about the lads with pick-axe handles. That type of entertainment wasn't hard to come by in Leith, but you rarely got the chance to enjoy it with a pint in front of you.

The barman clocked me instantly, let out a yelp. It was a familiar sound, but I wasn't registering any of his stream of words until a couple of big lads on barstools turned to face me. These were new faces to me, and I wasn't keen to get to know them any better.

'Pull your fucking necks in, boys,' I took out the revolver and pointed it at the pair of meatheads. They both sat down, as if on cue.

'You … get out here.' I called over to the barman and he shook his head.

Behind him was a massive mirror with a picture of a colourful, happy-looking toucan under the word *Guinness*. Normally, the advertising works perfectly on me, but I felt strangely immune to its effects this time.

I started to feel light-headed. It was hot inside the bar. I couldn't think clearly as I stared at the sweaty barman and he stared back, stupefied.

The room fell silent.

There's a phrase: "Could hear a pin drop".

I felt the burn of eyes on me and then the trance broke.

Ringing.

It was my mobi.

Ringing.

The sound annoyed me. So persistent.

Ringing.

They wouldn't give up.

Ringing.

Shit. I knew I had to answer.

But, I couldn't pick-up and still hold up the shooter.

Ringing.

I backed away, fled. The snoutcasts outside the pub scattered at first sight of me.

'Hello … Dury.' I managed a jog to the car, opened up.

'Hi … I mean, hello there … I don't know if you remember me?'

I didn't know the voice, bit, 'Who's this?'

I trapped the phone between my ear and shoulder and turned the ignition. As the engine revved, I put the mobi on speaker and flung it on the passenger seat.

'My name's Rory.'

Why did that mean something to me?

'We met a little while ago …' he sounded young, just a lad. 'In Newhaven, in the lock-up. You told me to call.'

I slammed on the brakes. 'Oh, Rory. Fuck, yes. Of course I remember you.'

'You said to call, if I ever saw any movement at the lock-up.'

'I did? I *mean*, I did. I'm sure I did.'

The line crackled a little, then settled again.

'Well, it's only that, there's someone there now.'

I felt a little flutter in my chest, like God had just whispered in my ear, 'Stay put, Rory! Stay just exactly where you are.'

I put the wheel on full-lock and turned back for Newhaven. Got a power of horns blared at me as I crossed the central reservation, some fingers pressed to windows, but wasn't giving two fucks.

Maybe, just this once.

Maybe, my luck was in.

CHAPTER 36

Time was, when none of this got to me. It was meat and drink, a rush. But, I knew those days were behind me. I didn't want to live like this anymore. I was too old. Too tired. And too fucking disinterested in the affairs of others to get, in any way, involved. The world, and everyone in it, could go to hell in a handcart — like I'd bat an eyelid.

My guts ached worse than they ever had as I pressed myself closer to the wheel, trying to control the vehicle with one hand. The bends were hellish, I now had a scorched palm to add to my woes; could imagine the piss-taking I'd get from Hod and Mac for that.

If it weren't for that pair, and for poor Stella and her unborn child, I'd have put a stop to this nonsense long ago. There was a film reel unfurling in my mind now, like someone showing holiday slides on a projector, of myself leading a normal life.

I was holding down a job, again.

Maybe even … *well*, yeah, Amy had worked her way into the picture too.

I needed change.

I needed out.

I'd kept Rory on the line for as long as I could, but the callbox ate all his cash way too soon. Where he found one of those

271

in Edinburgh, outside of the tourist traps on the Royal Mile, I'd no clue. They were never designed for calling mobiles, though, each coin only delivering a couple of seconds chatter.

Rory said there was a van. A white Bedford. And only one man there. It sounded like a parcel monkey — and I'd be seriously pissed to find out it was only Yodel.

I hit Newhaven in good time, but the sky was darkening. I checked the Casio on my wrist: I had about an hour or so to turn things around. The thought of Stella, in the same steading as Donnie, with only Jonny Ladd and his posse for company, didn't play well with me. Holy Christ, the girl was overdue to deliver her baby — how would that be dealt with? I remembered the expanse of greenery, the endless fields. Any number of bodies could be buried there already.

I spotted Rory up ahead. He had that jakey posture already, hunkered down at the side of a building, a blankie over the shoulders, he blended right in around here.

I pulled up to the kerb, 'Hello, lad.'

'Gus, did I do okay?' He just about stood to attention.

'You did. Jump in.'

I waited for him to close the door and drove the car over to the other side of the road, down a service lane. Rory was staring at my hand all the while.

'What happened?' he said.

I lifted my fingers, hadn't realised they were just about black all over now. 'I had a little accident.'

'A *little* accident?'

'Rory, trust me, in the scheme of things, it ain't that bad.'

I parked up. Now there was only a 6ft brick wall between us and Bunny's lock-up.

'Here, you take this,' I handed over my mobi. 'You know how to work it?'

'Of course.' That look, 'I'm not a total tard.'

'Once I get over that wall, it's showtime.' I pulled back my coat to show I had the Enfield in my waistband. 'If you hear this go off, and see your laddo in there running, then call Fitz and tell him what's gone down.'

I pointed out Fitz's number in my contacts.

'You mean, I'm not coming in,' said Rory.

'No chance.'

'But ... '

'No buts, either.' I patted the boy on the shoulder. 'Now, one more thing, Rory, if you see me leave in the van, then call Fitz, too. Tell him to get himself to Donnie's steading — he'll know what I mean. Do you understand?'

'I think so.'

Immediately, I wondered about putting my fate in the hands of a young homeless I hardly knew. He'd come good so far, but there was nothing to stop him heading straight to Cash Converters with my iPhone. 'When this is over, Rory, there'll be a good drink in it for you. Trust me on that. You've no idea how much you've done. It's not just my arse you've saved here — a lot of people will be very grateful.'

'I only made a call.'

'The right call.' I got out the Golf, was halfway to closing the door when a thought struck me, 'Rory, are you any good with engines?'

'Engines? Like car engines?'

'Yeah, and mechanics and that?'

He shrugged. 'Pretty decent, yeah. Why do you ask?'

'I think I might know a man with a vacancy in that line.'

'Really?'

'Yeah. Just don't ever ask what happened to your predecessor.'

I closed the door and started to drag a wheelie bin over to the wall. The up and over was harder than I thought, with aching guts and a number of broken digits, but I managed it.

My Docs landed soundly in the yard, with hardly a splatter of the surface water. I got right down to it, flung myself against the wall. Think I'd seen it done like this in Where Eagles Dare.

As I crept along I could hear movement in the lock-up. Something was being dragged over the cement floor. I eased my head round the door and risked one eye.

A man. Roughly my size, but with a black ponytail that would make Francis Rossi weep. I closed in. Slowly. It was a crawl from wall to wall. My mouth clamped tightly shut, my breathing just an occasional, still gasp.

The ponytail moved in and out of the mechanic's pit in a hurried motion. Little brick-sized cellophane packages were being piled on the floor of the van. There were dozens of them, sandy brown numbers with a bit of weight in them by the looks of things.

I edged closer, got a better feel for the lay of the land. It seems on my last visit I'd missed a false floor in the mechanic's pit. I wasn't alone, mind. Jonny Ladd's mob must have missed that too.

Now I could see that the floor was solid metal, as it leaned against the edge of the pit. One side of the floor was covered in a thin layer of concrete — a couple of bags of ready-mix, sparsely spread, would have done the trick. The sneaky bastard had hid his entire stash, or should that be Jonny Ladd's stash, in plain sight.

I watched Bunny complete the job, load up the last few bricks, and close up the back doors of the Bedford. As he went about the finishing touches, I stationed myself near the driver's door, shooter out front.

'Hello, Bunny?' I said.

He stopped still. His eyes widened. 'The fuck are you?'

'Well, well. Seems I have a Bunny in the headlights.'

He turned down the edges of his mouth, words were in there but he was holding them back. Now that I was at close range, I noticed the ears on him — the FA Cup didn't get a look in.

'Well, that's one mystery solved,' I said.

He showed palms, shrugged.

'The ears,' I pointed, 'what's up, Doc?'

'Are you trying to be funny?' he said.

'You can't try to be funny, mate, you either are or you aren't … That's the funny thing, don't you think?'

He looked at me like I was mental. I had him right where I wanted him. 'Keys. Get them over.'

He handed me the keys and I pointed him into the driver's seat as I backed round the front of the vehicle and into the cab. He stared at me for a moment, probably wondering why I hadn't shot him already, or just took off with the truckload of skag.

I leaned over, put the keys on the dash. 'Drive.'

'Where?'

'Wherever I fucking tell you,' I put the tip of the Enfield on his temple. 'Now get moving.'

He turned over the engine and drove out of the lock-up. As we went I looked in the rear-view mirror and caught sight of Rory watching us go. It was on my mind to remind him to keep trying Fitz if he didn't pick up, but the moment passed and we were on our way, heading for the wilds of East Lothian.

By the city limits the thought about the lad calling Fitz was still haunting me, and I hoped Rory would have the sense not to leave a message that could easily be intercepted by DCI McEwen. Now, that would properly fuck things up. And, not just for me.

'You're making a big mistake, you know,' said Bunny. He gripped the wheel so tightly I thought it might start to seep through his fingers.

'Is that right, now?' I said. 'You'll be telling me I don't know who I'm messing with next, I suppose.'

'Oh, you'll find out.'

He seemed so cocky, so arrogant. If he wasn't driving the van I'd have cracked the pistol over his puss, just to mind his manners.

'I've already found out about you and your piss-ant little crew, Bunny. I know all about your silly ambitions to run over Jonny Ladd and be the Big Man. You're a fucking joke. An utter laughing-stock by this stage, and it looks to me like you don't even know it.'

He turned to shoot me a couple of daggers. Like it bothered me. He could rage away inside, he was nothing but a bottom-feeder and he'd take the cards that fate, or more precisely, Jonny Ladd, dealt him. I could see those big Bunny ears of his getting made into a pair of carpet slippers, just for shits and giggles.

'You'll know then, that Donnie died through this way,' he'd spotted the signs for Dunbar. 'What makes you think that we'll fare any differently with Ladd?'

'Trust me, I know all about Donnie's sad demise. I know about your efforts to blackmail Stevie Fergusson as well, and I know about the little girl you set him up with. So, tell me, what kind of a strange, messed-up fuck do you have to be to associate with the likes of you?'

A tut. 'You're no better.'

'Is that so?'

'Who are you to judge me?'

'Trust me, Bunny, I'm no choir boy. But, compared to the likes of you, I'm as pure as the driven snow.'

'Bullshit. We're all the same … If the opportunity was put in front of you, you'd grasp it. Nobody turns down the poppy in my experience.'

'You've no idea what I've turned down, or lost already.'

He lifted a hand from the wheel. Pointed behind him with his thumb. 'That lot there, worth over a million. I could do you a split.'

I laughed. 'I wouldn't know what to do with it. You're wasting your time, man, would you just watch the road and quit fantasising. It's over, you had your little run, now you're done.'

'And you think you're so superior, sitting there with a smug grin on your face, when all you're going to do is put the lot in Jonny's lap!' He started to laugh, 'That bastard's a hundred times worse than me.'

'It's not a case of who's the baddest of the bad here, I could not give a flying fuck about either of you. Get me, Bunny? You're both trash. But there's a girl, and she's nine-months pregnant, with a baby that will never know its father, and they don't deserve any of this, or care about you and Jonny's pissing contest.'

He tried to talk again, but I cut him down.

'No. Shut the fuck up, Bunny, and no more of your ball-fanning either. Just drive the car. One more word and I'll fucking pop you, I swear it. Don't test me again!'

We drove in silence.

The darkness came down rapidly now. The night sky looked clear, but starless. I tried to follow the road to the steading that Fitz had described to me but we got lost, reversing and over-revving the heavily-loaded vehicle on a dirt-track.

The wheels were stuck, one of us would have to push. I knew Bunny would bolt into the night the first chance he got, so I guessed it would have to be me.

I opened the door and stepped out of the Bedford. Bunny watched, waiting for me to open my mouth but I found it difficult, if not downright unnecessary. I was in full sight of the steading now — the one where Donnie had been so brutally killed — but we weren't alone.

'Get those fucking hands in the air, Dury!' It was Sharky. He had a 12-bore in my ribs — well, it was the country after all.

I turned around, slowly, and spotted some more figures coming out of the shadows. Jonny Ladd was the only one without a long-barrel broken over his arm, instead he waved about a Maglite. It looked like a hunting party, minus the deerstalkers.

Sharky started to pat me down. He found Mac's revolver and held it in the Maglite's beam. The sight of it seemed to be a source of much hilarity to everyone but me.

'Jesus, Dury, you on your way to the *Antiques Roadshow*?' said Ladd.

'Come on now, Jonny, there's none of us getting any younger, but you're not that old yet.'

He made a feint towards me with his fist, then aimed the flashlight at my stomach, but stopped himself. 'How's the guts?' he joked, 'Man, that hand of yours looks bloody nasty, should get it seen to.'

I didn't answer. Flinching my stomach had taken the last of my strength from me.

I turned to see Bunny being dragged from the van, and frog-marched round to meet the Bad Ladd. Bunny's lip was burst, they'd decided to get their revenge in early. His mouth spooled blood onto the ground as he walked.

Sharky opened the slide-door on the van, 'Jonny, it's all here, look.'

Ladd positioned the Maglite right in my face. 'How?'

'The real question is: *Why?* We had a deal.'

Ladd turned towards Bunny and asked him one question, 'Is it all there?'

'Jonny, I want to say something …'

'I asked a question.'

'But …'

Ladd roared. 'No buts!' He snatched the 12-bore from Sharky and pointed it at Bunny's head. He held the Maglite next to the long gun-barrel and Bunny lit up in its full glare. He was a ghost of himself, trembling, dribbling blood from the tip of his chin.

'Jonny, please, I only want to say one thing …'

'You've already said too much, Bunny boy.'

'But …'

'The damage is done.'

'We can work something out, surely.'

'I'm afraid that's not possible now, Bunny.'

'Jonny, please …'

'The answer's no. And nothing will change my mind.'

The rifle's report went straight to my ears, set the universe ringing. One quick depression of the trigger and Bunny's white features were replaced by a bloody explosion. The two pugs nearest the victim were showered in brittle skull fragments, and splattered with blotches of blood down the sides of their faces. There was a second or so where shock set in, and then the noise of Bunny's corpse dropping to the ground. A second later another noise came from the grass, about twenty-feet away.

'The fuck was that?' said Sharky.

Ladd walked into the field, following the shot's trajectory. He leaned over and retrieved something from the ground that looked like a dead rat.

'Look at this,' he was laughing hard, trying to focus the item in the light of the torch, but his shoulders shook too much.

'What is it?' said Sharky.

Ladd walked back, laughing loudly, the item in his hand now coming into full view. It was Bunny's ponytail, still attached to a quarter of his skull and a good portion of grey matter.

'That's fucking hilarious.' The mob surrounded Ladd, slapping each other and wailing in gut-laughs. I couldn't believe what I was seeing. I started to pray that Stella be spared the same treatment — then the mood changed abruptly, everyone got jumpy.

'Wait, what's that?' said Ladd.

Guns were pinned to shoulders as a set of car-lights appeared on the dirt-track. It looked like a farm vehicle, as it got closer, I saw it was a 4x4. The high-vis police livery was impossible to miss.

'It's only Robbie,' said one of the biffers, 'he's on his own.'

DCI McEwan kept the engine running, and the lights on, as he proceeded down the track towards the group. He looked around, eyed Ladd cautiously, and then settled his gaze on me.

'What the hell is he doing out here, Jonny?' said McEwen.

Ladd walked over to the van and closed the door. He nodded to Sharky, who headed round to the driver's side. 'He's returning my investment, Robbie, keep the head.'

I watched the pair of them close in on me. Neither appeared to be interested in what I had to say, but I put it out there anyway. 'Now, don't fight over me, boys. I'm just fulfilling my part of the agreement.'

McEwan snapped. 'What agreement?'

'Never mind, it's over now.' Ladd was still waving about Bunny's ponytail.

'What the hell is that?' said McEwen.

'Just some pest control.'

The remainder of the mob laughed; I started to feel uneasy. Seeing McEwan and Ladd together like this sealed it for me that they were in cahoots over the cover-up of Donnie's murder. The rage inside me was building, thinking of Hod and Mac getting framed for a murder they had nothing to do with.

'Jonny,' I said, 'we had a deal, remember, now where's Stella?'

The DCI pointed a finger at me. 'I get it, you sent Dury into action to find your lost payload, Jonny.' he said. McEwan focussed his attention on the ponytail in Ladd's hand, 'And, by the looks of it, Bunny Veitch.'

Ladd walked over to Bunny's corpse and directed the Maglite to the bloody pulp on the ground, a seeping wetness was spreading over the dry track.

'Dury's one hell of an operator, I'll give him that,' said Ladd.

'Oh, Jesus ...' said McEwan. 'You realise this changes everything.'

I saw where this was going, said, 'Now hold up there, the only thing this changes is that you have some sweeping up to do, Detective. Stella and me are walking out of here tonight, and you no longer need Hod and Mac when you can pin the lot on the late Bunny, understand?'

McEwan's eyes slow-blinked. He was thinking, just not in the way I wanted him to. He turned to Ladd, 'Where's the girl?'

'In the steading?'

'All right.' He looked towards me, 'Get Dury in there too. This ends tonight, and we can't leave any witnesses.'

'Fair fucks,' said Ladd.

'Now wait a minute,' I yelled, but it was too late — a gun-barrel was forced between my shoulder-blades and the march to the steading had begun.

Many thoughts, many images, flashed as I walked towards the steading. This felt like it. The End. There was no way out now. I'd let everyone down.

Hod.

Mac.

Stella.

And her unborn baby.

In a moment like this, the most obscene calm settles on you. I'd lost. I could do no more. That was it. But this feeling, this calm, felt unnatural. It felt like I was enjoying a reaction that I had no right to.

I was a drinker, there was no escape from that either. No matter what route I took, it always ended in my capture. I was beholden to that bottle. But when I admitted this, to myself, a similar calm awoke in me.

The moment that bottle-top was turned, the concession was made. You'd conceded your fate. No one was in control now — except the man upstairs — certainly not me.

'Move it,' the barrel was poked in my ribs this time, forcing me into the steading.

There were lanterns inside. The old variety, burning kerosine. They painted a dull glow on the stone walls. Black shadows lurked there but they seemed friendly enough. The least friendly face was Stella's.

'You lied to me,' she said.

'I did.'

'About Donnie.'

I knew they'd told her. She had to find out, but telling that to a pregnant woman sickened me.

'Stella, I'm sorry, for everything.'

She didn't respond. Her gaze flitted off into the dark shadows and I lost her there. The girl wasn't herself — how could she be after all that had happened?

I wondered how they broke it to her? The savages. It was all a game to them. A high stakes game, but they never faced the consequences. They went about their business, about their daily lives, with no thought to the people that they preyed upon.

We were just a source of income and amusement to the likes of Ladd, and beyond that, we didn't exist. People like me, people like Stella and her baby, we were just collateral damage. An inconvenience along the way.

I watched one of Ladd's pugs as he roped my hands together. The broken fingers had ceased to bother me in the slightest, even as the rope tightened. That calm again, it was everywhere.

I thought of my mam, and all she had endured with my father. So much misery. So much suffering. Even after all I'd seen, that still haunted me the most.

I was glad I wouldn't have to think about it again.

Soon, it would be only a memory.

Dust.

'You've nothing to be sorry for,' said Stella.

Her words shocked me. 'What did you say?'

'It wasn't anything to do with you. None of it. I know you lied to protect me.'

Stella was putting the record straight, as we both ran out of time. I prayed they'd get it over with quickly. Not because I was afraid to die, but because I didn't want the girl to suffer any more.

'Jonny,' I called out to him. 'Let the girl go.'

He walked over to me. 'You heard the man, things have changed, Dury.'

'Jesus, she's pregnant. Have you thought what that will do to your soul?'

A smirk.

'What soul?'

As he spoke the entrance to the steading was lit up. Another torch through the darkness. Sharky appeared, his face flushed.

'The hell are you back here for?' said Jonny.

Sharky sounded spooked, blurting his words between gulps of breath, 'They're on the way. The roads are blocked. I had to turn back.'

'Who?' Ladd grabbed Sharky by the shirtfront, 'Who's on the way?'

He didn't get to answer. The flashing blue lights and the sirens did it for him.

Ladd freaked. 'McEwan, what the fuck's going on?'

'I don't know.' He turned to me, 'It's him and that Irish copper, Fitzsimmons. I checked the messages on his voicemail.'

'What message?' said Ladd.

'About tonight — how else do you think I found out what you were doing? But I don't know anything about this.' He raised his arms to his head.

The noise grew louder.

More lights, searchlights now.

Dogs barked outside. A bustle of boots on the road. Then, the best yet, a loudspeaker with Fitz the Crime's voice blaring through the night.

'Put down your weapons and step outside. We know you're in there, Ladd ... and McEwen ... Don't make it any more difficult for yourselves.'

Ladd turned to the DCI. 'What do we do now?'

'What do we do? We do fucking nothing, you idiot, there's a squad of marksmen out there. Do you want to be cut to shreds?'

'So, that's it?' said Ladd, 'We just chuck it in?'

The detective went for the door. 'You can do what you like. You're on your own now, Jonny.' McEwen took his jacket off and turned it inside out, made a white-flag with the lining, as he walked out, arms in the air.

'I'm unarmed,' he yelped. 'I'm coming out.'

Some of Ladd's mob followed in McEwan's wake but Sharky and Ladd stayed behind. As Ladd paced the steading, Sharky yabbered continuously.

'Shut up! Just shut the fuck up,' said Ladd. 'I'm trying to think.'

Sharky kept up the rapid chatter, making no sense, then ran for the door. He got about two steps into the spotlights before the police marksmen opened fire. When the shooting stopped, I saw the stupid bastard still held a rifle in his hands.

The sound of heavy gunfire had sparked fear in Jonny Ladd. But the sight of Sharky going down, a grand red arc of blood shooting in the air, and then splattering onto the cold cobbles, finished off the Bad Ladd.

He turned towards me, mouth open. I waited for him to say something but his eyes said it all. Without a word passing between us, Ladd put down his flashlight and waked out, hands behind his neck.

I started yelling.

'Fitz, get us out of here!'

I stopped mid-roar, turned to Stella. 'You okay, there?'

'No, I don't think so.'

My heart stopped. I didn't want to believe the worst, but the dark pool on the floor between us told me otherwise. 'Stella you've been shot?'

A group of uniforms appeared in the steading, assault rifles scoping the place. They checked the corners, all the exits, but ignored my pleas.

'I have a woman with a bullet wound, here!'

'Gus ... *Gus* ...' said Stella.

Fitz appeared in the doorway, the familiar houndstooth coat, even more of a giveaway in the bright searchlights.

'Over here, Fitz, Stella's taken a bullet ...' I tried to free my hands but I couldn't. I pulled harder but only added a dislocated wrist to my list of injuries.

'Gus,' she said.

'He's coming now, it's Fitz, it's going to be okay.'

'She's been shot?' said Fitz.

'No!' yelled Stella. 'I've not been shot ... My waters have broken.'

Fitz turned to face me, then back to Stella.

'I'll get an ambulance, right away,' he said.

She was breathing strangely now, lips pierced into a tiny aperture. 'It might be too late for that.'

'By the holy,' said Fitz. He started to loosen off his tie, caught my expression. 'What are you laughing at, Dury?'

'Nothing. Not a damn thing.'

Lightning Source UK Ltd.
Milton Keynes UK
UKHW040735051219
354823UK00002B/457/P